THE SEASIDE ICE CREAM PARLOUR

SARAH HOPE

Boldwood

First published in 2020. This edition first published in Great Britain in 2023 by Boldwood Books Ltd.

Copyright © Sarah Hope, 2020

Cover Design by Head Design Ltd

Cover Photography: Shutterstock

A CIP catalogue record for this book is available from the British Library.

Paperback ISBN 978-1-80549-096-8

Large Print ISBN 978-1-80549-097-5

Hardback ISBN 978-1-80549-098-2

Ebook ISBN 978-1-80549-095-1

Kindle ISBN 978-1-80549-094-4

Audio CD ISBN 978-1-80549-103-3

MP3 CD ISBN 978-1-80549-102-6

Digital audio download ISBN 978-1-80549-099-9

Boldwood Books Ltd
23 Bowerdean Street
London SW6 3TN
www.boldwoodbooks.com

For my children,
Let's change our stars
xXx

1

'Please don't start grumbling, Grace. You've already had something to eat, you just need to give in and go to sleep now.' Pushing the brake down with her foot, Jenny Weaver peered over the top of the buggy. Grace looked shattered. Not that she blamed her. They'd had to catch the coach at 6:45am, a time when they'd usually still be asleep. 'Not long now. Soon we'll be on the train and then hopefully you *will* fall asleep.'

Looking over at the departure board, she watched the updates flashing through. She smiled, it looked as though their train was still running on time. Another five minutes and they'd be out of the London smog and on their way to their new life. They'd done it. Well, almost. Their recent life of sofa surfing was over. In just a few short hours, they'd have somewhere they could call home again. Somewhere Grace could leave her toys scattered on the living room floor of an evening, ready to jump back into the same game the next morning. A place where they could finally start to put some roots down.

'Excuse me, miss.'

Shaking her thoughts away, she focused on the boy standing in front of her. Taking in his ripped jeans and blue baseball cap pulled down over his eyes, she shifted her weight, clicking up the brake to unlock it, ready to head further up the platform towards the suited office workers if she needed to. She wasn't in the mood for any trouble. Not today.

'You've been dropping your luggage. I think your suitcase might be broke.'

Turning behind her to where he pointed, Jenny cursed under her breath. T-shirts, underwear and a collection of other items littered the path behind her leading all the way back towards the lift. 'Thank you. I hadn't noticed.' Leaving the suitcase where it stood, Jenny turned the buggy and began picking up items of their clothing, balancing them on the hood of the buggy.

'Oi, you lot! Come and help.' The boy in the baseball cap whistled back at his friends who unfolded their long limbs from the bench and lumbered towards them.

Bending to grab another of Grace's tiny T-shirts, she watched as the five teenage boys ran the length of the platform picking up their pastel-coloured clothes. Pausing, she accepted the handfuls of clothes as she was handed them and glanced around the busy platform. Unbelievable. Every day the newspapers and the news told stories on knife crime, postcode gangs and the general disrespect of young people today, and yet, here she was, her suitcase having expelled her worldly goods, and who comes to her rescue? Yep, a group of wayward teenagers whilst the 'respectful' citizens happily stand around in their expensive suits, clasping briefcases and desperately trying to avert their eyes, pretending to be focused on the urgent text they had just received, or too busy staring at the empty railway line willing the train to come and rescue them from their uncomfortable stance.

Rolling her eyes, she wheeled the buggy in the direction of a pair of flowery pink leggings which were blowing across the platform perilously close to a group of office workers trying to ignore the commotion right in front of them.

'Excuse me.' Picking up some leggings, she jogged on to the next item.

'Here you go, miss.' The boy in the blue cap passed another armful of clothes to Jenny.

'Thank you.' Nodding, she took the clothes from him just as the platform filled with the noise of the approaching train.

'Do you want me to check the lift for you? In case there's more in there and upstairs?'

'No, no. You've done more than enough. You get your train.' Smiling, she stood and accepted the rest of their belongings as the teenagers ran towards the train. Heading back to the suitcase, she lifted the lid and chucked their luggage back inside. The zip must have worked loose. She'd known it was a bit dodgy but had assumed it would at least get them to Helen's.

'What are we going to do? Hey, Grace?' Dragging the suitcase towards the bench, she tilted her head towards the lift. It would be just her luck that she'd left a trail of clothes all the way from the bus stop outside the station. Looking back towards the train humming at the side of the platform, she drummed her fingers against the wooden seat. What was she supposed to do? Run to catch the train, which would no doubt leave any second now, or go and collect the rest of their clothes?

She'd get the train. They couldn't afford to miss it. If they did, they'd miss Helen and Jenny wouldn't have a clue what she would be doing for the next few months. Clothes she could replace, not right now, but they could muddle through until the end of the month and she was able to take a paycheck.

Yes, they'd get the train.

'One minute.' Trying to block out Grace's now high-pitched screaming, she yanked the zip to the suitcase up. Pulling the band out of her hair, she looped it through the small hole in the pull of the zip, and stretching it, tied it to the strap. She shrugged, it wasn't perfect but it'd have to do until they got there.

'Come on, Grace. We're getting on the train now.' Standing up, she pushed forward towards the track.

'Blankie.' Grace's voice broke into a series of hiccups as she cried. Holding her hands up, she tried to grasp the hood of the buggy.

'Blankie. Drat, drat, drat.' The damn thing had been in the suitcase. She'd packed it in there worried that it would get lost on the train. She hadn't seen it as she'd shoved the recovered clothes back in though. Looking from the train to the lift, Jenny cursed under her breath and turned the buggy back on itself. If she didn't find Blankie, she could wave goodbye to any sleep for the foreseeable future.

'Blankie!'

'OK, OK. Let's go and find Blankie.' Striding towards the lift, she kept her eyes on the floor, searching for anything familiar looking.

'There, it is. There's Blankie.' Bending down, Jenny retrieved the pink, holey scrap of material from where it had somehow wrapped its way around the leg of a bench. Giving it a shake, she inspected it before wiping it over her top and passing it to Grace who immediately leaned her head against the back of the buggy and pushed her thumb in her mouth, clutching her precious Blankie between her index and middle finger. Taking a deep breath, Jenny tried to push the image of a million germs marching their way from the blanket to Grace's soft cheek. She'd give her a bath later anyway. A few germs were nothing compared to her screaming herself to sleep. It would be fine.

An earth-shattering rumble sounded from the platform below. Peering down over the side of the footbridge, she rolled her eyes as their train inched forward, picking up speed as it left the station until it was just a dot in the far distance.

Great.

* * *

Leaning her back against the cool of the wooden bench, Jenny closed her eyes, her face turned up to the summer sun beating down. She'd twisted the buggy to face the wall behind, the hood pulled as low as it could go, so at least Grace was shaded. She could already feel her arms tingling with the heat. She hadn't bothered slapping the sun cream on this morning. After all, they should have been on the train most of the day.

The whimsical ringtone from her mobile screeched through the silent, empty platform. Opening her eyes, she grappled around in the bottom of the buggy until her fingers closed around her mobile. The last thing she needed was for Grace to wake up and get bored now. 'Hello?'

'Jenny, Jen. How's the train ride going? Is Gracie enjoying it?'

'Helen? We missed the train. The damn suitcase came open spewing our clothes everywhere. Luckily some teenagers came to the rescue and helped me collect it all, but we've missed our train. Sorry.'

'Oh no, did you manage to get everything back?'

'I think so.'

'That's something then. When's the next one?'

'Half an hour.' Glancing across to the departure board, she rolled her eyes. 'Scrap that. It's been delayed. The next train's in an hour and forty-five minutes.'

'You're still going to get here in time though, aren't you?'

'In all honesty, I don't know. I hope so, but it will probably be quite tight now.' Leaning forward, she picked at a loose thread on the knee of her jeans. 'Sorry.'

'Hey, no need to apologise. It's not your fault.'

'No, but it's just typical of my life right now, isn't it?'

'You need to stop this. It's just a delay on the line, no doubt a couple of leaves got blown into the track or something. It has nothing to do with you and the way your life is turning out. It's not your fault. You need to give yourself a break and start believing things will turn around for you and they will.'

'Umm, I believe you.'

'Well, you should do. You moving down here and running this place is going to be great. You'll love it. I asked around and checked out some toddler groups and stuff for you too. There's loads on. Parent and Toddler groups, singing and signing groups, all that type of happy-clappy stuff you like. There's even a sandcastle building meet-up on a Friday! Can you imagine that? You can actually take your toddler to a sandcastle building lesson! I mean, whatever next?'

'Thank you for checking them out.'

'You're welcome. More than welcome.'

'So, are you all set then?'

'Yep. I think so. Well, there's no going back now, is there? So I've kind of got to be.'

'You'll have a great time out there.'

'I hope so. I'm really looking forward to it. I'm looking forward to catching up with that side of my family again. Although it's not really catching up, is it? Not after fifteen years! It'll be more like getting to know them all over again. I keep worrying that they'll not like me or we won't get on for some reason, and then I'll be stuck there for three months with almost complete strangers who I don't really want to spend any time with, let alone be staying in their house with them.'

'It'll be fine. You'll be fine. And it's not like you don't know them at all. You've been skyping for ages.'

'I know, but it's not the same, is it? What if they don't really want me staying with them? What if they just feel like they should have me?'

'Now *you're* worrying over nothing. They wouldn't have offered if they didn't want you staying at theirs. Weren't *they* the ones who said you should go over to visit in the first place?'

'Yes.'

'There you go then.'

'I know. I know. I'm just being silly, aren't I?'

'Yes, you are. It'll be an adventure.'

'I hope so. It's just such a long way. I mean, I never thought for a million years that I'd be swanning over to the other side of the world to go and stay with people I hardly know and work out on their ranch.'

'It'll be amazing. You've always wanted to go to Australia and now you not only get to do that but you get to work with horses too. You'll be in your element! Stop worrying and enjoy it.'

'You're right. I will. I've just got a few hours to kill. It's the waiting around that's making me doubt myself. I wish you were here already.'

'I'm sorry.'

'No, no, don't be. I'll be OK.'

'Why don't you go for a stroll along the beach or something? Try to keep your mind off it?'

'Umm, I might do. Although I'm not sure what shift Nick is volunteering on.'

'Won't he be at work?'

'No, he takes Monday's off because he usually covers one day over the weekend.'

'Can't you just go for a walk in the other direction? You don't have to go past the lifeboat station if you don't want to, surely? Plus, if there hasn't been a call-out he'd still be at home, wouldn't he? I thought they only went out if there was a call-out?'

'Umm sometimes, but sometimes they hang around the station or patrol the beaches in case they're needed. Especially during the summer season. I can't wait to not have to try to avoid him any more.'

'I think this time away will do you good. Hopefully, you can just put him out of your head and then when you get back you won't have to worry about running into him or not because you won't care any more.'

'Hopefully. It's been so difficult these past few months. It takes all my strength just to forget about him, and then when I do manage to think of something else or go on a date with another guy, he just pops up, right there in front of me.'

'It must be really difficult living so close to him.'

'It is. It really is. Anyway, enough about me. How's your love life going? It's got to be better than mine, surely?'

'My love life? What's that?' Jenny swallowed. 'No, I'm really not interested in getting involved with anyone anytime soon, thank you very much. Grace keeps me busy. I don't need any distractions.'

'You're still hoping Anthony will want to get back together, aren't you?'

Twisting the loose thread around her index finger. Jenny pulled. It wasn't budging. 'No, he's happy with this Annie. I'm just dreading when Grace has to meet her...'

'I'm sorry, Jenny.'

'Hey, don't feel sorry for me. Me and Anthony weren't getting on for a long time and at least he left before he started seeing her. He's decent enough not to have an affair.'

Helen took a sharp intake of breath. 'It wasn't long before he got together with her though, was it? Do you think they knew each other before?'

'I've no doubt that they did, but at least he didn't start seeing her behind my back. I'm certain of that.' Jenny shrugged. She'd believed Anthony when he'd said he hadn't had an affair with Annie. It still hurt, hurt like hell, that he preferred Annie over her, but at least he had been honest. 'No, I really just want to focus on Grace while she's so young. Men can wait.'

'Good on you.'

Looking towards the empty train track and back down again, Jenny rolled her eyes. Why was everyone so pitying? Why couldn't they believe that she was actually happy being on her own? 'Anyway, are you OK leaving me out a list of instructions in case we do miss each other later?'

'Yep, already done. Besides, Ashley will be here so she can show you the ropes.'

'Thanks.'

'Right, I'd better get going. Customers.'

'OK. Hopefully, I'll see you later.'

'Oh yes, sorry, before I go, you haven't forgotten about Smudge, have you?'

'Smudge? Helen's cat, of course. She'd have to write a reminder on her phone to feed him. 'Smudge? No, of course I haven't. Grace can't wait to meet him.

'Yes. Great. See you later.'

'Bye.' Lowering her mobile to her lap, Jenny rolled it around in her hands. She'd really wanted to, needed to, catch up with Helen before she flew off. How was she supposed to figure out how to run The Seaside Ice Cream Parlour from a list of hastily written notes? Helen had built the parlour up from the ground. It was her business baby. What if Jenny ran it out of business? Anything could happen. She'd barely had any retail experience, unless you

counted the job she'd got in the local newsagents when she was
sixteen which had lasted all of six weeks. What if she wasn't cut
out to make and serve ice cream all day? And the accounts, she'd
have to do the accounts. What was she getting herself into?

'Shhh.' Pushing the buggy slightly forwards and backwards,
she shushed Grace as she began to stir. She was doing it for her.
She'd taken the leap for Grace. The other parents at Toddler
Group had begun asking about their living arrangements. She'd
needed somewhere to feel settled again.

Leaning her elbows on her knees, Jenny held her head in her
hands. She'd tried. Ever since Anthony had left, she'd tried to get a
job, tried to raise enough money for the rent, but she'd failed.
She'd failed them both. They'd had to leave their rented apart-
ment when she couldn't pay the rent, and so for the last five
months they'd lived in a total of seven different places. Her mum
had done her best to try to get Jenny's dad to agree for them to
move in with them, but he'd always believed children should stand
on their own two feet and had obviously preferred to see his
daughter and granddaughter sofa surf for months on end than
offer them the spare room.

It wasn't as though she wasn't qualified; she was. She'd been to
university. She'd got herself a nurse's qualification. She'd had a job
right up until she'd been thirty-seven weeks pregnant. She'd even
planned on returning to work after maternity leave but Anthony
had felt she should stay at home with Grace. And it had been
lovely being a full-time mum, it really had, but now here she was,
out of work for three years and not a job in sight.

Taking a deep breath, she rolled her shoulders back trying to
relieve some tension. It would be great living by the sea. It really
would, and she was so so grateful to Helen for giving them this
opportunity, but she was still petrified. There were so many doubts
whirring around in her mind. What if she couldn't cope being

miles away from everyone she knew? What if she struggled to balance running the parlour and motherhood? What if she just wasn't as business-minded as Helen and made the wrong business choices?

Anything and everything could go wrong. She looked across at Grace, she was now sleeping peacefully with her Blankie grasped to her cheek. There was so much that could go right too. So much. It was Grace that mattered. Nothing else. Jenny would cope being away from her family and friends, as long as she still had Grace with her.

Things would be fine. They had to be.

'Look, can you see it, Gracie? Can you see our new home?' Turning and dragging the suitcase down the short flight of steps from the bus, Jenny set it down on the pavement next to the buggy. 'Are you getting back in, or do you want to walk the rest of the way?'

'Walk.'

'OK. Hold on to the buggy then.' Looking both ways, they crossed the road. The Seaside Ice Cream Parlour stood proudly on the corner of the street lined with greasy spoon cafes, tiny shops stuffed full of holiday trinkets, and a collection of chip shops all vying for the tourists' attention. Its pink and white canopy flapped gently up and down in the warm breeze blowing inland from the seafront opposite. 'Look, over there is the sea. Shall we go and explore later?'

'Sea.'

'Yes, the sea.' Pushing the front door to the parlour open, she gently guided Grace inside before pushing the buggy in and yanking the suitcase up the step. The sweet and creamy aroma of ice cream hit her nostrils as the door swung shut behind them.

'Jenny! You're here!' Helen appeared from a doorway behind the counter, her arms outstretched.

'Helen. I'm so glad we made it before you left.' Allowing herself to be pulled into a hug, she watched as Grace stood still, her eyes transfixed on the tall, flamboyant lady hugging her mum.

'Me too! Only just though. My taxi will be here any minute.'

Stepping out of Helen's embrace, Jenny looked around. She didn't remember the brightly painted yellow and white walls or the typically British seaside blue plastic chairs and tables. 'You've done a lot to it since I was last here.'

'You can say that again! It wasn't easy, mind you, not painting over that dull purple colour. Do you remember it? It was awful, wasn't it?'

'It wasn't bright and cheerful like this, that's for sure. It looks great now. Really great. Just how an ice cream parlour should look.'

'Thanks. I think the makeover's really helped to get the customers in. And offering them somewhere to sit has too. It's made us different from the other hundred ice cream shops crowding the seafront.'

'It's great.'

'Right, I've written everything in here.' Helen held up a navy notebook. 'It's got everything from the recipes for the ice creams, although they are in the recipe book out the back in the kitchen as well, to instructions on how to keep the accounts and the details and prices for the parties.'

'Parties?'

'Yes, I started them a couple of months ago. Nothing special, just traditional party games, designing and making their own ice cream flavours and serving a bit of party food. That's all. They seem to be going down well, though. We've actually got one booked in for tomorrow. For a three-year-old actually, so you might be able to make some little friends for Grace.'

'A party? Tomorrow?'

'Yes, but don't look so worried, Ashley will be here anyway. She'll have it all under control. I've asked her to show you the ropes too.'

'Right, OK. Brilliant.'

'Oh, that'll be my taxi. I'd better get going. You'll be great. Use anything left in the cupboards, fridge and freezer. Basically, use this as your home now, OK?'

'Yes, will do. Thanks.' Jenny shook her head. 'You have a wonderful time in Australia. Don't worry about a thing here.'

'I won't. Oh, don't forget to feed Smudge. Bye! Bye, Gracie.'

And that was it. They were alone. Left standing in the middle of The Seaside Ice Cream Parlour without a clue how to run the place.

'Careful, Grace. Don't touch those, you'll have the whole display down.' Rushing across, she gently prised Grace's fingers from a bottle of ice cream sauce.

'I want eats.'

'Yep, me too, Gracie. Me too.' Slowly turning around, she took in the brilliant white counter positioned at the back of the parlour. The barstools drawn up underneath made her think of some old TV programme. To the left of the till an array of bottles of sauces and jars of toppings covered half the counter before it gave way to the long freezer which seemed to house a million different ice cream flavours. And she was supposed to make these ice creams? All of them? In the small kitchen out the back? What had she got herself into?

'Eats.'

'Come on then. Let's go and get something to eat.' Taking Grace by the hand, she led her out of the parlour, the buggy and suitcase still standing in the middle of the black and white tiled floor could wait for them. She could unpack when they got back. 'When we get back we'd best remember to feed Smudge.'

'Smudge.'

'Yes, Smudge, Helen's kitty. You'll like him.'

* * *

'These are yummy, aren't they? Do you want another one?' Holding Grace's cardboard cone of chips towards her, Jenny shrugged her shoulders as she was ignored. Grace preferring to draw a mismatch of circles and lines in the damp sand rather than eat the food she had so desperately needed only a few minutes before.

Letting the salt from the chips dissolve in her mouth, she inhaled the warm sea air. Her mum always said it was good for the lungs and maybe it was. It would make sense, wouldn't it? Being blown across thousands of miles of ocean must purify it somehow. Jenny shrugged, it certainly wasn't laced with exhaust fumes and hadn't been regurgitated by millions of other people's lungs before hitting hers, not like the air hiding in the London smog. This definitely smelt cleaner.

Hopefully Ashley would get into work early tomorrow. Yes, she probably would. She'd want to show willing to her new boss, she'd want to get things in order tomorrow so the transition between management could be seamless.

Management. It sounded so surreal. She was now managing the parlour. That's what Helen had said when she'd first asked if Jenny would look after the place for her. She'd asked if Jenny would consider managing the parlour for a few months. Jenny tried to ignore the gnawing feeling of apprehension rising from the pit of her stomach. She'd be fine. She used to save people's lives when she worked in Accident and Emergency. She could make sure a little ice cream parlour turned over a profit. She could, couldn't she?

Shaking her head, she picked up a shell next to her and pushed herself to standing. 'Grace, look what I've found. A pretty seashell. Shall we see if we can find any more?'

'Shell's pretty.' Peering at the small shell in Jenny's hand, Grace's eyes widened as she picked it up and clasped it in her fist. 'Look, more.'

'Yes, let's look for more shells.' Following Grace as she zig-zagged along the beach, Jenny held her chip cone as it was filled with seashells along with the odd pebble or two.

Soon Grace's attention was pulled towards the sea, the delicate waves lolling inland. Inching closer and closer, Grace stood watching as the white horses foamed towards her.

'Here, let's take our shoes off and go paddling.' Laying the chip cones on the sand, Jenny smiled as a brave seagull swooped down to help itself to Grace's unwanted chips. Turning, she helped Grace take her shoes off before slipping her own trainers off.

'Sea.'

'Hold my hand then and we can go paddling.' Grasping Grace's small podgy hand in hers, Jenny walked them into the shallow waves. Grinning, she listened to Grace giggle as the warm water tickled at her feet. She probably didn't remember them coming down last year with Anthony. She'd have only been two.

3

'No, that's fine. It can't be helped.' Swallowing the bile rising to her throat, Jenny kept her voice steady. Replacing the phone in the holder, she turned and leaned against the counter. Ashley was poorly. She wasn't coming in. Jenny would have to open up, serve customers, and prepare and implement a party. All on her first-ever day of ever doing anything like this. On her own.

'Mummy.'

'One minute.' Looking down at Grace's auburn curls, Jenny unhooked Grace's fingers from their grasp on her top. She needed to think. It was a quarter to nine now. The parlour was supposed to open at nine. She had fifteen minutes to work out what she was supposed to do. Fifteen minutes to learn a career Helen had been working on for the past five years.

'Mummy.'

'Grace, what's the matter? Mummy's busy at the moment.'

'Me toys.'

'Toys. Right, yes. I'll get you some.' That was the other thing, how was she supposed to keep a close eye on Grace whilst she was the only one running the parlour?

She'd get a heap of toys for her, that's what she'd do. Hopefully, that would entice Grace to stay behind the counter, and if it didn't she'd just have to bribe her to be strapped into the buggy. It wouldn't matter for a few minutes here and there if they got busy. That would be the safest option.

* * *

'Right, Grace, that's the door opened. Let's see when we get our first customer, shall we?' Leading her back behind the counter, Jenny settled her with her colouring book and some crayons before turning back to Helen's navy notebook. Flicking back to the pages detailing the parties, she read through the instructions again, deciphering Helen's cursive scroll was a little easier the second time around. In theory, it should be quite straightforward, the toddler parties only lasted an hour and a half, in which time they had some simple party games, ate party food and then had the opportunity to create their own ice cream with a mixture of ice cream flavours, sauces and toppings. Helen had left all the party food already prepared so all Jenny had to do was carry out the actual party.

She tapped her foot against the tiled floor. It sounded easy enough. Maybe she should just ring and check a few details with Helen, though? Picking up the phone, she stared at it. No, no. She could do this. It wouldn't be fair to call her over this, not something she should be able to work out for herself. She checked the clock on the wall, Helen would still be on the plane. She wouldn't be able to ring her, anyway.

The tinkle of the small bell above the door rang through the parlour, making her jump.

'Morning.' Smiling, Jenny closed the notebook and watched as a woman led a toddler towards the display of ice cream. 'How can I help you?'

'Hi. Sorry, we won't be a minute.' Bending down, the woman picked up a small boy and pointed to the various ice creams.

'That's OK. Just let me know when you've chosen.' Placing the notebook on the small shelf on the back wall, Jenny looked down at Grace, who was miraculously playing quietly with her doll.

'Can we have a small scoop of bubble-gum ice cream, please? In a cone?'

'Yes, of course.' Taking the ice cream scoop, Jenny loaded the cone with a mound of bright blue ice cream. 'Can I get you anything else? Sprinkles?'

'No, just that. Thanks.'

'OK.' Twisting behind her, Jenny checked the price on the display board. 'That will be £1.50 then, please?' She swapped the ice cream with the five-pound note the woman held in her free hand. 'Thank you.'

'Here you go, Max.' Lowering Max to the floor, the woman straightened, waiting for her change.

'Sorry, I won't be a moment.' Pressing the button on the till, Jenny swallowed. Why wasn't it opening? She'd followed Helen's instructions, it should be opening. Checking the wires leading into it, she rang the ice cream through the till again. 'Sorry, it's the first time I've used it. It should be opening by now.'

'Don't worry.' The woman took a serviette from the counter and bending down, she wiped a blob of blue ice cream from her son's nose.

Turning back to the shelf, Jenny grabbed the notebook, flicked through the pages, and scanned through the instructions Helen had left on how to work the till. She'd done everything right. She'd pressed the correct buttons in the correct order. Repeating the steps again, Jenny told herself it had to work this time. Nope. Nothing. The drawer still wouldn't budge open. If she had the coins in her own purse she'd use that, but she'd used the last of her change to buy their chips last night.

The tinkle of the bell above the door penetrated the uncomfortable silence. That's all she needed, another customer. She'd have to close, or else tell anyone who came in that she couldn't take cash today. There was a card machine, people would just have to pay by card. 'Look, I'm sorry. Here have this one on the house.' Passing the five-pound note back to the woman, she smiled.

'If you're sure? Thank you.'

'She won't like that.'

'I'm sorry?' Tilting her head, Jenny looked across at the man who had just come in.

'Helen. She wouldn't want you to give away her profits.' Lowering himself on a stool at the counter, the new customer wiped his hand across his chin, his skin rasping against the dark stubble.

'Well, I wouldn't have to if I could work out how to open this thing. Helen would understand and, besides, it's my call to make for the next few months, anyway.' Feeling the heat rise from her chest to her face, Jenny pursed her lips and glared at him. Who did he think he was? Coming in here and telling her what Helen would or wouldn't want her doing? Helen certainly wouldn't begrudge giving a little boy a £1.50 ice cream for free.

'I'm just saying,' Mr Stubble retorted.

'Yes, well. Anyway, what can I get you?'

'I'll have a tub with a scoop of berry and meringue surprise and a scoop of cookie dough and vanilla please?'

'Right.' Picking up the ice cream scoop, she ladled the ice creams into a small tub before placing it carefully on the counter in front of him. 'That will be three pounds then, please?'

'OK.' Standing up, he rummaged in the back pocket of his

jeans and took out a debit card, laying it on the counter before counting out precisely three pounds in a mixture of fifty pence and ten pence pieces. 'You don't mind the change, I take it?'

'Not at all.' Sighing, she counted out the coins.

'Do you need any help?' Sitting back on the stool, he took a spoonful of ice cream, letting it melt in his mouth before pointing the spoon at the till.

'I'm fine, thank you.' He was going to sit there until he finished it, wasn't he? Looking towards the door, she willed someone else to come in. Anything to distract him from the fact that she hadn't attempted to put the money in the till yet.

'Can I have a receipt when you're ready, please?'

Was he being serious? Who asked for a receipt for an ice cream? What was he going to do with it? Put it through the accounts wherever he worked? Claim the tax back on it? 'Of course.'

'Thank you.'

Taking a deep breath, she punched the buttons on the till and waited for the drawer to open. Nothing.

'Are you sure you don't need any help?'

'I'm fine.' Clenching her teeth together, she tried again. He was doing this on purpose.

'Look, if you just...'

'I said, I was fine.' Glaring at him, she shook her head. She shouldn't have snapped at him. However infuriating he was, he was still a customer. 'Sorry, it's my first day.'

'I know. Helen said you were coming.'

'She did? You know Helen?'

'There's a knack to it, you just need to...' Leaning across the counter, he tapped the corner of the till. 'Like that, see?'

Jumping back, she narrowly missed tripping over Grace's colouring book. 'Thank you.'

'You're most welcome.'

'Mummy, eats.'

'OK, do you want another breadstick?' Taking a breadstick from the box on the shelf behind her, Jenny passed it to Grace. 'Ta.'

'You've got a child behind there?' Standing up from the stool, he peered over the counter.

'Yes, my daughter.' What business was it of his anyway?

'Right.' Shaking his head, he sat back down.

Narrowing her eyes, she turned away. Maybe if she made herself look busy, he'd get the hint and leave. Kneeling down, she looked through the cupboards until she found a shelf labelled 'Party'. Yellow plates, bowls, and mugs were organised into neat piles. Taking the pile of plates out, she placed them on the back counter under the shelf and began counting them out. Eight children were coming to the party. Would she need plates and bowls for the adults? Would they be expecting to eat too? No, she was sure they wouldn't. Whenever she'd been to a party with Grace, the adults didn't have food prepared for them, they usually just ate the leftovers. Yes, that's what they'd do.

'You've got a party this morning?'

Replacing the spare plates and bowls, she stood up. 'Yes.'

'I hope you've got enough sauce. Kids always use way too much sauce.'

'You've got children?'

'No, not me. I have a niece though. I sometimes bring her in here.'

'Oh, right. That's nice then.'

'Yes, she likes it.'

Jenny nodded.

'Right, that's me done. Good luck with your party.' Twisting around, he slipped off the stool. Holding his hand up as he swung the door open, he waved as he disappeared onto the street.

Shaking her head, Jenny chucked his small cardboard tub into the recycling bin. 'I guess we were bound to have at least one awkward customer today, hey, Gracie?'

* * *

Standing in the middle of the room, Jenny looked around. She'd arranged the tables into one long line, small chairs tucked under and party hats placed on top of the plates. The parcel for pass-the-parcel and a bag of small treats were on the counter and nursery rhymes played in the background. Yes, everything was prepared. They just needed the birthday girl and her guests to arrive now and they could begin.

'Grace, come here, poppet.' Kneeling down, Jenny held Grace's small hands in hers. 'Now, do you remember I told you some other children are coming here for a party?'

Grace nodded, her tiny bunches flicking up and down with the movement of her head.

'Well, I need you to be a super good girl and play behind the counter, OK? And if you are super good we can have our own ice cream party after they've gone, OK?'

Grace nodded again, before running back behind the counter to the dolls scattered on the floor. Jenny shook her head, trying to force the image of Mr Stubble and his disapproving looks out of her mind. It wasn't ideal; she knew that. It was probably against some rule or something too, but what other choice did she have? Hopefully, Ashley would be back in tomorrow and things would be easier.

Peering over the counter, she watched as Grace hurtled one of her small dolls across the tiled floor, within seconds the other one raced to rescue her, flying Superman-style before coming to a painful landing. She still seemed so young, too young to go to nursery, but Jenny supposed she'd have to send her. Life here wouldn't be sustainable if she didn't get some form of childcare.

'Shall we go and have a look at some nurseries when Ashley is feeling better?'

'Yay.' Standing up, Grace jumped up and down, her small feet pounding against the floor.

'That's right.' Jenny smiled. It was amazing how enthusiastic Grace could be over something that she had no idea about. Did she even know what a nursery was? She certainly didn't realise that she'd be left there, Jenny was sure of that. After three solid years of always having her mum at home with her, or being with her dad, it would certainly be a shock being left in a complete stranger's care.

'Is it party time, Mummy?' Grace looked up at Jenny.

'Almost, but remember you need to be super good, don't you?'

Nodding, Grace's hazel eyes sparkled.

'Oh, look, I think this must be the birthday girl coming now.' Shaking out her arms, Jenny plastered a grin on her face and held the door open as a little girl ran towards the parlour, shortly followed by her parents. 'Morning, you must be the birthday princess, is that right?'

A small girl dressed in a pale pink glittery T-shirt teamed with a bright pink tutu style skirt was ushered through the door pulling a large foil unicorn balloon which bounced across the doorframe behind her.

'Hi, I'm Sasha, Peony's mum. I don't think we've met. I booked this party whilst Helen was here.' A tall lady with a bleached blonde bob stuck her hand out before introducing her husband, Dave.

'Nice to meet you both.' Taking Sasha's hand in hers, Jenny smiled before turning to Peony. 'So, are you all ready for your party?'

Peony nodded, slipped her hand from her mother's grasp and ran towards the counter, promptly sticking her hands on the glass of the ice cream display.

'Mind your sticky fingers, Peony.'

'Don't worry, she's fine. Is that the cake? Do you want me to take that? I can display it on the small table at the side if you like?' Indicating the large cardboard box Dave was carrying, Jenny stepped forward.

'Thank you.'

Turning her back, Jenny gently opened the box and lifted out the large unicorn head cake decorated in more edible glitter than she had ever seen on one cake. She pushed it towards the back of the table, hopefully it would be out of the reach of small children there. 'It's beautiful.'

'It should be, it cost enough.'

'These things do, don't they?'

'Not usually as much as Sasha likes to pay.' Dave laughed and walked across to join Peony who was still transfixed by the abundance of ice cream.

'I thought we could play some party games when everybody gets here and then do the food, ice cream and finish off with the cake, if that's all right with you?'

'Sounds perfect.'

'Who's that?' Peony pointed towards the end of the counter.

Turning her head, Jenny laughed. 'That's my little girl, Grace. Grace, say hello to Peony.'

'Hello.'

'Sorry, we only arrived yesterday so I haven't had the chance to sort childcare out yet and then the lady who works here too rang in sick so, unfortunately, I've got this little rascal in tow.' Jenny shifted on her feet. She knew it looked completely unprofessional having Grace here, especially when Sasha and Dave had booked the parlour out for Peony's party.

'We've all been there. Try having to take your screaming baby into work in an accountancy firm when the nanny has rung in sick at the last minute. Now, that wasn't fun.' Sasha shook her head.

'Still, I know how unprofessional it looks.'

'Honestly, don't worry. Are you going to join in with Peony's party, Grace?'

'Oh no, she'll be fine.'

'Honestly, it's fine. It seems silly her having to watch other children have fun when she can make some new little friends.'

'Thank you. I'm sure she'd love to.' Holding her hand out, she waved Grace across to her. 'What do you say, Gracie?'

'Thank you.' Clasping Jenny's hand, Grace hid behind her before running across to Peony.

'Right, it looks as though your friends are coming, Peony. Shall we go and welcome them?' Taking Peony's hand, Jenny led her towards the door to greet her friends.

* * *

Wiping her forehead, she looked around at the group of expectant children standing in front of her. She'd just about depleted her bank of go-to party games. They'd enjoyed pass-the-parcel, pin-the-tail-on-the-donkey and had worn themselves out after a few rounds of musical statues and musical bumps, although she was sure the lure of a sweet as a prize had kept the energy up. She looked around at the parents who were all clustered around the counter sipping mugs of tea and coffee. She still had ten minutes to fill if she were to keep to the party schedule Helen had outlined in the notebook.

'What game's next?' One of Peony's little friends, Molly pulled at Jenny's T-shirt.

'Let me have a think.' What could they play? She couldn't think of any more party games. Why hadn't Helen written a list of games that should be provided for the parties? If she'd done that, Jenny could have just followed the plan knowing that what she was doing was right. Taking the hairband out of her hair, she shook her head before tying it back up into a messy bun. There must be another game that a group of nine three- and four-year-olds would enjoy, surely?

'Mummy, more games.'

Looking down at Grace, Jenny watched as she jumped up and down, holding hands with another child. She really did need to find a nursery or playgroup around here. That was it! At Toddler Group, the organisers always initiated a short time of nursery rhymes for the children to sing. They always enjoyed it. Lowering her voice and bending down to their level, Jenny ushered the children towards her. 'OK, we're going to sing some nursery rhymes now. Who knows "Dingle, Dangle Scarecrow"?'

'Me! Me! Me!' Peony ran towards the middle of the group, hastily diving to the floor and closing her eyes.

'Brilliant. Right, everyone, copy Peony then. Lay down and close your eyes. Here we go. While all the cows were sleeping...'

Scooping Grace's limp body from the chair, Jenny carried her to the buggy. It was already half-past two, well past Grace's nap time, but she'd been so excited after the party she'd refused to settle. Jenny shrugged, she assumed there would be an influx of customers after school pick-up so that would no doubt wake Grace up, that along with a nice play on the beach and she was sure she'd drop at bedtime anyway.

Stroking Grace's cheek, she gently tucked a strand of loose hair behind her ear. Grace had loved the interaction with the other children at the party, and the other mums had given Jenny a list of recommended nurseries and playgroups, so she'd ring to arrange some visits if Ashley was back in work tomorrow.

Jenny straightened her back and went back behind the counter. Drumming her fingers against the counter, she looked around. There wasn't anything to be done. She'd tidied up after the party and refilled the cones and bowls. She supposed she should relish the quiet lull before it got busy again. No doubt, when the schools broke up for the summer holidays next week, she'd be craving some quiet time.

The sharp ringtone of her mobile interrupted the silence and Jenny grabbed it from the back shelf before it woke Grace. 'Hello?'

'Jenny? It's me, Anthony.'

Drat, she should have looked at the display and checked who was calling before she'd picked up. 'Anthony. Hi.'

'I just rang to speak to Grace.'

'She's just gone down for her nap. I can ring you back later though, if you're free?'

'You got there safely, then?' The sarcasm in his voice leeched through the mobile.

'Yes, sorry I completely forgot I'd said I'd let you know when we got here. Sorry, the train was delayed and when we finally got here, I was just busy with Grace.' She bit down on her bottom lip, there was no way she'd admit to him that she'd missed their train because of the suitcase incident. He didn't need any more reasons to think she was a total failure.

'Right.'

'So, shall I ring you later so you can speak to her?'

'Yes, please do.'

'OK, I'll speak...'

'You do know how upset my parents are, don't you? My mum didn't get a wink of sleep last night.'

'Sorry to hear that.' Rolling her eyes, Jenny realigned the bottles of water on the counter, smoothing her finger against a promotional sticker telling prospective customers that the bottles only cost 99p. As if Gwen hadn't had a wink of sleep because her granddaughter had moved away. Yes, she doted on her when she saw her and basically cared for her when Anthony had her, but she'd never been one for going out of her way to visit or see her.

'I'm upset too. I can't believe you've gone through with it.'

'Gone through with it? I've not moved her to a different country, we're only a couple of hours away by car.'

'It doesn't feel like that.'

'Well, it is. It's not far. You know that. We used to come down every once in a while before Grace was born. And we came last year. You must remember that?' OK, they had probably only visited Helen twice, maybe three times in the eight years she and Anthony had been together, but he knew where the ice cream parlour was. For goodness' sake, he travelled enough with work anyway, driving a couple of hours to see his daughter shouldn't be that much of an issue for him.

'It certainly feels far. You wouldn't like it if I had her and moved so far away.'

Jenny took a deep breath. 'You only see her a couple of times a month, anyway. You can still do that.'

'Annie thinks I should have taken you to court to stop you going.'

Flaring her nostrils, Jenny picked at the sticker. How dare she? It was none of her business; she wasn't Grace's mum. Plus, things probably wouldn't even last between her and Anthony, anyway. He'd jumped straight into bed with her as soon as Jenny and Anthony's relationship had broken down. Annie was probably just a rebound distraction. Jenny nodded. Yes, that was probably what she was. Shaking her head, she forced the niggling voice in her head back in its box. Despite the overwhelming evidence that Anthony had been seeing Annie behind Jenny's back for months before they had decided their relationship wasn't working any more, she couldn't bring herself to think that of him. No, for all his faults, Anthony wasn't a cheat. 'Well, good job it's not up to Annie, isn't it?'

'Maybe I should have. Maybe I should have stopped you taking her.'

'Seriously? You'd rather your own daughter was still sleeping on someone else's living room floor every night? You'd really have preferred us to have carried on sofa surfing rather than have taken this opportunity? Here, we have a flat, a whole flat, to ourselves and we can finally settle.'

'Yes, well, you should never have put her in that situation either.'

'Me?' Jamming her elbows on the counter, she placed her chin in her free hand. 'You know exactly why we were sofa surfing. You can't place the blame for that on me alone.'

'You should have tried harder to find a place to rent. There are loads of places around here up for rent.'

'Not to rent to a single mum with no income, there isn't. You know how it works, and you know the estate agents wouldn't touch me.'

'You could have held out for a council house.'

'For how long? When I applied when we had to move out of our place, they told me the average wait was two years, at least.'

'You could have declared yourself homeless.'

'And ended up in one of those B&Bs? No chance. You know the one the council uses in the centre of town opposite the pub? You must have heard the horror stories?'

'I'm sure it wouldn't have been all that bad.'

'No, I'm sure it wouldn't have been, not for you anyway.'

'There's no need to be like that with me. Grace is my daughter too. I wouldn't want to put her in any danger either. Stop making out as though I don't care.'

'I'm not. I'm just saying you know what it was like for me, and you know I was in no position to turn down Helen's offer of running this place.' Drawing a breath, Jenny grabbed a cloth and made her way around the counter. Scrubbing the sticky finger marks from the glass on the front of the ice cream display, she waited for his response. It may have been a mutual decision for them to walk away from the relationship, but it had been Anthony who had made it impossible for them to be together. It had been him who had stayed out every night 'working late' or 'catching up with old friends'. He, who hadn't shown any interest in helping her with Grace. At all. And she knew that she had been the one at home, that it had been her 'job' to care for Grace, but it had been Anthony who had insisted she'd given up work when Grace had been born. He had insisted they fall into the more traditional roles of breadwinner and homemaker.

What he had forgotten was that she hadn't had a break. Not once had he offered to put Grace to bed so she could go out and meet up with friends or taken her to the park on a Sunday morning so Jenny could have a much needed lie-in. No, the parenting had all been left to her, and if she was honest, she'd half expected contact to dwindle. She was sure the main reason he still wanted to see Grace was to impress Annie.

'It's been difficult for me too.'

'I know.' Jenny gritted her teeth. It must have been awful to move from their pokey two-bed flat straight into his parents' comparatively palatial four-bed detached house with a hot tub. Peering closely at the glass, she used her fingernail to pick off a bit of dirt. Maybe she was being too harsh. He loved Grace. She knew that. It was evident in the way he looked at her, and to be fair, since they'd split he had actually been spending time with her. She was sure Grace now had more quality daddy-daughter time than when they had been living together.

'Anyway, I've been thinking, I think that being as you're now living so far away it seems to make more sense for me to have her for a couple of nights every other week rather than just one night.'

'Two nights?'

'Yes. It makes more sense. Otherwise, I'm going to be spending most of the time I'm supposed to have her travelling. If I drive down and collect her on a Friday evening after work and bring her back on Sunday afternoon it will mean that I have the whole of Saturday to spend some proper time with her.'

'It just seems like a long time. She is only three still, remember.'

'I know, but I'm her dad. I appreciate it will be difficult for you to get used to, to begin with, but we've got to think what's best for Grace. It's not about us any more.'

Jenny coughed and reeled back, leaning against the table behind her. '*Not* about them any more.' Really? He really had the audacity to say that? When had it been about anything other than him during their relationship? It had never been about Jenny or about them spending time together as a couple, or even as a family. Was this even Anthony talking? Or had the perfect Annie or his parents put him up to this?

'Jenny?'

'I don't know. It just feels like a long time. She's never been away from me more than one night at a time. She's still not in a decent sleep routine and more disruption will only make it harder to get her into one.'

'Disruption? I'm her father. Not a "disruption".'

'That's not what I meant. You know what I meant.' Maybe she *had* meant he was a disruption, after all, he'd well and truly disrupted her life.

'I should hope not. You need to realise that we both have parental rights. If we can't agree, maybe we should go down the legal channels and get a court order for contact?'

He'd love that, wouldn't he? Making out that he was in the perfect position to care for Grace. Chucking the cloth on the counter, she dug her nails into the palm of her hand and steadied her breathing. 'It's fine. It makes sense you having her for two nights.'

'Thank you. I'll pick her up on Friday then.'

'This Friday?' Surely he'd want to give them some time to settle in first?

'Yes, I'll message you to let you know what time I'll get there. Bye.'

And he was gone. That was why he had rung then. To discuss, or more fittingly tell her, the new childcare arrangements, not to speak to Grace. That had just been a cover. Sitting down in a chair, she sank her head in her hands. How was she ever going to get through two nights, almost three days without Grace? How would Grace cope?

He knew exactly how to get his way. He always had. Threaten her with court and he had her agreeing to all sorts. Leaning back, she shook her head. It was better this way though, not going to court. If they did, Anthony would probably file for fifty-fifty custody or something. No, she'd just have to get used to Grace going there Friday to Sunday every other weekend. It wasn't what she'd signed up for when she'd had her though. She hadn't signed up to be a part-time parent. Her life wasn't supposed to have turned out like this.

4

'Thank you. Hope you have a nice rest of the day.' Waving, Jenny watched the little girl she'd just served hold her mum's hand as she walked out onto the street. 'Hey, you OK, Gracie?'

'Mummy, eats.' Standing up from the floor, a collection of crayons fell from her lap, scattering across the tiles.

'Yes. I'll get you some lunch now. Do you want some toast and cucumber?' Picking her up, Jenny placed her on her hip and carried her through to the kitchen behind the counter. She'd set up a little toaster and brought some food down from the flat so she could keep the parlour open as well as look after Grace.

'Mummy, I want apple.'

'An apple. Let's have a look.' Popping the bread in the toaster, she opened the cupboard where she'd stashed Grace's favourite foods. 'Yes, here you are. Here, let's sit you down at this table while I get your toast.' Placing Grace at the small table in the kitchen, she smiled. Although she'd been worried when Ashley had rung in sick again today, it had probably been good for her. Having to open up and run the shop on her own had been a huge learning curve, but she'd done it. She'd managed it herself.

'Hey, anyone around?'

Twisting her head, Jenny looked out towards the parlour. She hadn't heard anyone come in, she'd have to check the little bell above the door hadn't got caught on something. 'Here's your apple, Grace. Two minutes and I'll be back to butter your toast.'

'Anyone?'

'Coming.' The voice sounded familiar, a deep voice with an almost intangible northern twang. Placing her hand on Grace's shoulder as she hurried past, she went out, stopping still as soon as she saw him. It was him, Mr Stubble. Plastering a smile on her face, she wrung her hands on the tea towel and took her place behind the counter. 'Hello again, how can I help you today?'

'Today, I have this little one with me.' Leaning down, he picked up a blonde girl dressed in denim short dungarees and placed her on the stool next to him.

'Hello, what's your name then?'

'Darcy.' Kneeling up, Darcy leaned across the counter, pulling the jars of toppings towards her.

'That's a beautiful name.'

'Give those back to Jenny please, Darcy.' Gently prising Darcy's small fingers from the two jars she was clasping to her chest, he slid them back across the counter towards Jenny.

'Thank you.' Jenny twisted the lids back on, slightly tighter this time. How did he know her name? Instinctively, she looked down at her shirt, but she hadn't put a name badge on. She'd known she hadn't. She shook her head, she didn't even think Helen had brought her one. Why would she when Jenny was only managing the parlour for a few short months? She must have told him yesterday. Although she was sure she hadn't introduced herself to him. Why would she have when he had made her feel so uncomfortable?

'Right, what do you want then, Darcy? And remember, try not to order everything in sight as usual please.'

'One scoop strawberry, one scoop chocolate, one scoop fudge and lots and lots and lots of unicorn sprinkles.' Holding her arms out, she stretched them as wide as she could.

'OK, what the young lady asked for then, please? She's got her uncle wrapped right around her little finger, haven't you, Darcy?' He grinned at his niece.

'Coming right up.'

'Thanks. You wouldn't think a three-year-old would be able to eat that much, would you?'

'I'm almost four, not three, silly.' Holding four fingers up, Darcy giggled.

'Almost four-year-old, I stand corrected. Obviously, those few extra months make all the difference.'

Scooping the ice cream into a tub, Jenny smiled. Maybe she had got the wrong impression of him yesterday. Maybe he'd just been having a rubbish day. She shrugged, it was none of her business anyway. 'Here you go, Darcy. Do you want to do your own sprinkles?'

Nodding, Darcy lunged for the jar of sprinkles, almost knocking her tub of ice cream to the floor.

'Careful!' Steadying the tub, Mr Stubble licked a blob of ice cream from his finger. 'How are you coping with Ashley being off?'

Taking the jar of sprinkles back from Darcy, Jenny wiped the scattered sprinkles, mounding them in a heap at the edge of the counter before pushing them onto her hand. He knew Ashley then. And he knew she was off, so he must know her quite well. Jenny narrowed her eyes at him, looking him over. He wasn't seeing Ashley, was he? From what Helen had told her, Ashley was quite young. She'd always pictured her as being in her early twenties at the most. Whereas Mr Stubble was more her age. She shrugged, good on her. He was cute, she'd give him that. His stubble covered chin gave off just the right amount of 'I'm a bloke, I don't have time to shave everyday' vibe whilst defining his chin, and the way he kept running his hand absentmindedly through his black hair gave him an almost vulnerable air about him. 'Fine thanks.'

'Glad to hear it.'

'Mummy, toast.' Grace's small voice drifted through from the kitchen.

'Coming.' Shaking the excess sprinkles from her hand into the bin, Jenny glanced at the open doorway to the kitchen. She really would have to ring around some childcare providers tomorrow, whether Ashley was back or not. It wasn't fair on Grace to have her mum so distracted. Plus, she must be getting bored being holed up in the parlour all day. 'Excuse me, please.'

'Toast.'

'Yes, I'm getting it, Gracie.' Taking the now cooled toast from the toaster, Jenny buttered it and passed it to Grace. 'Shall we go for a walk on the beach again today?'

'Now?'

'No, not now, when we close the ice cream parlour.'

'Chips again.'

'Not chips. I'll make us some pasta before we go.' As tempted as she was to get chips for the second night in a row, she knew if she didn't get in the routine of making dinner as soon as the parlour closed, relying on takeaways could easily become a habit.

'Jenny, you've a customer.'

Closing her eyes momentarily, she tried to feel grateful to Mr Stubble for alerting her to a customer instead of feeling annoyed. 'Coming.'

'OK.'

'Hi, what can I get you today?' A small group of teenagers

dressed smartly in black blazers and white shirts leaned against the counter.

'A butterscotch cone, please?'

* * *

'Thank you.' Handing over change to the final teenager of the group, Jenny wiped the counter over.

'Mummy?'

'Gracie, come over here and do some more colouring.' Holding her hand out, she waited until Grace had ambled across the tiles before settling her at her drawing.

'Are you going to be able to manage?'

'Manage what?' Jenny looked across the counter at Mr Perfect Stubble. What was he suggesting? That she couldn't cope? She'd managed this far.

'The school run rush.'

'I'll manage. I did yesterday.' It was a shame he didn't have the good manners to keep his nose out of other people's business to go with his good looks.

'I wasn't suggesting you wouldn't.'

Jenny shook her head and turned away, focusing her attention on the small queue of customers, mostly teenagers, which had now formed. 'How can I help you?'

Twenty minutes later, most of the customers had dispersed. A few sat at the tables but most had just wanted an ice cream for the walk home from school. A few parents with young children trickled in, presumably having stopped off at the swing park and who wanted a snack before they commenced their journey home.

'How can I help you?' Smiling at the woman in front of her, Jenny tried to ignore Grace's pleas for attention which were growing increasingly louder.

'Can I have a strawberry cone and a vanilla one, please?'

'Of course. Sorry, one moment.' Bending down, Jenny gently pulled Grace's tiny fingers from her leg. 'Here, come and sit over here while I get this lady and her little boy an ice cream.'

'Sorry, is it a bad time?' Ruffling her son's blonde hair, the woman peered over the counter.

'No, no, it's fine.' Picking Grace up, Jenny sat her back down in front of her colouring book. 'Sorry, I'm new to the area and just need to sort childcare.'

'I see. Ladybirds Nursery is lovely and just a couple of streets away.'

'Is it? I think someone else recommended that one too actually.'

'That's where you went, wasn't it, Ellis?'

Ellis looked up at his mum and grinned. 'I liked it there. I didn't have to do proper work like at school, and they had an awesome climbing frame.'

'There you go. High praise indeed from the boy who normally only interacts with the characters on his tablet.'

Jenny laughed. 'I'll have to check it out. Now, it was a chocolate and a strawberry cone, wasn't it?'

'No, a vanilla and a strawberry, please?'

'Of course, sorry.' Rolling her eyes, she bent down again and lifted Grace up. 'Please, Gracie, just let me get the ice creams.'

'Here, pass her here. She can sit with me and Darcy.' Holding his arms out across the counter, Mr Stubble nodded to the empty stool next to them.

'Oh. No, it's fine, I can cope. Thank you though.'

'Mummy, let me sit.' Clapping her hands together, Grace looked from Mr Stubble to Jenny and back again.

'No, you'll be fine here.'

'Mummy, there.' Pointing at Mr Stubble, Grace's voice grew in volume.

'Come on. I'm only here. It's not as though I'm going to run off with a random child whilst I've got my niece with me, is it?'

Darcy looked up from her task of scraping the last of the sprinkles from the edge of her tub and laughed.

'No, I guess not.' Jenny looked across at Mr Stubble. Maybe they'd just got off on the wrong foot. Maybe he wasn't so bad after all. And he was right. Grace would only be sat on the other side of the counter from her. She'd be less than two feet away. She shook her head and looked down at Grace. 'You be super good then.'

'Come on.'

'Thank you.' Jenny passed Grace to him before washing her hands and returning to serving. 'Here you go, one vanilla and one strawberry ice cream. I've popped an extra scoop in there for the delay.'

'Thank you. What do you say, Ellis?'

'Thank you.'

'You're very welcome.' Watching Ellis follow his mum out onto the street, Jenny smiled. It felt good to be working again, good to be socialising, speaking to other adults instead of taking Grace to parks or out on her own all day trying to give whoever had let them stay on their sofa that night a bit of space. Turning to Grace, she held out her arms. 'Are you coming back to Mummy now?'

'No, me wants ice cream like Darcy.' Pointing to Darcy's empty tub, Grace kicked her little legs against the stool.

'She's fine here for the moment. You'll run the place out of business if you carry on giving ice cream away, though.'

'Umm... I think Helen would have minded more if I'd put them off coming in here again.' Why did he have to spoil things? He'd only just demonstrated that he had the capacity to be a decent human being, why disqualify himself from that title so soon? This was the second time he'd hinted at her not having the right to throw Helen's money away, why did he care so much? Narrowing her eyes at him, she turned her attention to the elderly couple who had just walked in. 'Good afternoon, how may I help you?'

'Afternoon, love. Could we just have a couple of coffees and two vanilla cones, please?'

'Yes, of course.' Turning her back, she placed a mug underneath the coffee maker, pressed the button and crossed her fingers. This was the first time anyone had ordered coffee, she should have had a trial run. Shrugging her shoulders, she pressed the button again.

'Hey.'

Twisting around, Jenny glanced at Mr Stubble and raised her eyebrows. What now?

Coughing he pointed to the back wall. 'You need to turn it on at the wall first.'

Following his finger, she looked towards the plug socket. Damn, she'd just assumed everything had been left on. Taking a deep breath, she hit the switch and mouthed, 'Thank you'. Keeping her back turned, she pressed the button again, hoping the familiar heat rising up her neck and across her cheeks would subside by the time the coffee machine had worked its magic.

'Oh, hello, Nick. I didn't see you there. How's life treating you?'

Nick? That was the name of Helen's ex, wasn't it? He had some nerve coming in here. Just because Helen was away, it didn't mean he would be welcome. Keeping her back turned, she swapped the coffee mugs and pressed the button again. She'd give him the two minutes it would take for the machine to spurt out the frothy liquid and then she'd tell him where to go.

'It's OK, thanks. I can't complain, the business is doing well and we've taken on more staff which gives me extra time to help Nancy out with Darcy.'

Picking up the two coffee mugs, Jenny turned around. Why was Mr Stubble answering in place of Nick? Unless the elderly couple had just got his name wrong?

'Can I have a milkshake now please, Uncle Nick?' Pushing her empty tub away from her, Darcy looked up at Mr Stubble.

'You're Nick?' Slamming the mugs onto the counter, she ignored the brown liquid as it rolled down the sides of the white ceramic, pooling around the base of the mugs. 'You didn't tell me you were Nick?'

'Oh, didn't I? I thought I'd introduced myself.' Shrugging his shoulders, he turned back to the elderly couple.

'No, you didn't. I'd have remembered if you had.' Holding her arms out, she leaned across the counter towards Grace. 'Pass her to me, please?'

'OK.' Squeezing his eyebrows together, his forehead scrunched, he picked up Grace. 'Are you all right?'

'Of course.' Was that why he'd been spending so long in here today and yesterday? Had he been making some point? Had he been hoping she'd report back to Helen that her ex had been hanging around and there was nothing she could do about it from Australia?

'No, Mummy.' Grace screeched as Nick passed her across the counter, her small legs flailing against Jenny's stomach as she clung on to her.

'Come on, I'll get you some ice cream. Stand there and choose which flavour you'd like.' Lowering Grace to the floor, she turned back towards the elderly couple, who were thankfully seemingly oblivious to how tense the atmosphere had become. 'I'm sorry, I'll wipe that right up.'

'It's no bother, love. I'll get a napkin. Here you go.' The elderly woman smiled as she slid the coins across the counter.

'Thank you.'

'See you soon, Nick, love. At least you don't have to worry about paying for Darcy's little treats in here.'

'See you later, Edna, Bill.' Nodding at the couple as they took their place at a table by the window, Nick looked back at Darcy. 'Which milkshake do you want then? The mint-choc-chip one as usual?'

'What did she mean?' Why had Edna implied, no, stated, that Nick wouldn't have to pay? Had he not told her that he and Helen were over? Or was it because of Ashley? Jenny shrugged, Ashley must have been giving free ice cream and drinks to him maybe. It wasn't right. It was completely wrong. If Ashley had been the reason Helen and Nick had split up, surely giving away food to Nick was just betraying her over and over again. Well, she'd soon put a stop to that. Helen didn't deserve her staff taking advantage of the fact that she was halfway around the world.

'What did who mean?'

Slumping her shoulders, Jenny rolled her eyes. He knew exactly what she meant. 'What did Edna over there mean about you not paying in here?'

Shifting in his seat, Nick straightened his back and clasped his hands in front of him. 'Helen hasn't told you, has she?'

'Told me what?' So Helen knew about him and Ashley? Even if she did, she wouldn't agree to Ashley giving out free stuff to him. She knew Helen, and Nick may have driven her away to Australia but she wouldn't want her business to be taken advantage of.

'I own half the place. I'm a silent partner.'

Jenny laughed and pursed her lips. 'Yeah, right.'

Looking away, Nick shook his head. 'She didn't tell you?'

'No, she didn't and do you know why? Because you aren't. She'd never have signed half her business across to you. I'm not some gullible idiot that you can walk all over just to get back or prove a point to her or something. Don't you think you can use me to play your games.' Picking up the coins Edna had left, she tapped them against the counter.

'Woah!' Holding his hands up, palms facing Jenny, Nick stood up. 'I don't know what she's been saying to you and I'm sorry she hasn't been upfront with you before you came down here to look after the business, but there's no need to get like that. It's down to Helen what she tells people. Although I have to be honest, I did expect her to have told you. After all, it does affect things.'

Turning her back away from Darcy and keeping her voice low, she glared at him. 'I don't know what sick game you're playing, but please leave.'

'I'll leave, but I'll be back tomorrow. I suggest you ring Helen and speak to her.' Standing up, he held his hand out for Darcy. 'Come on, Darcy, Mummy will be picking you up soon.'

'What about my milkshake?' Pouting, she jumped down from the stool.

'I'll get you a juice on the way home.'

Narrowing her eyes, Jenny watched as they left. Shaking her arms out, she took a deep breath. Who did he think he was? And why play games like that? They weren't in the school playground now. It was probably a good thing he and Helen hadn't worked out, Helen deserved better. Much better.

Looking behind her, she checked the clock. It was almost a quarter to five. What time would it be where Helen was? She should know this. Sydney would be well into the night, wouldn't it? She was sure she'd learnt that somewhere, probably from the past few New Year's Eves spending the evening in with Grace. But Helen was in Perth or somewhere, wasn't she?

Jenny shrugged. Helen never slept anyway. Plus, if she was asleep she'd probably have her mobile on silent and if she didn't, well, she should do. 'Right, come on, Grace. Let's shut the parlour up, we'll only be a few minutes early anyway and then I'll get that ice cream I promised you.'

Looking across at Grace, who had finally settled at a table to eat her ice cream, Jenny leaned against the counter and picked up her mobile. She was probably being daft telling Helen about Nick claiming things that weren't true, but she had a right to know. It was her business after all, and she'd want to know if her ex was trying to spread rumours about it.

'Hi, Jenny! How's it all going over in sunny old England?'

Jenny smiled, it was good to hear Helen's voice. It was good to hear a familiar voice full stop, if she was being honest. She missed the friends she'd left behind. She'd have to find some time to catch up with them at some point too. 'Hey, Helen. How's it going? What's it like? How are you settling in? What are they like?'

'It's great! So great! It's hot, very hot but apparently you get used to that after a few days and the house has air conditioning anyway so it's really nice inside. They've got a pool! A pool! I've spent most of my time since landing just lying by it.'

'And they're nice? Your cousins? How are you getting on with them?'

'They're awesome. They've made me feel so welcome. Anyway, enough about me, how's it going there? Has Ashley been showing you the ropes?'

Jenny tugged at a loose strand of hair. 'She's been off. She rang in sick yesterday and today, but it's been fine. The party yesterday went OK. Well, the parents were happy enough and the kids seemed to have fun.'

'Oh, I'm so sorry. I didn't realise Ashley had been off. Are you sure it's all been all right? How have you managed by yourself with Grace too?'

'It's been a juggling act but I've coped and Grace has been really good.' Jenny looked across at her where she still sat eating her ice cream. 'Most of the time anyway. I'll sort some childcare out as soon as Ashley's back anyway. I was going to ask you...' Jenny paused as Helen's muffled voice interrupted her.

'That's great. It sounds like you're doing great and thanks again for looking after everything. I'm really sorry but I'm going to have to rush off, we're off to the beach. I'll speak...'

'Hold on! Just one question and it's probably nothing, but Nick's been in and he been spreading rumours that he owns half the parlour. I tried to have a word but I don't think he listened.' Jenny ran her hand through her hair, she shouldn't have bothered Helen with grief from Nick. That's probably what he wanted anyway, to upset Helen whilst she was trying to get away from it all. 'I'm sorry, I shouldn't have said anything. I can handle it.'

'It's true.'

Jenny shook her head. Helen's voice had become barely a whisper. 'What did you say?'

'I said, it's true. Nick is telling you the truth. He owns fifty per cent of the parlour.'

'What? Really? How did he manage that? He didn't threaten you to sign it over or anything, did he?' She knew he wasn't a very nice person, she'd gathered that much from what Helen had said about there being another person involved in the break-up of their relationship, but to somehow coerce Helen into signing away half of the business she'd spent the last five years building? Well, that was another thing entirely.

'Nothing like that. I was in a bit of a fix financially and he helped out.'

'By buying half the business? You never said you were having money worries. I thought the business was doing really well?'

'It was. It is. No, it wasn't anything to do with the business. I just needed the money. Look, I'm sorry, I've really got to go now. I'll explain it all another time. Bye.'

Staring at the now silent mobile in her hand, Jenny closed her eyes. Why hadn't Helen told her about Nick owning half? Jenny had been downright horrible to him and accused him of lying. Opening her eyes, she stared at the promenade opposite as people wandered up and down looking out to the sea. Helen had said Nick had helped her out but that didn't mean he hadn't acted out of spite. Half the business must have been a heck of a lot of money; Helen wouldn't have been in that much money trouble, not if the accounts were anything to go by. He must have taken advantage and demanded the ridiculous share in the business.

Walking towards the windows, Jenny lowered the blinds. He'd be in again tomorrow, she was sure of that, and what was she supposed to say to him? She certainly wouldn't be apologising for not believing him, he may technically own half the business but she sure as hell didn't believe it had been as straight forward as that. Especially not if Ashley had been the reason him and Helen had split.

5

'Come on, Grace. Let's just pop these on and then we can get some fresh air before opening up.' Slipping Grace's bright pink boots onto her tiny feet, Jenny pulled her to standing.

'Go to beach.'

'Yes, that's right. We'll go and have a paddle and make a sandcastle, shall we?' Jenny glanced at the clock. They had half an hour before they were due to open up. That would give them plenty of time to have a wander along the beach. Hopefully, if she could wear Grace out now, she'd actually have her nap late morning instead of falling asleep in the afternoon and not being able to settle at bedtime.

Pulling the front door closed behind them, Jenny took a deep breath, letting the salty aroma fill her lungs. She'd never tire of this, of literally having the beach on their doorstep. She knew that Helen would be back in three months, but maybe Jenny could find a job down here and rent a small house or flat in the town. If they could put some roots down, they could make their home here. 'You like living by the sea, don't you, Gracie?'

'Yay!' Clapping her hands, Grace jumped up and down.

'Good. Here, take my hand and we'll cross the road.' As she felt Grace's small hand slip into hers, she stepped off the kerb.

'Mummy, me build sandcastle.'

'Yes, of course, sweetheart. We can build the biggest sandcastle ever, if you like?'

'The biggest one ever.'

'Oh, what's going on here?' As they stepped on to the promenade, they could see a group of people clustered at the water's edge. There must have been at least ten people, mostly dog walkers or runners, and the beach was filled with raised voices and an air of excitement.

'Sandcastle, Mummy.'

Jenny looked down at Grace as she tugged on her hand. 'One moment. Come here.' Swinging her up into her arms, Jenny walked towards the shoreline and looked out across the vast expanse of water. She couldn't see anything.

'Mummy?'

'Hold on, Gracie.' Looking across at the other people lining the shore, she tried to catch the eye of a woman holding two pink leads, her golden Labradors sniffing the sand. 'Excuse me please, is everything OK?'

Momentarily glancing at Jenny, the woman pointed into the far distance. 'You see that boat, right past the buoy, out there?'

'Just about.' Using her hand to shade her eyes, she looked towards where the woman was pointing. She could just about make out something. She wouldn't have been able to tell it was a boat though.

'They sent a flare up a few of minutes ago, and Stan, here,' the woman nudged the man standing next to her, holding the leads of two more Labradors. 'He rang the coastguard. If you keep watching you'll see our boys coming out from the estuary in a moment.'

'Oh no, I hope everyone's all right.'

'Ah, they will be. Our team of lifeboat volunteers do a grand job. The coastguards will have already sent them out, no doubt.' Stan looked across at Jenny and stuck his hand out. 'You're new here, aren't you? I haven't seen you about on our walks. I'm Stan and this here is my better half, Christine.'

'Good to meet you, Stan, and you too, Christine. Yes, we're new. We've only been here a couple of days. I'm looking after the ice cream parlour over there for my friend.'

'For Helen? Oh, you must be Jenny then, and you my little sweetie must be Gina, is that right?'

'Grace.' Jenny lifted Grace's small body further up on her hip. 'Say hello, Grace.'

Grace waved before turning and burying her face in Jenny's T-shirt.

'Hello, Grace. What a beautiful name for a beautiful little girl.' Stan patted Grace on the head before turning back to look out to sea. 'Here they come. I knew they wouldn't be long.'

A hushed silence fell through the group as the unmistakable orange of a lifeboat flashed across the ocean, white clouds of water following it as it sped towards the boat in the distance.

'Look, Gracie, can you see the lifeboat going out to rescue the people?'

Grace turned her head and eyed Stan before deeming him safe and twisting around in Jenny's arms to get a better view of the rescue.

'If we walk up towards the estuary we'll be able to see them tow the boat in.' Turning, Stan pointed further up towards the estuary.

'It always gives me goose bumps, thinking of those brave men and women who are willing to risk their lives for others.' Christine, wiped her eyes with a tissue.

'It sure does, love. It sure does.'

Following the group, Jenny walked alongside Stan and Christine as they made their way back up the beach to the promenade and along to the estuary.

'Look, Gracie, stand and hold on here and you'll be able to see the lifeboat towing the other boat.' Lowering Grace to the floor, Jenny patted the metal railing in front of her. Straightening up, Jenny kept her hand on Grace's shoulder and leaned forward to get a better view.

'Here they come.' Patting Grace's head again, Stan pointed towards the mouth of the estuary.

The orange of the lifeboat bobbed up and down in the near distance, tugging a small fishing boat behind them. Squinting against the low morning sun, Jenny could just make out the crew, one woman and three men by the looks of it. As they neared, the small crowd which had grown in size cheered.

Blinking back tears, Jenny swallowed hard and bent down to Grace. 'These people have just rescued the people on the boat they're towing. Shall we clap them?' The crew members deserved all the praise they could get, rushing off into the sea to help complete strangers as they had done so.

'Yes, clap, Mummy, clap.' Jumping up and down, Grace clapped her podgy little hands together. 'Look, man.'

'Yes, three men and a lady who rescued the boat.'

'No, man. Ice cream man.'

'Ice cream man? What do you mean, Gracie?' Shading her eyes with her hand, Jenny squinted at the volunteers. Nick. That's who Grace meant. Nick was in the boat. He was a lifeboat crew member, of course. Breathing heavily out through her nose, Jenny quickly averted her eyes. 'Right, we'd best get on. Nice to meet you, Christine and Stan.'

'Nice to meet you too, love. We'll probably see you in a bit. Might treat ourselves to an ice cream for the way home.'

'OK, great. See you soon then.' Holding out her hand, she waited until she felt the warmth from Grace's hand in hers before turning back to the parlour. 'Come on, Gracie. Let's go and open up.'

'Go beach, Mummy.'

'Not now, we went to have a look at the lifeboats instead. We need to get back and open the parlour now, sweetheart. Maybe we can go for a walk on the beach this evening.'

'Beach, Mummy, beach.' Tugging her hand free, Grace ran towards the beach.

'No, Grace.' Grabbing her hand before she stepped into the road, Jenny pointed to a shop a few doors from the parlour. 'Look, Gracie, that shop sells buckets and spades. If you're a good girl today do you want Mummy to get you a bucket and spade so we can build proper sandcastles?'

'Yes, sandcastles. We can build them big and big and big.' Stretching her hands out as wide as she could, Grace tipped her head back and grinned at her mum, all thoughts of running towards the beach gone.

'Yes, we'll make super tall sandcastles, shall we? Bigger than the biggest one ever.' Standing still, Jenny tilted her head to get a better view of the parlour's large front window a few doors up. That was strange, she was sure she hadn't opened the blinds before they'd gone out and yet they were pulled right up and the light was on. Scrunching her forehead, she frowned. The A-frame pavement sign depicting a collection of their most popular ice creams stood proudly outside in its usual spot. She was certain she'd taken it in last night. Yes, she had.

She remembered because Grace had been screaming for her bedtime milk and she'd had to run out to drag it inside because she'd forgotten to when she'd closed up. 'Come on, Grace. Let's hurry up a bit.'

'Look, Mummy, me run.' Tearing away from Jenny's hand again, she ran ahead, almost immediately tripping over a dip in the pavement, falling on her knees and screaming out in pain.

'Oh, sweetheart. Let's have a look at your knees.' Bending down, Jenny sat Grace up and held her leg.

'No, hurts.' Cupping her knees with her hands, Grace sniffed as tears ran in streams down her cheeks.

'It's OK, I'll be gentle. Just let Mummy see.' Gently lifting Grace's tiny hands, she peered at her knees. 'Hey, it's all right, Gracie. They're just grazed. Come here and we'll get back and clean them up.' Holding out her hands for her, Jenny waited until Grace had wiped her cheeks with the palms of her hands before lifting her onto her hip.

'It hurts.' Burying her face in Jenny's T-shirt, Jenny could feel the wetness from fresh tears soak through the thin material.

'I know, sweetheart. I'll pop some magic spray on them and they'll feel as good as new, OK?' Walking the last few steps to the parlour, she could see someone was definitely inside, and more than that, whoever it was seemed to be in the process of opening up. As she neared the front door, it swung open.

'Morning! Are you coming in for some ice cream?' A young girl, if she was twenty Jenny would be surprised, held the door open for them.

'Oh, hello. You must be Ashley?'

'Yes, that's right.' Grinning, Ashley pulled her long dark hair over her left shoulder.

'Hi, I'm Jenny, and this is my daughter, Grace.'

'Jenny! So nice to meet you. Sorry, I assumed you were still upstairs in the flat or something. I hope you don't mind me opening up? I mean, I can close it up again if you're not ready?'

'No, no, that's great you've opened up. Thank you. We went for a walk to the beach and got a bit distracted.'

'Oh, by that rescue mission? Did you see the lifeboat, Grace?' Touching Grace's cheek, Ashley smiled. 'It always makes me think I should join up or do something. I mean, it's great working here and making people smile by serving them ice cream, but I think it would be cool to make a difference to someone's life. You know, by saving their lives or something. Don't you think?'

'Yes, it would. Well, I guess there's nothing stopping you from volunteering.' Jenny shifted Grace to her other hip.

'I might do. I'd need to train, though. I mean, I can swim, but not to the level you need to as a volunteer.'

'Well, at least you've got something to work towards.' It must be nice to be part of a team volunteering, especially volunteering on the lifeboats or something equally as life-risking. They must trust each other explicitly. Although after feeling such a burden on all her friends for the past few months, it would just be nice to feel part of any group and be seen as an equal rather than being pitied or treated as a charity case. Jenny shook her head, she was being unfair to her friends, they probably didn't really view her like that. It was more likely her own feelings of failing as a mother, failing to provide for her daughter that made her feel that way. In a couple of weeks, once they'd settled into life here, she'd invite some of them up. Yes, they could stay over at the flat. She was sure Helen wouldn't mind, and it would be a chance to try to repay them a little for putting her and Grace up and helping them when she was most in need of their support.

'Anyway, ignore my ramblings. I'll pick Nick's brains when he comes in later.' Pushing the doorstop into position with her foot, Ashley turned towards the counter.

'You know Nick then?' Popping Grace up on the counter, Jenny searched in her bag for the antiseptic spray she kept handy and sprayed her knees clean.

'Ouch, Mummy.'

'That's my brave girl. Now, shall we get you a strawberry and banana smoothie?'

'I'll get her one. Quite fancy one myself, how about you?'

'Umm, yes why not? That'd be great, thanks.'

'No worries.' Ducking into the small kitchen, Ashley came back out with a bag of frozen fruit. 'Course I know Nick. He's part of the furniture here now.'

'Right, of course.' She'd just have to wait until he came in, which knowing him wouldn't be a long enough wait. She couldn't very well ask Ashley if she had jumped into the spot of girlfriend with him as soon as he'd finished with her boss. No, she'd be able to tell when she saw them together.

'Hello again, love. Ouch, have you got a poorly?' The bell above the door tinkled, announcing Christine's arrival.

'Hi. Yes, she fell over on the way back.' Jenny lifted Grace down and led her around the back of the counter. 'Did they finish towing the boat in OK?'

'Yes, yes. Turns out they were a couple of holidaymakers in the boat. Apparently, they'd borrowed it from their uncle or someone whose holiday home they were staying in. Anyway, they didn't think to check how much fuel they had and ran out a few miles offshore.'

'At least everyone was all right then.'

'Yes, apart from a couple of very bruised egos I should think!'

'Definitely! What can I get you?'

'I'll have a fudge cone and I'll get Stan a vanilla, please?' Christine tilted her head towards Stan who was waiting outside with the dogs.

'No problem. So, have you lived around here long then?' Jenny washed her hands and picked out a cone.

'I've been here forty or so years, but Stan was born and bred here.'

'I can see why he's never left.'

'I know, and take that as a warning to you, once you come and experience life here with the seaside on your doorstep and the beautiful countryside surrounding the town, it's a struggle to leave.'

Jenny smiled and placed the fudge cone in the holder. 'It is beautiful around here.'

'It sure is. Us locals are quite welcoming too. I hope you've met enough of us to realise that?'

'I've met a few.' Placing the vanilla cone next to the other one, Jenny looked out towards the promenade opposite, most of the locals had been nice enough. There had only been one she wouldn't have described as welcoming, and unfortunately she was expecting him to pop back in at any moment.

'Good, good. Right, I'd better get this to Stan. See you soon. Bye, Ashley.'

'Bye.' Turning around, Ashley grinned and waved as Christine left.

'Smoothie. Mine. Strawberry and banana.' Grace tugged on Jenny's apron.

'Here it is, you little darling.' Bending down, Ashley gave Grace a small cup of smoothie before passing Jenny hers. 'I'm so sorry I missed your first couple of days.'

'It couldn't be helped. We managed, didn't we, Gracie? The party seemed to go well.'

'Awesome. I still can't believe Helen's jetted off halfway around the world.' Ashley whistled through her teeth. 'Have you spoken to her yet? She sent me a text saying she was having a great time but didn't go into any details.'

'I spoke to her briefly yesterday, but she was in a bit of a hurry. By the sounds of it, she's enjoying being over there though and she's getting on well with her cousins.'

'I'm so pleased for her, especially after all she's been through this year.' Dipping her head, Ashley sucked the thick pink liquid through her straw.

'Oh, you mean breaking up with Nick?' Jenny fixed her eyes on Ashley's face. Did Helen know it was Ashley who Nick had been seeing behind her back? If so, how come she was still working here? Jenny shook her head, maybe she'd got it all wrong. After all, Ashley was only young and Nick was more Jenny's own age, he was almost old enough to be her father. OK, maybe not quite, but he was still a lot older than her.

'More all the other stuff. Talk of the devil.' Ashley put her hand up to wave as Nick and a group of others came through the door. 'That's him now. And those people he's with are the rest of the volunteers from the lifeboat.' Grinning, Ashley clapped her hands. 'Well done, you guys! You're total heroes.'

'Hey, Ashley. It was just a couple of guys who ran out of fuel, so nothing too taxing.' Nodding at Jenny, Nick slipped onto one of the stools. 'Morning, Jenny.'

'Ah, I bet you were still heroes to them. They'd have been swept out into the sea by now if you hadn't towed them in. Jenny, you saw it, didn't you? You saw them tow them in.'

'I saw a bit of it, yes. Well done, everyone.'

'Here, let me introduce you. This is Gabi, David and Stephen.' Ashley indicated the other crew members who had gathered around the counter.

'Nice to meet you.' Smiling, Jenny shook their hands. 'What can I get everyone?'

'Usual? I'll bring them over.' Ashley nodded to the table by the window and waited until they'd strolled over before turning to Jenny. 'Gabi and Nick each usually have a strong coffee, David a berry smoothie and Stephen normally has an orange juice.'

'OK, I'll make a start on the coffees then. Do they usually have anything to eat?'

'Helen normally makes them a plate of toast after a call-out.'

'I don't think we've got any bread in.' She'd used the last of the loaf from the flat for Grace's lunch yesterday and she hadn't seen any in the downstairs kitchen.

'It's OK. Helen always keeps a loaf of wholemeal in the freezer in the bottom drawer. I'll pop this on and go and get it.' Tipping frozen berries into the smoothie mixer, she turned it on, its gentle whir quiet compared to the smoothie maker Jenny and Anthony used to own.

Pouring milk into a small milk jug, Jenny placed it on a tray. So Helen was still friendly with Nick then? She must be if she kept a loaf of bread in the freezer for him and the rest of the crew. Unless it was just a habit, a ritual after a rescue and he'd kept it up not caring about any ill feelings between them. Jenny drummed her fingers on the counter and watched him across the parlour. He was laughing and joking with the other crew members, he didn't look in the least bit uncomfortable after his announcement yesterday.

'Jenny, have you got those coffees?'

'Sorry?'

'The coffees? For Nick and Gabi?'

Shaking her head, Jenny turned back to the coffee machine and placed the mugs on the tray. 'Sorry, I was miles away.'

'He's quite nice, isn't he?'

'What? Who?'

'Well, let's be honest, any of them but I was thinking Nick in particular.' Ashley picked up the tray and made her way towards the window, calling over her shoulder. 'Don't worry, Helen knew exactly what I thought.'

Jenny frowned, she hadn't been thinking that at all. In fact, the thought hadn't even crossed her mind, not even when she hadn't known who he was. Grabbing the dishcloth, Jenny wiped the surface over, trying to distract herself from the fierce warmth flushing across her cheeks.

'Me toast too, Mummy.' Opening the cupboard door, Grace pulled out a plate.

'Careful.' Swooping over to her, Jenny grabbed the plate as it fell from Grace's hand. 'I'll get you some toast. Why don't you come and play with your dolls while I make it?' Placing the plate on the counter, Jenny took Grace's hand and led her to the small table at the side of the parlour, pulling her dolls from the shelf as she did so. 'Here you go.'

'Yay, dolls, Mummy. My dolls.'

'That's right, your dolls.' Hurrying back behind the counter, Jenny placed a slice of the frozen bread in the toaster. Ashley's laughter rang through the air. Looking across at the group, Jenny noticed that Ashley was perched on the table next to them, clutching the tray in her lap. So Helen had known that she'd had feelings for Nick. Maybe something had gone on then.

'Mummy, where my toast?'

Jerking her head away from Ashley, Jenny buttered the toast. She'd try to pop out later, take Grace into a couple of nurseries and see if any had spaces. It wasn't fair keeping her cooped up in here all day, every day. Any child would get bored and frustrated, least of all a three-year-old who was used to having her mum's undivided attention. It would be difficult for Jenny to see her being looked after by someone other than herself, but it would definitely be the best thing for Grace.

* * *

'See you guys.' Nick waved off Gabi, David and Stephen before taking a seat on a stool at the counter.

'Haven't you got to get off to work too?' Jenny looked up from the dishwasher.

'No, I'm on night shifts this week. Are you trying to get rid of me?'

'Not at all.' Jenny coughed.

'So you spoke to Helen then? She told you I wasn't making things up?'

Pulling at a strand of loose hair, Jenny pretended to check the signs in each tub of ice cream. 'She told me you were a shareholder, yes.'

Nick nodded.

Straightening her back, Jenny looked around. Where was Ashley?

'Everything OK?'

'Of course. I was just wondering where Ashley was.'

'She popped out to get some more milk I think. She did say.'

'Oh right.' Did she? She must have mentioned it when Grace was playing up. Looking across at her, Jenny frowned, she was engrossed in a game with her dolls. Why was it she was always good when Jenny needed the distraction but always begging for attention when Jenny was busy?

'Look, I realise you weren't aware I was a shareholder until you spoke to Helen, and I understand why you didn't just take my word for it. After all, I am a complete stranger to you, but I'm not here to make your life difficult.'

'No?' Looking at him, Jenny circled her shoulders. 'I mean, no, maybe you're not.'

'I'm not. I just wanted to see who was running the place while Helen was away.'

'Well, now you know.' Holding her arms out to her sides, she frowned. She could understand why he'd been hanging around and why he wanted to check her out. Especially being as Ashley had been away. Who wouldn't want to know who was running their business? But now, surely he could leave her, by now he knew who she was and that, yes, she was quite capable of running the place.

'I do.'

Shaking her head, Jenny glared at him. Why was he still here then?

'Hey, I'm back!' Coming through the door, holding two bottles of four pinters, Ashley bustled in. 'This should last us the rest of the day, but then one of us will have to pop to the wholesalers in the morning. Helen left you her membership card, right?'

'Umm, I'm not sure.' Drat, she hadn't even thought about going to the wholesalers. Standing on her tiptoes, she pulled down the notebook filled with instructions and scanned the handy contents page Helen had scribbled on the first page. Wholesalers, page 18. 'It's in the till.'

'Cool. I bet she's hidden it under the drawer inside then. I'm happy to pop there on my way in, if you like?'

'Yes, that'd be great, please? I haven't got a car so...'

'It's cool, I can go. The manager's quite fit, I'll have to think of a reason to talk to him.' Placing the milk on the counter, Ashley leaned her elbows next to the bottles. 'Umm, what could I have to talk to him about? I need a query.'

'Why don't you just ask him for a drink? You've been making excuses to speak to him for months now.' Shifting on his stool, Nick turned to look at her.

'Nooo, I can't do that!' Holding her hand over her chest in

mock horror, Ashley peered at the ice cream. 'We probably need to make a bit of ice cream tomorrow too. Helen left us some in the freezers but I think we'll definitely need some more mint-choc-chip and fudge for the weekend, at least.'

'OK, are the recipes in the notebook?' Jenny glanced at Nick. They clearly weren't together then, not the way he was encouraging Ashley to go out with that other guy.

'Yes, but I know them anyway. I'll show you.'

6

'You're not going to sleep in there, are you, Gracie?' Stopping and tipping the buggy back slightly, Jenny peered over the hood. 'Gracie, wake up, sweetie. It's not time for bed yet.'

'Me tired.' Reaching her small hands up, Grace pulled the hood down.

'Hey, are you trying to hide from me?' Laughing, Jenny walked around to the front of the buggy and bent down, stroking Grace's cheek. 'Gracie, let's get you home and get you some dinner and then you can go to sleep.' Standing up, Jenny carried on pushing the buggy, picking up the speed. If Grace slept now, she'd be awake by eight o'clock and then probably stay awake until twelve. A nap at this time of the evening really wasn't worth the five minutes of peace.

'Not hungry.'

'OK, how about we just have a bit of toast then?' Folding the hood back, Jenny ruffled Grace's hair. 'Did you enjoy the nursery?'

'Yes. When is me going again?'

Jenny smiled. They'd popped to the nursery in town and the Ladybird's Nursery that one of the customers had recommended, and it had wiped Grace out. Although they had been able to book an appointment to visit the nursery in the centre of town tomorrow, the staff at Ladybird's had been really welcoming and had invited them in. They'd then given them a tour and even let Grace play with the other children while they had discussed details. They opened at 8am with the last pick-up time being 6pm and they said they could be quite flexible with times, to begin with anyway, so that she could wean Grace in slowly. It was good they were open so long even if she didn't plan on putting Grace in there all day every day; it was good there was that option, and really useful they had the option of adding in extra one-off sessions if they had the space too. 'Shall we go on Monday and you can have a bit of time there without me so you can enjoy playing with your new friends?'

'Yay.'

'What did you like about it the best?' The bonus was it was only just around the corner, so they'd be no time wasted getting there and back either.

'The slide. The slide. I liked the slide. Me go on there Monday?'

'Yes, of course, you can. You can go on the slide on Monday and can you paint me a lovely picture too? Then we can put it up in the ice cream parlour, would you like that?'

'Yes, I paint you a butterfly.'

'Ooh, a butterfly would be lovely.' They were almost there now. If she could just keep Grace awake until they got back, she'd be able to get her to bed after her dinner. 'Are you looking forward to making lots of new friends to play with?'

'Yes, lots and lots and lots of friends.' Yawning, Grace stretched her arms upwards.

'Look, we're almost home now. Can you see the parlour?' Tipping the buggy back, she pushed it up the kerb.

'I see it.'

'Good. When we get in, I'll make you some nice cheesy pasta. Do you want some sweetcorn and peas too?'

'Umm.'

'Grace, do you want sweetcorn and peas with your pasta?' Jenny jogged the last two metres to the parlour door and pulled out her keys. 'Gracie, stay awake, sweetheart. We're here now.'

'Ashley?'

'Ashley's gone home now. We'll see her again in the morning.' Pushing the door open, Jenny pulled the buggy up the front step and into the dim parlour. Locking the door behind her, she unclipped Grace.

'Ice cream now, Mummy?' Sliding out of the buggy, Grace ran across to the ice cream cabinet, tapping on the glass.

'No, not now. We'll go upstairs to the flat and I'll get you your cheesy pasta.'

'No! Ice cream not pasta!' Stamping her feet, Grace looked over her shoulder at Jenny.

Locking the front door, Jenny took a deep breath and joined Grace at the counter. 'Come here.' Picking her up, Jenny climbed the stairs to the flat.

'No, Mummy, ice cream.' Kicking against her mum's legs, Grace squirmed in Jenny's grasp.

'Ooh look, let's see what's on TV. Do you want to watch the sparkly ponies?' Sitting down, Jenny twisted Grace around on her lap. 'Here they are.'

'I like the sparkly ponies.' Leaning her head back against Jenny's chest, Grace stuck her thumb in her mouth, all thoughts of ice cream abandoned.

'I know you do. Right, you sit down here and I'll go and get you your pasta.' Sliding her off onto the sofa, Jenny watched Grace curl up with her head on the arm before heading into the kitchen.

Turning the oven ring on, Jenny turned and leaned against the work surface and circled her shoulders. She was doing the right thing, putting Grace into nursery, wasn't she? Anthony had always made such a big deal of her staying at home with Grace until she was old enough to go to school, but things had changed and that wasn't possible any more. Plus, it would be good for Grace to mix with other children. She'd loved joining in the other day at the party, she'd revelled in the attention she had got from the other children. Jenny nodded, it would be good for her, and definitely much better than having to hang around downstairs while she worked all day.

The water bubbled over the rim of the saucepan. Mixing in the cheese, Jenny ladled the pasta, peas and sweetcorn into a bowl as she listened to the voices from the TV floating in from the living room. She couldn't hear Grace at all. Hopefully, she was just watching her programme and hadn't drifted off to sleep. Ten more minutes and it wouldn't matter if she went to sleep, but if she hadn't eaten anything there would be absolutely no chance of her sleeping through.

'Here you go, sweetie. Try to have a bit to eat.' Balancing the bowl on the arm of the sofa, Jenny sat down next to her and gave her the fork.

Sitting up, Grace rubbed her eyes and took the spoon.

'That's it. You eat up.' Pulling her legs up, Jenny settled back against the sofa cushions and watched Grace eat. Tomorrow evening Anthony would be picking her up for the weekend. Feeling a lump rise to her throat, Jenny swallowed and blinked back the tears threatening to spill. She'd not been away from Grace for a whole weekend. Not ever. She did understand Anthony's point of view, that it was a long way to travel, and it did make sense for him to hold on to her for that bit longer, but... Jenny shook her head, it didn't matter what she thought or how she felt about the whole thing. She knew she had to tread carefully because if he went to court he could easily walk away with fifty-fifty and she couldn't imagine how people coped only having their children for half the time. No, she had to keep him sweet. She had to let this happen, however much it hurt.

Sitting on the side of the bed, Jenny watched as Grace drifted to sleep. She yawned, she should probably go to bed herself even though it was still ridiculously early. She was sure the sea air made her more tired than usual. Although in reality it was probably the long working hours and the fact that even with being stuck in the parlour all the time, she was on her feet the majority of the day and then they had been taking an evening walk along the beach. She was definitely doing more exercise than before.

Lifting her legs up, she let her eyes close, she'd just have a five-minute nap before feeding Smudge and locking up. Just five minutes.

Twitching her eyes open, Jenny looked across at Grace. She was still asleep. Shaking the muzziness from her mind, she lifted herself up on her elbows. Something had woken her up. Maybe it had just been something she'd been dreaming about. All was quiet now.

Laying her head back down, she turned over.

Nope, there it was again. Jenny closed her eyes, it was probably a grisly baby being walked past on the promenade, probably in the hope that the sea air would send it to sleep. That's what it sounded like. Although it was so loud, it almost sounded as though the parent was holding the poor baby underneath their window. Yanking the pillow from under her head, she covered her ears.

It was no good. Sighing, she stood up and wiped her hand across her face. She could have done with a few more minutes.

The wailing continued, more frequently now with hardly a breath between each unearthly shriek. Maybe it wasn't a baby crying. Now she was fully awake it didn't sound right, not like she remembered Grace sounding even as a newborn, anyway. This noise was different. It might be a fox. Did foxes live near the beach? They probably did. Foxes lived anywhere there were easy pickings, didn't they? They'd probably get quite a lot of food from careless tourists, the beach was probably awash with leftover picnic food and dropped chips. They'd more than likely be quite happy here.

Taking the short steps towards the window, Jenny peered out. The bedroom window overlooked a small courtyard with parking spaces behind. They'd not been out there yet, hadn't needed to, not with the beach being across the road.

Holding her hand up, she shielded her eyes from the glare of the setting sun. She couldn't see anything, but it definitely sounded as though it was coming from the courtyard or just behind. Glancing back at Grace, Jenny checked she hadn't been disturbed by the noise and went downstairs.

The noise was louder outside, a mixture between a bloodcurdling screech and cry. It must be a fox. They were supposed to sound unearthly. Whatever it was, it sounded as though it was in pain. Ducking down, Jenny gently shifted the branches of the hedge in front of the back wall, peering into the shadowy space underneath.

'Smudge!' Curled up at the back next to the wall, Smudge was sat, his leg stuck out at a strange angle. What had happened? How had he done that? Kneeling onto the cool slabs, Jenny reached to the back of the gap, twigs and leaves scratching her arm. 'Come here.'

Dragging him out slowly, Smudge squealed in pain again. 'I'm sorry, buddy. I've got to get you out though.'

With the small cat lying on the slabs at her feet, Jenny could see his leg was more than likely broken and blood had dried around his nose. 'Have you been hit by a car, Smudge?'

Shrugging out of her cardigan, Jenny wrapped him up, careful not to touch the damaged leg. 'Come on. Let's get you some help.' Carrying him inside, she tugged a towel hanging next to the sink, let it drop to the floor and carefully laid him on it.

Taking her mobile out of her back pocket, Jenny quickly googled a local vet and ordered a taxi.

'Gracie, Gracie, wake up.' Lifting a still floppy Grace into her arms, Jenny kissed the top of her head.

'Sleepy, Mummy. Me sleepy.' Momentarily opening her eyes, Grace looked at her mum before burying her head in Jenny's T-shirt.

'I know, sweetheart, but Smudge is poorly and needs to go to the vet, so we're going to take him in a taxi. That will be exciting, won't it?' Gently lowering Grace onto the bottom step, Jenny slipped her tiny pink sandals on.

'Where's Smudge?' Looking around, Grace wiped sleepy dust from her eyes.

'He's having a little rest. We'll go and wait for the taxi in the parlour and then I'll go and get him, OK?'

* * *

'Thank you. Don't worry about the change.' Flinching, Jenny handed across the ten-pound note hoping a twenty pence tip would be enough. They'd only been in the taxi for less than five minutes and it had cost nine pounds eighty. She'd have to pay out again for the journey back to the flat, she just hoped they wouldn't be kept waiting too long and they could get a taxi back before the fares went up at eleven.

'This way, Gracie.' Holding Smudge in her arms so that his leg wasn't touching her, she nudged Grace towards the door, a luminous sign shone above the glass announcing that it was indeed a twenty-four hours veterinary practice. 'Keep walking.'

Getting to the door, Jenny carefully manoeuvred Smudge so he was balanced in one arm and pulled the door open, holding it with her foot so she could usher Grace in whilst returning her hand to Smudge. 'Quick, through you go.'

'Where are we, Mummy?' Looking back at her, Grace slowly inched through the doorway.

'We're at the vet's, aren't we? The nice vet is going to make Smudge all better, isn't she?' Jenny let the heavy door swing shut. At least she hoped they'd be able to make Smudge better, she was already dreading telling Helen. If she had to tell her they couldn't fix him... Jenny shook her head, she was being silly, he just had a broken leg. They'd be able to put a cast on it or something and he'd be just fine.

'Evening, are you the lady with Smudge? The little cat who may have broken his leg?' A young veterinary nurse bustled around the desk, holding her arms out towards them.

'Yes, that's right. I found him in the courtyard like this so I'm not really sure what happened.'

'I'll take him from here. Take a seat and I'll have the vet speak to you once he's got him settled.' Putting her hand on Jenny's shoulder, the veterinary nurse smiled reassuringly.

'Right. Thank you.' Nodding, Jenny carefully handed the small cat across to her, his light body stiller than it was before and his meows weaker. Without a backwards glance, the veterinary nurse disappeared through a door behind the desk leaving Jenny and Grace standing in the empty waiting room. 'Let's go and find a seat, Gracie.' Taking Grace's hand, Jenny led them towards a cluster of blue plastic chairs.

'Mummy, me tired.' Clambering onto the blue chair next to her mum, Grace sat back, her short legs barely reaching the edge of the chair.

'I know, Gracie. Come here.' Holding her arm out, Jenny waited until Grace had slid across the hard plastic and leaned into her side before cuddling her arm around her and kissing the top of her head. 'Try to get a bit more sleep while we wait, sweetie.'

'Night, Mummy.' Snuggling her head into Jenny's side, Grace closed her eyes.

'Night.' Stroking Grace's forehead until she had drifted off to sleep, Jenny leaned her head back against the stark white wall behind her. Please be OK, Smudge, please be OK. Should she ring Helen now? Or wait until she knew more? What if the worst happened, and she hadn't informed her? Jenny closed her eyes, there was nothing Helen could do, anyway. Not from Australia, she'd only worry. She'd ring when she'd spoken to the vet, at least then she'd have all the facts. Yes, that was what she'd do. She'd wait.

* * *

Opening her eyes, Jenny looked out of the window in front of her, the darkness frequently being punctuated by the bright headlights as cars swung around the corner. It seemed busy for this time of the night, especially for a relatively small town. Jenny sighed, she supposed it wasn't that late, people could still be travelling back from work if they'd worked a late shift.

Closing her eyes again, she shifted in the chair, the hard rim of plastic between her and Grace's chair digging into her thigh. He'd be OK. Smudge would be fine. Concentrating on the slight rise and fall of Grace's body, she tried to match her slow breathing.

* * *

Jolting awake, Jenny looked towards the door, another patient was being brought in. A dog, this time, being carried by its frantic owner.

'Please, please, someone help me?' Running towards the desk, the owner repeatedly dinged the small bell set on the side until the veterinary nurse emerged from the door behind.

Jenny couldn't hear what was being said, but the soothing voice of the veterinary nurse seemed to do the job and the small dog disappeared into the back rooms leaving the owner standing near the desk.

Glancing around and spotting Jenny, the owner smiled weakly. 'We've only had her three weeks. The kids will be devastated if something happens to her.'

'I'm sure she'll be fine.' Nodding, Jenny watched as the woman pulled her mobile from the handbag slung across her shoulder and disappeared outside.

Rubbing her eyes, Jenny focused on the wall clock to her left. They'd only been here half an hour. It felt a lot longer. Still, she had expected the veterinary nurse to keep them updated.

Closing her eyes again, she rested her head back against the cold wall behind her.

* * *

'Excuse me? Smudge's owner?'

Opening her eyes, Jenny nodded and slipped her arm from underneath Grace's head, gently laying her down on the chair before standing and approaching the desk.

'I'm sorry it's taken a while, but the vet has now stabilised Smudge and is ready to discuss the next steps.'

'So he's alive? He's all right?'

'He's stabilised. The vet will be able to discuss the details with you.'

'OK, OK. That's good he's stabilised, right? It means he's out of the woods.'

'If you'd like to come this way.' Holding the door open, the veterinary nurse waited for Jenny.

'My daughter. She's asleep.' Glancing back at Grace and then at the front door to the veterinary surgery, Jenny bit her bottom lip. She didn't want to wake her, not now, but she couldn't just leave her unattended in a strange place where anyone could come in.

'She'll be fine. I'll show you through and come out and sit with her.'

'OK, thank you.'

'If you just go to the end of the corridor and take the last door on the right, the vet will be with you shortly.'

Jenny nodded and walked through before the veterinary nurse closed the door and disappeared back to the waiting room to keep an eye on Grace.

Making her way down the short corridor, Jenny pushed the last door on the right open as directed and entered the small sterile room. Walking towards the black table which dominated the small space, she tapped her fingers against its surface. Grace would be fine. The veterinary nurse had said she'd sit with her, and it wasn't as though there was anyone else about. The woman who had disappeared outside on her phone hadn't returned, and if there were any other patients brought in, the veterinary nurse would bring Grace through to her. She'd be fine.

Circling her shoulders, she tried to relax. Smudge had been stabilised. That could only be a good sign. He'd be fine. The vet was taking his or her time though. She looked around. She was in the right room, wasn't she? The veterinary nurse had said the last door on the right, she was sure she had. Unless she'd said the first on the right? That would make more sense. It would definitely make more sense that the room closest to the waiting room was the room being used by the vet. She must have heard her wrong.

Turning on her heels, she took the few short strides to the door and turned the handle. She'd go and check.

'Evening. You must be Smudge's owner.'

Pausing, Jenny let go of the handle and slowly turned around. She knew that voice. She'd heard it before. Heard it a lot since moving down here. 'Nick.'

'Jenny?' Looking up from his clipboard, Nick looked at her.

Making her way back to the table, she stood opposite him. 'I didn't know you were a vet?'

Glancing down at his green scrubs, he looked back up at her. 'Well, I am.'

'Umm, I can see that.' Placing her hands palm down on the table in front of her, Jenny shook her head. 'How's Smudge doing?'

Clearing his throat, Nick shifted on his feet. 'I've managed to stabilise him. He was in a pretty bad way and will need an op on his leg.'

'It is broken then? Why does he need an operation? Can't you just put a cast on it and let it heal naturally?'

'Unfortunately, it's often not that easy with cats. If he'd come in straight after breaking it, that may have been an option but because it looks like he's been in this way for a couple of hours and has tried to walk on it, the bone has been displaced and will need to be repositioned.'

Looking down at her hands, Jenny picked at a bit of dried blood on her fingertip. She hadn't noticed it before. It must have come from Smudge. 'I brought him in as soon as I could, as soon as I heard him wailing in the courtyard. If I'd known earlier, I would have brought him in then.' She wiped her eyes dry, flicking her hair from behind her ears to cover her face. She hadn't meant to cause any harm to him. Had she made it worse when she'd picked him up? She probably had. And during the taxi ride. She should have rung the vets to come out.

'Sorry, that came out wrong. It's nothing you've done. It's just their nature. Cats are independent creatures. It looks as though he was more than likely hit by a car. He would have dragged himself home. He may have even jumped over the wall in the courtyard unless the gate was open.' Placing his hand on top of hers, he sighed. 'You haven't caused the complications.'

'It was closed. The gate was closed. He must have jumped over.' Taking her hand from under Nick's, she pinched the bridge of her nose. 'Will he be OK?'

'The next few hours are critical, but we've got him stabilised so the odds are in his favour. When he's got a bit of strength back, I'll operate and set the leg. He will likely need pins in there to give the leg the best chance of healing. If he can get through the operation, then we'll be on the home run.'

'What do you mean, if he can get through the operation?'

'Well, he's a small animal, the anaesthetic can be risky.'

'Right.'

'We'll do our best for him. We're an experienced team, we operate on small animals every day but I need you to be aware of the risks before you sign the consent form.'

'He's not mine.'

'I know. I assumed he was Helen's. I knew she'd got a cat, but she'd insisted on taking it to the vet in the next town. I'm assuming in order to avoid me. But, as acting guardian, the consent will need to come from you.'

Umm, I wonder why she wanted to avoid you. Jenny gritted her teeth. No doubt he'd been breathing down Helen's neck ever since he'd invested, just like he had Jenny's. No wonder Helen had decided to register Smudge at a different vet.

'Does she know?'

'No. I haven't rung her yet. I was waiting to find out how he was before I rang.'

'It might be a good idea to ring her now then and let her know what's happening.'

'Yes, of course.'

'I'll give you a few minutes. You can ring her from the phone here if you want.' Glancing at her, he turned to the door he had come through.

'Wait. No, I need to check on Grace. She's in the waiting area.'

'I'll go and check.' Indicating the phone next to the computer, Nick left the small room.

Drumming her fingers against the table, Jenny pushed back. She knew she had to call her. She knew Helen would want to know what had happened to Smudge. Looking around the stark space, Jenny made her way around the other side of the table and towards the phone. Picking it up, she held it against her ear, the dialling tone clouding her thoughts.

No, she couldn't do it. She couldn't ruin Helen's holiday. Not like this, and certainly not when it had barely begun. She'd meant to have been looking after Smudge. Helen had entrusted his care to Jenny. She shouldn't have let this happen.

Replacing the receiver, Jenny stared at the poster on the opposite wall. A photo of an owner grinning at her kitten stared back at her. Helen would want to know. She would. She loved Smudge. She hadn't stopped pinging photo messages to her when she'd first got him.

Setting her jaw, Jenny picked up the phone again and dialled Helen's number before she had a chance to change her mind.

'Hello?'

'Hi, Helen. It's me, Jenny.'

'Jenny! Hi. Sorry I didn't recognise the number. How's it all going? It must be really late there now. Is everything OK? Is Grace all right? Has anything happened to the parlour?'

'It's Smudge. I think he's been run over.'

'Oh no. He's been killed, hasn't he? He's only young. I should have kept him as an indoor cat, I knew I should have, but everyone kept telling me it was cruel and not to.'

'No, no. he's still alive. We're at the vets now. The vet thinks he's broken his leg.'

'Thank goodness for that. Just a broken leg? That's not so bad then. Does he need a cast? Of course, he will. But he'll be fine after a few weeks then, won't he? You really scared me for a moment back then. I thought that was it, I thought you'd rung to tell me he'd passed away, that you'd found him on the side of the road somewhere.'

Jenny closed her eyes. Helen had gone from being frantically upset to being quite calm about the whole thing in a matter of seconds. She had to tell her the risks. She couldn't just let Helen think everything was OK, that Smudge would just need a cast and then he'd be fine. She had to prepare her for the worst. 'Actually, it's a bit more complicated than that. He needs an operation and, apparently, the anaesthetic can be quite risky for cats.'

Silence.

'Helen? Are you still there?' Holding the phone away from her ear, Jenny checked the receiver, the lights were still flickering indicating it was still connected. Swallowing hard, she shifted on her feet. 'Helen?'

'Sorry. I'm still here.'

Helen's voice was quiet, too quiet. Ever since Jenny had known her it had been Helen who had been the one who had always been outgoing, confident and loud. She didn't recognise the wary, worried Helen who appeared to be on the other end of the line. 'I'm sure he'll be just fine. I mean, so many cats have operations every day, hundreds, thousands probably. The vet will do his best.'

'No, listen, I want you to take him to Nick. He works at the vets in town. For all his faults he's the only one I'd trust with Smudge's life. I should never have registered him at the other one. Please take him to Nick's.'

'I'm already here. I panicked and couldn't remember the name of the vets you usually take him to. I didn't realise Nick was a vet until tonight though.' Biting her bottom lip, Jenny picked up a pen from the desk.

'Thank you. Nick will look after him. I'm sure of that. Look, you'll ring me as soon as he gets out of the operating theatre, won't you? Whatever happens, you'll let me know?'

'Yes, of course, I will.'

'Thank you.'

Replacing the receiver, Jenny tapped the pen against the surface of the desk. Poor Helen. Being stuck thousands of miles away from Smudge tonight.

'All done? Look who's woken up.' Grace clung onto Nick's shoulder as he carried her through the doorway.

'Gracie, sweetheart. What are you doing awake?' Stepping forward, Jenny held her arms open, taking Grace from Nick. Sinking her nose into Grace's hair, she took a deep breath, the sweet smell of watermelon kids' shampoo and sleep filled her nostrils. 'Thank you. Yes, all done. I told Helen what had happened, and the risks involved in the surgery. She seemed pleased you were looking after him.'

'Well, what can I say? I'm a brilliant vet.' Looking down, he ran his hand through his hair.

'What happens now?'

'Now, we wait. We give him a few hours to get his strength back and to keep an eye on a couple of things and then we'll operate, probably in the early morning all being well.'

'What do you mean "keep an eye on things"? Is there something else that's wrong with him?'

'His blood pressure is lower than we'd hope. It could be a sign of an internal bleed somewhere but hopefully, it's just the shock of the accident. We just need to make sure we can get it under control before we operate.'

'But I thought you said he was stable?'

'He is in every other way and if I felt he needed the operation immediately, I'd be happy to operate. But as it is, we have a small window so I feel it's best to give him a little time and see if we can get his blood pressure up to give him the best chance we can.'

'Right. Sorry for all the questions.' Looking down at Grace's head, she kissed her sweat damp hair.

'It's completely understandable. Now, if you agree, I just need you to sign the consent form.' Placing a clipboard on the table, he pushed it across to Jenny.

'OK.' Picking the pen back up, she bent over the table, careful not to let Grace's sleepy body flop backwards, and signed her name. 'What about money? Do I pay you?'

'Not now, no. I'm assuming Helen has insurance?'

'Cat insurance? I have no idea.' Straightening her back, she placed her free hand behind Grace's head.

'I'm sure she will have. In which case, she'll need to give you the details so you can fill in a form. There'll be an excess but we can sort that out another time.' Picking up the clipboard, he opened the door into the corridor. 'I'll call you once he's through the operation.'

'Thank you.'

'You're welcome. Don't worry, he's in good hands.' Placing his hand on Jenny's shoulder, he spoke quietly, his eyes fixed on hers.

Nodding, Jenny smiled and lifted Grace up higher on her hip. 'Thank you.'

Pushing the heavy glass door open, Jenny stepped out into the cold night air. As the cold breeze whipped her cheeks, she finally felt the uncomfortable warmth drain from her face. Why did he make her feel this way? It wasn't the first time he'd caught her off-guard, been uncharacteristically kind. She shook her head; it was just an act. He was a professional; he had to be seen to be kind and, heck, he probably did care for the animals he treated. Just because he looked at her like that and touched her shoulder it didn't mean he was being anything but professional.

'Tired, Mummy.' Grace snuggled into the fold of her top.

'I know, sweetie. The taxi will be here in a minute and we'll be home and back in bed before you know it.' He wasn't kind, he had cheated on Helen. Kind people didn't cheat.

7

'Don't worry about him. Nick will take care of Smudge. Has he rung yet to tell you how the operation went?' Hanging her jacket up on the back of the kitchen door, Ashley joined Jenny at the counter.

'Not yet. Do you think that's a bad sign?' Rinsing the dishcloth under the tap, Jenny continued to scrub the raspberry milkshake syrup she'd split.

'No. No, I don't. If anything, it's a good sign. It means that he was stable enough to wait for the operation. Plus, if anything bad had happened he would have rang you straight away.'

'I guess you're right.' Jenny shook her head, she had so many thoughts whirring around she really couldn't focus.

'Is it today that Grace is going to her dad's?' Tying her stripy apron around her middle, Ashley began emptying the float into the till, the coins tinkling their way into the correct compartments.

'Yes. Anthony is picking her up after lunch. He's got the afternoon off work.' Swallowing hard, Jenny pinched the bridge of her nose. Had she packed Grace's pink sandals? She'd wear her canvas shoes in the car, but she might need her sandals when she got there. Had she packed them?

'You OK?' Pausing, Ashley looked across at her.

'Yes, I'm fine.' Shaking her head, she replaced the dishcloth on the side of the sink. 'I'm just going to put the sign out on the path, can you keep an eye on Grace, please?' She looked across at her daughter who was sat swinging her legs at the table by the window, munching on the last of her breakfast.

'Of course.'

'Thanks.' Dragging the heavy A-frame sign through the parlour, she poked her tongue out at Grace as she walked past.

Letting the door swing shut behind her, Jenny pulled the sign into position and straightened her back. Taking a deep breath, she let the salty air fill her lungs. It was warm already and the humidity was high. The parlour would be busy today. Circling her shoulders back, she tried to loosen her stiff muscles. She'd hardly slept a wink last night. Between worrying about Grace going to Anthony's for the weekend and Smudge, if she'd got three hours it would have been a miracle.

'Morning.'

'Morning.' Jenny smiled at the small group of joggers who passed her. They'd more than likely pop in on their way home. They had for the last three days, anyway. They'd order two caramel milkshakes and one iced green tea. Jenny was sure whatever calories they burnt from their morning jog was replenished as soon as they got to the parlour, but never mind, it was none of her business and they were doing far more exercise than she had time to do these days so she couldn't really judge. She smiled, the green tea girl must feel smug.

Turning around, she went back inside and plastered a grin on her face. She would get through today, she'd have to get used to Anthony taking Grace for the weekend. She didn't have any choice.

What she could do though was to make this morning fun for her. 'Right, are you done with your breakfast, Gracie? Because I thought you could help Mummy and Ashley today. What do you think?'

'What me doing?' Pushing her bowl away from her, milk dribbled from the sides, pooling on the plastic tabletop.

'Let me see. How would you like to begin by making some new ice cream flavours for us?'

'Yes, Mummy. Yes. Lots of flavours.' Slipping from her chair, Grace followed Jenny behind the counter.

'Great. What will you need?' Taking bowls from the cupboard, Jenny scooped flavour after flavour of ice cream into each bowl.

'Sprinkles!' Jumping up and down, Grace clapped her hands, her tight curls dancing around her face.

'Sprinkles? Do you really think you'll need sprinkles?' Looking down at her, Jenny tried to keep her face serious. 'Umm, I guess you probably will. I bet you'll need fudge pieces, chocolate chips, and mini marshmallows too. Just in case, of course.'

'Yes, yes. Lots and lots and lots.'

'OK. Go and sit at the table nearest the counter then, and I'll bring them over.'

'Hurry, Mummy.'

'I will.' Jenny watched as Grace clambered onto the plastic chair before decanting the bowls from their tray onto the table in front of her. 'So here are all of the different flavours: bubble-gum, vanilla, mint-choc-chip, raspberry meringue, toffee popcorn and the rest. I'll just go and get you the toppings and some empty bowls and then you can start mixing.'

'Grace, don't forget to make me a special ice cream, please?' Ashley called over from behind the counter.

'OK, Ashley.' Turning her head, Grace grinned.

'Here you go. Here are the toppings and lots of empty bowls for you to mix it all up in. Can you make me one too, sweetie?'

'Yes, Mummy.' Biting down on her tongue, Grace began scooping small amounts of ice cream from one bowl into another.

'That should keep her occupied for a while at least.' Wiping her hands on her apron, Jenny made her way to the door and switched the sign to 'open'.

'It should do. Great idea! There's nothing better than lots of ice cream and permission to mix as many flavours as possible.' Laughing, Ashley turned the coffee machine on at the wall.

'I'll miss having her around when she starts nursery.' Tilting her head, Jenny watched as Grace licked the excess ice cream from her fingers.

'It will be weird. I've gotten used to having her here now. When is it she starts?'

'Monday. Just for the morning though. They suggested she goes every morning next week and see how she gets on before upping her hours.'

'That makes sense. I'm sure she'll enjoy it. You said she loved interacting with the other kids at the party, didn't you?'

'Yes, she did. I'm sure she'll be fine.' And she was, she was certain Grace would be just fine. It would be her, Jenny, who wouldn't be. Maybe she should have delayed starting her at nursery until Tuesday at least? Otherwise, she'd go straight from being at Anthony's all weekend, coming home for a night and then going back out to nursery. Filling up the cone holder, Jenny sighed, it was probably best to get Grace into her new routine as soon as possible. Best for Grace anyway.

'Here come our first customers.' Nodding towards the door, Ashley turned and began making the caramel milkshakes the joggers would likely order.

'Thank you. Enjoy the rest of your day.' Jenny placed the coins in the till and rung it shut, watching the perfect family of a mum, a dad and two small children exit the shop carrying their cones. Turning her attention to the elderly couple in front of her, she smiled. 'Morning, what can I get you today?'

'Just a couple of teas and two vanilla cones, please?'

'Coming right up.' Turning her back, Jenny pulled two cups from the shelf.

'You're busy today.'

'Nick! You made me jump!' Swivelling around, Jenny winced.

'Sorry.'

'How's Smudge? Did he get through the operation OK?'

'Yes, he's fine.' Twisting his head, he looked at the queue. 'I'll explain everything when you've got a minute, but he'll be fine.'

'That's great news. Thank you!' Turning back to the couple in front of her, Jenny loaded a tray with cups and saucers, a teapot and milk jug. 'I'll just get your cones.'

* * *

'That was crazy! Is it normal for us to get that busy?' Leaning against the back counter, Jenny yawned.

'Oh yes. That's nothing. You wait until the weekend. The schools finished for the holidays yesterday so we'll have all the tourists to contend with as well.' Laughing, Ashley took her apron off. 'Are you OK if I pop on my break? We should have a bit of a lull before the lunchtime rush now.'

'Yes, of course. You go.' Jenny checked Grace was still playing with the now melted ice cream and stepped towards Nick. 'Did the operation go as expected then? Is Smudge really going to be OK?'

'Yes, the operation was a success. I had to pin his leg because of the position of the break, but he'll make a full recovery.'

'Thank goodness for that. Will he have to have the pins taken out?'

'No, they'll stay in there for the rest of his life.'

Jenny shuddered.

'Don't look like that! That's what they're designed to do. It's perfectly normal. It'd be even worse if we had to open him up again and go digging around to take them out.'

'I guess so.' Jenny rubbed the back of her neck. 'When can I come to get him?'

'We'll give him a few days to recover and get him back on his feet before we discharge him, so probably early next week sometime, depending on how he's doing. Here, let me see that.' Slipping from the stool, he made his way behind the counter.

'What?'

'Your neck, you keep rubbing it. Have you strained it?'

'Do I? Yes, it does hurt. It's probably your fault. I turned around too quickly when you came in.' Holding her hand to the back of her neck, she winced. It did hurt.

'What can I say? I do tend to have that reaction from people.' Grinning, he put his hands on her shoulders and turned her around to face away from him.

'Haha. Very funny. You know what I meant. You made me jump. I didn't expect you to come in.'

'Come here. Let's see if we can sort it out.' Placing his hands on her shoulders, he gently massaged the back of her neck with his thumbs. 'Is that OK?'

Jenny closed her eyes, the warmth from his skin melting the pain in her muscles. It was more than OK. 'Much better thanks.' Stepping forward, she bit down on her bottom lip.

'Don't. Just give me time.' Gently pulling her back, he continued to massage the back of her neck.

Closing her eyes again, she held her breath, hoping he wouldn't notice the blush speeding across her face.

'There you go. How does that feel?' Letting his hands fall to his sides, he stepped back.

'Great. Much better. Really. Thank you.' Tightening her ponytail, she looked towards Grace again, who was still sat taste-testing her melted creations.

Nick looked down at his hands before holding them up and waving them at her. 'These hands aren't just for healing animals, you know!'

'Hey, I'm back!' Swinging the door open, Ashley walked in carrying a bundle of food in her hands. 'Got my lunch. Do you mind if I go and sit out in the courtyard? I need to work on my tan.' Pausing, she looked from Jenny to Nick and then back to Jenny. 'Sorry, did it get busy? Do you need me to have my break later?'

'No, no it's fine. Nick was just helping me out with something.'

'Oh, right.'

'All sorted now.' Coming out from behind the counter, Nick slipped back onto his stool.

'OK.' Ashley frowned before turning on her heels and heading out the back.

'Anyway, what can I get you?' Feeling the heat fade from her cheeks, she turned back towards Nick.

'I'll have a strong coffee and...' Twisting his head, he looked across at Grace. 'What have you got Grace?'

'Lots and lots of sprinkly stuff.'

'Oh. Sprinkly stuff sounds good. I'll treat myself to raspberry meringue ice cream with the sprinkly stuff Grace has, please?'

Jenny laughed. 'Your wish is my command. Though how you can justify it as treating yourself when you come in here every day, I don't know.'

'Hey, what are you trying to say?' Frowning, Nick looked down at his svelte stomach. 'No, I deserve a treat. I've been up all night if you didn't know. Rescuing poor little cats who have been run over.'

'Haha. Super strong coffee it is then. And, seriously, thank you for what you did for Smudge.'

'Stop with the thank yous already. You'll only complain when I turn into some arrogant idiot.'

Jenny tilted her head and grinned. 'I shan't ask if you're one already.'

'Oi!' Leaning across the counter, Nick grabbed the wet dish-cloth and sent it flying towards her.

'Hey!' Laughing, Jenny bent to pick it up from where it had landed at her feet and chucked it back at him. It landed with a heavy splash on the counter. 'I think you need to practice your throwing skills!'

'Look who's talking!' Laughing, Nick took a sip of his coffee.

'Can I play? My turn!' Running across from her table, Grace pulled herself on her tiptoes and clung onto the edge of the counter, her eyes barely level with the top.

'Aw, Gracie. We were being a bit naughty. We shouldn't be throwing things in the parlour. You tell Nick off for Mummy, won't you?' Placing her finger on Grace's nose, Jenny grinned.

'Naughty Nick. No throwing.' Turning, Grace wagged her finger at Nick, her small forehead creased in seriousness.

'I'm very sorry. I won't throw again.' Turning towards Jenny, he mouthed. 'How come I get all the blame?'

'He won't throw again, Mummy.'

'Good. Let's hope that's the last of it, please, Nick?'

'Of course. I promise. No throwing in the parlour.' He turned back towards Grace. 'Now, can I see what ice creams you've been making, please?'

'Yes. They're a bit melted and splashy now.'

'I bet they still taste nice though.' Leaving his coffee on the counter, Nick followed Grace back to her table.

* * *

'I dread to think what Saturday will bring if it's going to be busier than this!' Throwing the tea towel on the counter, Jenny looked around the parlour. Every table was full, even Grace had had to abandon her table so a group of teenagers could sit down.

'Don't worry, as long as we have coffee on tap, we'll get through it!' Ashley refilled the ice creams.

'We'll need lots of coffee by the sounds of it.'

'Yep, but then we have Sunday to look forward to.'

'Oh yes. I keep forgetting we open up late on Sundays.'

'Yep, not until after lunch so at least we'll get a lie-in.' Ashley got herself a coffee. 'Do you want one?'

'Yes, please? I could do with the caffeine.' Stepping over Grace, who was busy colouring in pictures of unicorns behind the counter, Jenny went into the kitchen area. 'I'm just going to grab Grace some toast, you all right for a minute?'

'Yep, that's fine.'

* * *

Cutting up some cucumber while the bread toasted, Jenny blinked back the tears stinging her eyes. Anthony would be here in a couple of hours. He had said he'd got the afternoon off work so he would probably get here anytime from three.

She knew loads of people did it. Loads of people waved off their children every other weekend. She'd heard that was the standard way of dealing with divorce or separation. She knew she wasn't alone in what she was going through, how she was feeling, but still, it wouldn't feel right without Grace here this weekend. It wouldn't feel right at all, not for two nights.

She shook her head and began to butter the toast, letting the heat from the crusts seep into her fingers. Just like everything else she would just have to get used to it.

'Right, here you go, Gracie. I've got your lunch.' Pausing, Jenny looked around the parlour, the tables were still full and she didn't feel comfortable making her sit out in the kitchen away from her view. 'Nick, do you mind if she sits with you at the counter?'

'Of course not. Come on, Grace.' Standing up, Nick leaned forward and took Grace from Jenny's arms, popping her down on the stool next to him. 'Yum, toast and cucumber.'

'Mine.' Giggling, Grace crossed her arms over her plate, hiding her food from him.

'Thanks. Do you actually have a home to go to or do you hang out here all day to save on rent?'

'Now there's an idea. Maybe I could bring my sleeping bag and hole myself up in the larder. Nah, it just takes me a while to unwind after a night shift. Though I'll have to go home and get my head down for a few hours soon, the lads from the rugby team keep insisting I need to go out tonight. To be honest, I'd rather not, but somehow I don't think any excuse is going to crack it.'

'I didn't know you played rugby?'

'I don't. I used to, years ago. I sometimes go and watch a game if they're playing against anyone interesting, but apart from that we just hang out, the old team and me.'

'I see.'

'You see? What do you see? Someone past it in rugby terms?' Nick raised his eyebrow and smirked.

'Well, I wouldn't like to say.' Laughing, Jenny turned her back and took her coffee from Ashley.

'Daddy!'

Freezing, her coffee mug halfway to her lips, Jenny slowly turned around.

'Hey, gorgeous girl. Hello, Jenny.'

'Anthony, I wasn't expecting you until later.'

'Yes, well, I got off work earlier than planned, so I thought I'd come and pick this precious bundle up early.' Holding his arms out, he waited for Grace to stand up on the stool before taking her into his arms. 'That's not a problem, is it?'

Jenny placed her mug down on the counter. 'It would have been nice to have known.'

'Aw, there's nothing like a surprise though, is there, Gracie? Is it a nice surprise to see Daddy earlier?' He tickled her under the armpits, looking over at Jenny as Grace threw her head back in laughter. 'I think there's your answer.'

'Umm, well, next time can you let me know a proper time, please?'

'Sure thing. I will.'

'Thanks.' Who did he think he was? Swanning in here two, almost three hours earlier than arranged and being so blasé about it? *Sure thing?* She wasn't a mate of his. He hadn't arrived at the pub five minutes late or something. Taking a deep breath, Jenny plastered a smile on her face. She wouldn't show him it had bothered her. He hadn't won.

'Where's this munchkin's things? Have you got a bag, Gracie? Shall we go and find it?' He shifted her higher up in his arms as he walked towards the door to the flat.

Walking quickly ahead of him, Jenny put her hand on the door handle. 'I'll get them. You can stay here.'

Taking the stairs two at a time, Jenny reached the top and paused. Why had he turned up so early? Without telling her? Was he trying to let her know that he had the upper hand or had he simply forgotten to message her and tell her about the change of plan?

Yes, he had always had a tendency to play games and to be more flexible with the truth than the average person, but to not let her know to expect him early? She shook her head; it didn't really matter why he had done it, did it? He had, and that was it.

Going through to the bedroom, Jenny lifted the rucksack she'd packed for Grace up onto the bed. She just needed to check she'd put everything that she might need in. Rummaging around inside she counted out the clothes, two outfits, two pyjamas. Nappies, she hadn't packed nappies. Going into the living room she grabbed the bag of nappies. How many was she supposed to put in? How many would Grace need for the weekend? It depended on so many things, how much she drank and whether Anthony would change her when she needed to be. It had always been Jenny who had done that sort of thing. It had been her who had been the primary carer. Even when he'd had Grace overnight before they'd moved, it had been his mum who had helped him.

She shrugged, she supposed it would be Gwen who would be doing most of the caring anyway. After all, Anthony had moved in with his parents so she'd be there anyway. She stuffed a handful into the bag, if they ran out they could get some more from the shop.

Bending down, she picked up Blankie. Holding the holey, thin material to her face, she inhaled Grace's sweet scent. She had planned on coming upstairs and spending some time with Grace after the lunchtime rush. She'd arranged it with Ashley and she had said she didn't mind running the place solo for an hour or so. They wouldn't be able to do that now. She wouldn't have her special time with Grace before she left.

'Jenny! How long are you going to be?'

Anthony was irritated, she could hear the all too familiar strain in his voice. She needed to hurry. Not that she should have to. It was him who was early, not her who was late. But small details like that had never seemed to bother Anthony much, she was sure they still didn't.

Taking a final deep breath in, Jenny tucked Blankie into the top of the rucksack before heading back downstairs.

Before pulling the door to the café open, she fixed a smile on her face. Grace didn't need to see how upset she was.

'You took your time.' Huffing, Anthony moved Grace onto his hip and took the rucksack.

'Not really, I had to pack her things. I didn't think you were coming until later, did I?'

'I suppose so. Anyway, Grace, say bye-bye to Mummy.'

'Hold on, let me say bye properly.' Holding out her arms, she took Grace from him. There was no way she was letting him take her without at least giving her a cuddle. Glancing towards the counter she realised the toast and cucumber had hardly been touched. 'She's not finished her lunch. Let her finish that quickly before you go.'

'Lunch? No, it's fine. I'll get her something on the way back.'

'But I've already made it. It won't take her long. It seems silly you having to stop and get something.'

'No, really. I don't want to get stuck in the traffic on the way home so we'll just get going.' Holding out his arms for Grace, he glanced towards the door.

'Traffic? It's barely past lunchtime.' Why was he being so awkward? Letting a slow breath out, she looked at him. He probably thought *she* was being awkward, but she wasn't. She just wanted to spend a little more time with her daughter. What was ten minutes when they'd agreed a later time anyway? Taking Grace, she kissed her on the forehead and reminded herself that they had to get along for Grace's sake. 'OK, hold on a minute and

I'll pop it in her lunchbox.' Lifting Grace higher on her hip, she picked up the plate.

'Anthony, what's taking so long?' A tall, woman, wearing denim shorts which seemed to elongate her already long legs, waltzed into the parlour, swishing her long dark hair behind her.

Jenny smiled to herself, Anthony was such an unusual name nowadays. It was weird to hear it down here. Most people shortened it to Tony or Ant or something. Grace's dad, Anthony, was the only one she knew who liked people to refer to him with his full name.

Frowning, Jenny watched as Anthony flinched and turned around. She watched as his face fleetingly softened in recognition before raising his eyebrows and crumpling his forehead. He knew her. She was referring to her Anthony. She shook her head, not her Anthony. Grace's dad, Anthony. That's what she had meant to think.

'Annie, I thought I'd asked you to stay in the car?'

'I did, honey. You were just taking so long, I thought I'd come and see what was happening.'

Annie? She was Annie? What? Jenny didn't understand. Why would she be here? Why would he have brought Annie to the seaside? To pick Grace up? She has nothing to do with Grace.

Quickly making the few short strides towards Annie, Anthony bent his head close to her and spoke quietly. Glancing across at Jenny, Annie nodded before turning and waltzing back out of the parlour, her head held high.

'Jenny, I can explain.' Walking towards the counter, Anthony spoke, his voice hushed.

'Is that Annie, Annie? The Annie you're seeing?'

'Yes, it is.'

'Why on earth is she here? You've got Grace this weekend. Why is she here?'

'Look, I didn't want to have this conversation today, but clearly, we're going to have to.'

'Go on then...'

Anthony looked around him. The parlour was only about half full now, most of the customers had finished their ice creams and drinks and hurried back into the sunshine to continue their perfect days. His eyes darted from Nick to Ashley and back to Jenny. 'Shall we go and talk somewhere more private?'

'Here's fine.' Stroking Grace's hair, she kissed the top of her head. She knew what was coming. She felt it in her bones, but she still needed to hear it from him.

'OK.' Anthony shrugged and lowered his voice. 'I've moved in with her.'

'What? You've moved in with her?' Staggering back, she gripped the counter behind her, holding herself still. She hadn't been expecting that. Not that. She'd thought he was going to say that she'd wanted to come along to see the seaside, to perhaps have a little trip to the beach. 'You've only just met her.'

'Hardly. I mean, we've been split up ages now and I knew her before that. You know I knew her through Pete.'

'We've been split up just over five months. That's not ages.' Admittedly, it had felt like ages on the numerous occasions she'd had to pack her and Grace's things up to move to another sofa in another friend's house, but it wasn't really ages. It was barely a blink in time.

'She has a three-bedroom house, and I was staying with my mum, as you know. It just seemed silly. Plus, this way Grace has her own room.'

'Her own room?'

'Yes.'

'So you're going to take Grace back there for the weekend?'

'Where else would we go?' Shaking his head, Anthony spread his hands in front of him as though it were a silly question.

'Grace hasn't even met her yet.' How could he possibly think it was OK to introduce Grace to someone for the first time and then go back to hers for the weekend?

'Yes, she has. She knows Annie.'

'What? When? You never told me you'd introduced her to Grace? We'd agreed not to introduce partners until we were certain we'd be with them for a long time. We agreed not to confuse her. And, we agreed that we would meet the other person before they were introduced to Grace.' She could hear her voice getting louder, higher in pitch. In what way was this whole situation right?

'Look, Jennifer...'

Jenny flinched, he hadn't called her that in years, not since they'd first met. Had she been downgraded to a total stranger already?

'Grace knows her and likes her, for that matter. They get along. Annie would do anything for Gracie. It's immaterial when they first met. Plus, to be honest, it's not really any of your business any more. The main thing is, Grace likes her.'

Jenny cupped Grace's head in her free hand, shielding her from Anthony's words. 'Of course, it's my business. She's my child.'

'Just like it was my business you dragging her down all this way to sit in the corner of a shop while you serve ice cream? I don't remember you asking my permission to move away with our daughter.'

'I did.'

'You didn't. You told me, but that's a completely different thing. When someone asks you, you generally have the power to stop them. You made it perfectly clear you were coming whether I liked it or not.'

'That's different and you know it. I had no choice but to come, I couldn't very well carry on crashing on other people's sofas. Plus, you never even told me about Grace meeting Annie.' Would he really have chosen to keep his daughter homeless over letting Jenny move her to the seaside and being able to offer her stability? Jenny took a deep breath and tried to stop herself from shaking. He couldn't compare the two situations, he couldn't.

'I know you felt like you had no choice. I had no choice either. Annie and I are together and we're staying together. I love her. And she loves me. All we want is to be able to give Grace a happy home when she comes to us.'

He loves her? Lowering her nose onto Grace's soft hair, she breathed in the sweet smell, a mixture of toddler sweat and shampoo. How could he have moved on so quickly? She didn't love him any more, but she certainly wasn't ready to move on. Had she meant so little to him that he could transfer his love for her to another woman just like that?

'You can't deny Grace's happiness, can you?' Anthony held out his arms across the counter.

Looking from Grace to Anthony it felt as though she had tunnel vision. The parlour seemed to virtually disappear, her vision focused only on Grace in her arms and Anthony standing across from her. She was vaguely aware of a hubbub of noise from customers filtering through the parlour and the scraping of a stool as Nick came around behind the counter to help Ashley serve. Lowering her voice to a harsh whisper, she looked Anthony in the eyes. 'All I asked of you was to let me meet any future partners before you introduced our daughter.'

'I know. I know. It was wrong of me, especially after we'd agreed, but it just kind of happened. I'd gone to pick Grace up one day and when I got back to my parents' Annie was there. She'd popped in. I couldn't very well leave Grace in the car while I went to ask her to leave, could I? There was no point. She would have had to meet her one day, anyway.' Running his hand across his closely shaven head, Anthony shifted from foot to foot. 'You're making a scene, just give me my daughter. It's my weekend to have her.'

Shaking her head, she glanced around, refocusing on the queue of customers to her side. They weren't bothered by her and Anthony. They were chattering amongst themselves, a mother and three children, two women who she was sure she recognised from the other day and an elderly man and his grandson, probably on an errand to fetch ice creams while the rest of the family lounged on the beach. No one was even paying attention to the fact that Jenny was having her heart ripped out once again.

'It's my time with her. We agreed.'

'Yes, well, we agreed we wouldn't introduce her to future partners without consulting the other parent too. Look how that ended up.' A dry, cold laugh escaped her throat. She knew it wasn't the same, but it felt good to show him that he expected her to keep 'agreements' when he was clearly so incapable.

'That's not the same and you know it. You're upsetting her. Just give her to me or do you want us to go to court? Get everything in writing?'

Narrowing her eyes, Jenny shook her head. Who the hell did he think he was?

'Thought not. Come on, Gracie. Come to Daddy.' Holding his arms out again, Anthony pursed his lips.

'Just let me say bye to her.'

'You've had enough time for that. Just give her to me, Jenny. Give me my daughter.' As his voice became louder, more demanding, he leaned further across the counter, his fingers almost touching Grace.

'Excuse me, mate. Let her say bye to her daughter.' Stepping towards Anthony, Nick crossed his arms, his voice low and authoritative.

Pausing, Anthony stared Nick in the eye before taking a step back.

'All right, Gracie, you have a lovely time with Daddy this weekend and Mummy will see you again on Sunday, OK?' Whispering in Grace's ear, she kissed her forehead.

'Love you, Mummy.' Cupping her mum's cheeks in her small hands, Grace kissed her on the nose.

'Love you too, sweetie, more than life itself.' Looking across at Anthony, Jenny gave Grace a final squeeze and passed her over the counter into his arms.

'Thank you. She'll be fine.' Lifting her onto his hip, he turned away. 'Say bye-bye to Mummy.'

'Bye-bye, Mummy.' Waving, Grace leaned her head against Anthony's shoulder.

'Bye-bye, sleepyhead.' She was still tired from their dash to the vets last night. Hopefully, she'd have a nap in the car on the way to Anthony's parents' house. Jenny shook her head, Anthony and Annie's house. That's where she was going to spend the weekend, not at her grandparents' house, at her father's new girlfriend's house. Swallowing hard, she looked away from the now empty doorway and stepped towards the now small queue. 'Hi, what can I get you?'

'One vanilla cone with extra fudge pieces, please?'

'Coming right up.' Smiling at the young girl in front of her, Jenny turned to scoop the ice cream out. He really was taking Gracie to stay at Annie's place, wasn't he? He was. Her Gracie would be staying at a virtual stranger's house. What if she was horrible to her? She hadn't seemed particularly nice when she'd strode into the parlour hurrying Anthony along. What if she treated Grace like that? What if she had a criminal record? Turning back, she passed the cone across the counter.

'Could I have the fudge pieces on top, please?'

'Sorry. Yes, you did ask. I'll get them now. Extra, wasn't it?'

'Yes, please.'

Turning back, Jenny scooped a heaped spoonful of fudge pieces from the glass jar and carefully sprinkled them over the ice cream. Catching the ice cream with the edge of the spoon, the scoop was dislodged from the cone and fell to the floor. 'Drat.'

'You OK?' Ashley called over her shoulder from the coffee machine.

Watching as the pale ball of ice cream splattered across the tiles, Jenny sank to her knees, grabbing a cloth from the counter as she went. Wiping the floor, she only seemed to smear more of the now melting mess across the tiles.

What if Grace wasn't safe at Annie's house? Did she even have stair gates? Had Anthony prepared for her stay in any way at all? She needed to ring him, remind him to put stair gates up at the top of the stairs as well as the bottom. She might wake in the morning and stumble down the stairs. What if he hadn't done that?

'Ashley, are you all right for a minute?'

'Sure thing.'

'Stand up, Jenny. Let's go and get some fresh air.'

Momentarily closing her eyes, Jenny felt Nick's hands cup her underneath her shoulders, gently pulling her up. Opening her eyes again, she weaved out from the counter and through to the kitchen, being gently guided by Nick's strong arms.

'I need to get that lady her vanilla cone with extra fudge pieces.' Still being led by Nick, she walked through the kitchen into the small courtyard, the warm summer sun seeping into her skin.

'She'll be fine. Ashley is making her another one as we speak.

Here sit down.' He gently lowered her to the bench that sat against the back wall.

Breathing in the delicate fragrance of the mock orange which sprawled along the flower bed, Jenny lowered her head to her hands.

'Are you all right?'

Lifting her head, she tried to smile. 'I will be. It was just a bit of a shock to see Anthony with Annie. Did you hear, he's living with her now? Gracie will be staying with them this weekend and every other weekend from now on. They'll look like a proper little family.'

'You and Grace are a proper little family.'

Jenny looked across at Nick and shook her head. No one understood. 'You don't understand. I know we are, but it's not the same. They'll look like we should have done. They'll be the family Grace deserves.'

'You're the family Grace deserves. You're a great mum. I've seen the way you are with her.'

'I can't give her what they can. They can give her a proper two-parent family.'

'That's rubbish. Annie isn't her mum, you are. Grace will always need you. When my parents split up, my dad found someone else quite quickly and moved in too. I remember my mum crying and overhearing her telling people exactly what you've just said to me, but I didn't understand. I didn't understand why my mum didn't know that my dad's partner wouldn't ever replace her. She was my mum, and she was home. I didn't need anything else when I was with her. Yes, I enjoyed going to my dad's house but not for the reason my mum thought, and certainly not for his partner. And coming back to my mum was always coming home.'

'I didn't know your parents had split up. How old were you?'

'Well, I don't talk about it much now. I guess it's just my normal so it doesn't tend to come up in conversation. I was ten, so quite a bit older than your Grace, but I don't ever remember comparing my two homes. I had my dad's home and I had our home, where my mum was.'

'I just worry that because she's so young, Annie will take my place and Grace will see her as mum too.'

'I wouldn't worry about that. Besides, she didn't seem particularly motherly when she barged into the parlour, did she?'

'No, I guess not.' Jenny chuckled. No, she definitely hadn't.

'There you go then. You're worrying about things that don't need to be worried about.'

'It's just difficult to think of Gracie there, with them, when she should be with me, her mum.'

'Dads need time too.'

'I know, I know. And I know I'm being selfish wanting to keep her all to me, but he never bothered with her when we did live together and even when me and Grace were sofa surfing before we came here, he hardly saw her and when he did it was his mother taking care of Grace. I just don't understand why he wants her for a long weekend every other week, not when he hadn't wanted to see her for so long before.'

'Maybe she's a good influence on him as a father then? This Annie? Grace will be spending some quality time with her dad. That might be good for her, especially if she hasn't had that in the past.'

'I guess that's one way of looking at it.' Looking down, Jenny picked at her cuticles. She knew it was in Grace's best interests to spend time with Anthony, she just didn't see why Annie had to be involved, but maybe, as Nick said, for whatever reason she's the driving force behind his decision. Whether Anthony was trying to look like the 'good dad' in front of her, or he actually thought he should be more involved probably didn't matter. What mattered was that he was taking more notice of Grace.

'It certainly is. And a better way of looking at it than thinking the worst.'

'You're right. I know you are. I guess, if I'm completely honest, I'm worried that Grace will prefer it there, that she'll prefer Annie over me. Or that Anthony and Annie will be able to provide a better life for her. What if they try to take Grace off of me, or Grace wants to live with them and not me?' Jenny used the pads of her thumbs to wipe her eyes. There, she'd said it, and she knew how daft she probably sounded. How paranoid she sounded, but still, she couldn't help it. She couldn't get rid of the fear in the pit of her stomach. The fear of losing Gracie.

'Has he ever said he wants to try for custody?'

'No, but...'

'There you go then. He just wants to see her, that's all. You've not only just split up, have you? How long have you been apart?'

'Umm, five months now.'

'There you go then, if he'd wanted to try for custody then he would have by now.'

'Yes, but what if Annie pushes him into it? Or even just suggests it and gets him thinking?'

'But she's been with him a while now, hasn't she? Why would she suddenly do it now?'

'Yes, she has, and I guess she's already met Grace. According to Anthony, anyway. So I know I'm probably being daft but I can't help myself. I can't stop thinking the worst.'

'You're not being daft. It's only natural to feel the way you do, but I honestly don't think you've got anything to worry about.'

'I hope not.' Patting some colour into her cheeks, Jenny nodded. She needed to try not to worry so much. She'd ring Anthony this evening and check in on Grace and hopefully even say 'goodnight'. 'Thank you for listening and for stepping in earlier.'

'Anytime. You're not alone, you know. I'm here for you.' Nick placed his hand over Jenny's.

'Thanks.' The heat and heaviness from Nick's hand upon hers was strong and reassuring.

'I mean it, I'm here anytime you need to talk.' Leaning forward, he wiped a tear from Jenny's cheek, tucking a loose hair behind her ear.

'Thanks.' Biting down on her bottom lip, she looked at him. His face was so close to hers, she could almost feel his deep blue eyes searching hers. They were barely a centimetre apart, she could feel the warmth from his lips reaching hers. Shaking her head, she pulled away, stood up, and brushed her apron down. 'I'd better get back, Ashley will need me.'

'Sorry, I...' Standing up, he shoved his hands in his pockets and looked at the floor. 'I'd best get home and get my head down for a few hours, anyway.'

'OK.' Jenny watched as Nick let himself out through the back gate, letting it swing shut on its creaky hinges. Sitting back down on the bench, she traced the outline of her lips with the tip of her forefinger. What had just happened? What had just almost happened?

Kicking at the edge of a crack in the slab in front of her, Jenny frowned. There had definitely been something between them, some physical attraction at least. She was sure she hadn't imagined it, the tingling, the electricity. Had he felt the same thing? Maybe he hadn't, maybe that's why he had pulled away.

She shook her head; it hadn't been him who had pulled away; it had been her. She'd made up the excuse that Ashley had needed her help. Why had she done that? She had wanted to kiss him. She had wanted him to kiss her. It had felt right.

Standing up, she brushed her apron down again. She needed to forget what had happened. She needed to go and help Ashley. Nick was Helen's ex, and he had treated her terribly. Once a cheat, always a cheat. That's what everyone said, didn't they? Plus, he was off-limits. She'd never date a friend's ex, and definitely not Helen's ex. It wasn't right.

* * *

'I'll just go and get the sign in.' Calling over her shoulder, Ashley made her way to the front door.

'OK, thanks.' Rinsing out the dishcloth, Jenny continued to wipe down the coffee machine. She could still feel Nick's hand enclosed upon hers, the tingle she had felt from their skin touching and the warmth that had emanated from him. Pausing, she closed her eyes, she needed to get Nick out of her head, she needed to remind herself that he wasn't a particularly nice person. She knew she'd only felt like she had because she'd been in a state over Anthony bringing Annie to collect Grace. Nick had stuck up for her in front of Anthony and, yes, that meant something, meant a lot, but it didn't erase how he had treated Helen.

'You all right, Jenny? You look a million miles away.' Having positioned the sign just inside the front door, Ashley returned to the counter.

'Sorry, I'm fine.' Smiling across at Ashley, she hoped the blush she could feel creeping across her face wasn't noticeable.

'Me and a few mates are going into town for a few drinks this evening, why don't you come with us?'

'Me? It's OK, thanks for asking though. I've not been out drinking since before I got pregnant with Grace.'

'It'll be a cheap night out for you then! Come, it'll be fun.'

'No, I'm all right.' Jenny shook her head firmly. She must be at least ten years older than Ashley, she'd just feel out of place.

'Aw, are you going to be OK? On your own, I mean.'

'I'll be fine. I'll probably have a night in front of the telly. I might even treat myself to a takeaway.' Or should she save the treat of a takeaway for when Grace was at home? Maybe she'd settle for one of those instant noodle pots she'd seen lurking at the back of Helen's kitchen cupboard. Yes, she'd save the money and get a takeaway when Grace was home, that way Grace could try something different for once. Plus, it would give her a night off cooking for the two of them. Yes, that's what she'd do, a noodle pot and a spot of TV.

'Why don't you just come out for a couple then? Early doors?'

'No, honestly, I'll be fine. I'm shattered anyway so could do with an early night.'

'Well, if you change your mind, just text me, won't you?' Ashley slipped on her light jacket and threw her bag over her shoulder.

'I will. I promise.'

8

Picking the small plastic pot of noodles up from the coffee table, Jenny stirred the congealed yellow lump again. Maybe it was out of date. That would explain why she couldn't separate the minimal hard green balls trying to pretend they were real peas from the mess of stodgy noodles and matted powder. She'd thrown the lid straight in the recycling bin and really didn't have the energy to fish it out to check the date. Putting it back on the coffee table, she curled her legs up underneath her and switched through the TV channels. There was nothing on and she hadn't got around to setting up any series links to record her favourite programmes, so there was literally nothing she could watch, or at least nothing she could be bothered to watch.

Taking her mobile from the pocket of her thin fabric dressing gown, she punched in Anthony's number again. She'd already tried to ring him three times to say goodnight to Grace, and he hadn't answered. He probably wouldn't answer this time either, but it was worth a go. Just in case.

Tapping her fingers against the arm of the sofa, she listened to the dialling tone and jumped when he actually answered.

'Hello?'

'Anthony, hi. It's Jenny, I just wondered if I could speak to Grace, please?' She raised her voice to be heard above the music seeping through from his side. Where was he?

'Hold on, I can't hear you.' His voice, almost a shout, suddenly muffled as the sound of the music faded. 'Sorry, we're just at the footie club. What's the matter?'

'Oh, right. Is Grace with you?' Where had he left her? Had he left her with his mum? After all the fuss he had made about spending time with her, had he dumped her off at his parents so he could go out to the footie club drinking with Annie? Jenny's stomach churned. Or even worse, had he left her with Annie? Had he left little Gracie with an almost total stranger? She could feel the burning sensation of sick rising in the back of her throat just thinking about how scared Grace would be.

'Yes, she's here. Well, she's inside with Annie. She's been dancing her little heart out, bless her. She's been up on the dance floor since the DJ started.'

Grace was with him? Glancing at the clock on the mantelpiece, Jenny saw it was eight thirty. Grace normally went to sleep at seven. She'd be shattered. 'She's been dancing?'

'Yes, we've come with Darren, Jane and their kids. She's loving all the attention.'

Darren and Jane had been her friends too before she and Anthony had split up. To be fair, they had been Anthony's friends before Jenny had been a part of his life, but she'd got on really well with them and had known them for years. She'd even babysat their children, multiple times, and now they were out spending the evening with Anthony and his new girlfriend. They hadn't even called or messaged Jenny to see how she had been after the break-up. Annie had not only replaced her when it came to Anthony but it sounded as though all their old friends had forgotten Jenny so easily and accepted Annie too. Jenny swallowed. She didn't care. Not really.

'Are you still there, Jen?'

'Yes, I'm here. I'm glad to hear she's having a good time. Can I speak to her?'

'Umm, I don't know. She's pretty happy at the moment. It seems a shame to stop her, doesn't it?'

So she wouldn't be happy speaking to her own mother, is that what he meant? Jenny closed her eyes. She knew that wasn't what he had meant. He'd just meant Grace might get upset after speaking to her, she knew that's what he meant but it didn't make it any easier. 'I guess so.'

'Ring in the morning if you like?'

'OK, thanks. I will. Bye.' Ending the call, Jenny picked up the cushion to her side and lowered her face into it. She let the tears flow. The tears over missing Grace, the tears for missing what she used to have with Anthony, the tears for the way things should have been. She shouldn't be apart from her daughter, not now. Not for this long. She should be there, watching Gracie dancing her funny little half run, half gallop around the dance floor. She should be the one holding Anthony's hand and chatting away to Jane and Darren. Not Annie. Annie was the imposter there. Annie was the one who had wiped any memories of Jenny away and filled the hole.

Wiping the tears away with one hand, Jenny stabbed at the button on the TV remote. As long as Grace was enjoying herself, that was the main thing. It had sounded as though she was happy. Jenny would just have to deal with her own insecurities, and fast. If this was the new 'normal' for them, then she'd just have to learn to live with all the feelings of inadequacy and loneliness.

It was going to be hard, though. It had been bad enough when Anthony was having Grace before and she was going to his parents' house. Now that Jenny knew she was going to be spending the time as a happy little family with Anthony and Annie, it was even tougher. She shrugged, it was only normal, she guessed. It had to be. Every single mum, or dad, must feel the same way when their ex began playing happy families with someone new.

She shifted on the cushions. Yes, she felt jealous. Mind numbingly jealous, but not jealous of Annie for having Anthony, she was over him, but jealous that now every other weekend Annie would be living the life she was supposed to have. Annie would be playing mother to her daughter. It just didn't feel right. It wasn't fair. It just wasn't fair.

Taking a tissue from her pocket, she dried her cheeks. She needed something to focus on, something to take her mind off Grace. However awful that sounded, she needed to have something else to think about or the pain would cripple her.

Switching the channels again, she finally found a rerun of an eighties comedy offering her the comfort of her childhood. Pulling the sofa cushions into place, she laid her head down and tried to remember what was going to happen next. Did the chandelier fall? Narrowly missing them? Was it that episode?

Her mobile pinged, bringing her away from guessing the plot. Sitting up quickly, she grabbed her phone from where it had fallen to the floor. It was Ashley, not Anthony. She was just asking if she'd changed her mind about going out.

After texting a short reply, she let the mobile drop to the floor again. She was in no mood for going out. It was sweet of Ashley though, to invite her.

Closing her eyes, she shut out the ping of another text message coming through. It would probably be Ashley again, telling her to let her know if she changed her mind or something. Dragging the thin throw from the back of the sofa, she wrapped it around her body and let the familiar rise and fall of voices and canned laughter wash over her.

Chucking the throw from her knees, Jenny sat bolt upright. Something had woken her. She blinked into the semi-darkness, the sun setting outside the window providing enough light for her to glance around. Muting the TV, she kept still and listened. There it was again, a loud ring, followed by someone calling her name. Who could it be? It wasn't as though she knew anyone around here, not to say anything past small talk, anyway. Pushing herself to her feet, she walked through to the window and peered through the gap in the curtains.

It was Ashley. She was sure it was. She could see her waving up at her now, she must have spotted Jenny looking. Turning around, Jenny made her way down the stairs and through the parlour.

'Hi.' Jenny cleared her throat. 'Hi, I thought you were going out?'

'Hi, Jenny. Yes, we are.' Letting herself in, Ashley surveyed her. 'Shall we find some more suitable clothes?'

'What for?' Looking down at her scruffy black jogging bottoms and grey T-shirt, she pulled the thin dressing gown tighter.

'For going out. You're coming out with us, right? You got my message?'

'Your message? Yes, thanks for inviting me but I'm really not feeling it tonight.'

'Ah, yes, you replied to my first message, but you did read my second one, and third and fourth one, didn't you?'

Blinking her eyes, Jenny shook her head.

'Oh well, I'm here now. Hold on one second.' Running towards a taxi which was parked in front of the parlour, Ashley leaned into the car, returning soon after and waving the taxi on. 'Right, they're going to meet us there. I'll come up and help you get ready.'

Turning around as instructed, Jenny made her way back up to the flat. 'Ready for what?'

'For coming out with us.' Frowning, Ashley put her hands on her hips. 'You really didn't read my messages, did you?'

'No, I really didn't.'

'Drat. I told you I wasn't taking no for an answer and that we'd call round to pick you up on our way into town.'

'Oh, right. Well, don't worry about me. I don't fancy going out if I'm honest. You go and have fun.'

'You've been crying, haven't you?' Ashley's tone softened as she passed Jenny a tissue.

Wiping her face, Jenny nodded. 'I've just been missing Gracie, that's all.'

'Exactly. And that's why I'm not taking no for an answer. Come on, come out with us. You'll have fun. The girls are a blast. It might even take your mind off things for a while if it doesn't do anything else. Plus, I'm here now.'

'I don't know...' She really didn't want to go out for a night on the town, but it was really sweet of Ashley for caring, and she had sent her friends ahead already. If she didn't go, Ashley would have to get to the pub on her own.

'Come on. I promise it will be fun.'

'We've got to open up early tomorrow, though.' It was the first Saturday of the summer holidays and she didn't fancy trying to contend with a hangover while serving a million customers.

'It'll be fine. That's what paracetamol is for.'

'OK, just for a couple of drinks though.'

'Awesome. Let's have a look through your clothes and find something for you to wear then.' Grinning, Ashley clapped her hands together.

* * *

Standing in the queue, Jenny glanced up and down the line of people snaking down the path. They'd been waiting ten minutes already and there was still a fair number of people in front of them. They'd come straight to the club because Ashley and her friends had begun drinking at home which made for a cheaper night out, apparently.

Jenny pulled her top down. Ashley had dressed her in a pair of dark denim jeans and one of Helen's tops because none of Jenny's had been suitable. It was pretty, navy with a cowl neck, but it wasn't as long as Jenny liked to wear them and it was riding up above the belt of her jeans. Standing next to Ashley and her three friends, Scarlet, Poppy and Tara, she felt old and frumpy. She looked back down the line; she wasn't the oldest person queuing. Not quite anyway. There was a group of women towards the back who were probably her age or slightly older and a divorce party with the leading lady wearing a 'Just Divorced' glittery sash much like a traditional hen would wear on her last night of freedom before marriage. Maybe she should have celebrated her break-up with Anthony? A night on the town would have certainly beaten crying into the raw cookie dough she'd binged on when they'd first split up.

'So, Jenny, how are you finding living here?' One of Ashley's friends, Scarlet, a tall girl with stunning cheekbones and dark brown hair leaned in to talk to her.

'I'm really enjoying it. It's great to live by the sea.' Speaking loudly, Jenny hoped Scarlet could hear her above the drum and bass of the music seeping through the windows of the club and the excited chatter and laughter from the tipsy line of punters. 'Have you lived here long?'

'Yep. All my life. I can't imagine not living by the beach. I mean, what do people do when it's hot and sunny if they don't have a beach to go to?'

'I guess we make do.' Jenny smiled and shook her head. It would be nice for Grace to grow up here. She'd have to start looking into renting a place for the two of them when Helen decided she'd had enough of life down under. For now though, she'd just try to make the most of life and enjoy it.

As more people were let into the building, the queue jostled down the path. Jenny watched as a girl, teetering on high heels, stumbled over, her friends grabbing her by the arm and pulling her upright again amid a barrage of light-hearted laughter. She'd forgotten what the nightlife atmosphere was like, everyone happy and sociable, at least until something annoyed them. Hopefully, there wouldn't be any mindless fighting tonight.

'We're getting closer!' Ashley linked arms with Jenny as they moved forward, closer to where the bouncers stood, their muscular arms crossed across their barrel chests. 'When was the last time you went clubbing?'

'Probably about five years ago.' Jenny grimaced. It was quite possibly a lot longer, Anthony had preferred to go and drink down the local footie club rather than venture into town. Yes, it was probably more like seven or eight years since she'd entered a club.

'Oh, wow! I was expecting you to say a couple of years, but not five!' Ashley giggled. 'You're so going to love it! I know you are! It's really good here too. There's not too much trouble, not like the big one in the next town along. Plus, they do a two for one deal on cocktails before eleven so it's always worth getting them early and lining your drinks up.'

As they were shifted closer to the entrance, Jenny looked across the road. There was a taxi rank almost opposite, and three taxis were waiting, she could be back at the flat in fifteen minutes, back in her scruffs in front of the TV in twenty. She picked at her cuticles, Ashley seemed excited to show her the nightlife on offer here, and she hadn't been properly out in such a long time. Heck, she hadn't just been out for a drink in at least three and a half years so maybe she should just relent, go into the club, have a few drinks and try to enjoy it. She couldn't drink much anyway, not with having to open the parlour by nine, so maybe she should just stay for an hour or so and go back. Jenny nodded, yes, she'd stay for an hour and get back to the flat. That was a good compromise, she'd please Ashley by having a couple of drinks but she could be back relaxing soon.

'Come along, ladies.' The bouncers waved them in. 'Be good tonight.'

'Yay, we're in. Here, give me your jackets, girls, and I'll go and pop them in.' Scarlet held out her hands.

Slipping out of her lightweight summer jacket, Jenny passed it to Scarlet. 'Thanks.'

'Right, come on, let's go and get some cocktails!' Slipping her arm through Jenny's again, Ashley led the group of them over to the bar which snaked the length of the vast room. 'What are you having, Jenny?'

'Oh, um, I'll have a gin and tonic, please?'

'Don't you want to start off with a cocktail? It's two for one until eleven, remember.'

'Oh yes, sorry I'd forgotten. I'll just have what you're having, please?' Passing across her money, Jenny stood with Tara and Poppy and watched as Ashley expertly weaved her way through the crowd to the bar.

'Hey, coats are in and safe. Here are your tickets.' Scarlet returned, beaming. 'Gav and his mates are here.'

'Where?' Poppy looked around.

'Don't look! Over there in the corner.'

'Who's Gav?' Jenny tucked her ticket into her small handbag.

'He's an old mate from college and Poppy's long-term crush.' Tara grinned.

'Ah OK.' Looking across at the group of boys Scarlet had indicated, Jenny felt even older than she had in the queue. They must only be twenty if they were that old.

'Here we go, girls.' Approaching them with a tray full of plastic cups holding various brightly coloured liquids, Ashley paused before leading them to a table. 'This one looks good. It's close to the dance floor.'

Sitting down, Jenny shuffled around on the dark cushioned bench. From here they had a full view of the dance floor which was already quite busy despite it being early.

'These are your ones, Jenny.' Ashley placed two glasses of pale creamy yellow cocktails on the table in front of her. 'I got us both pina coladas, is that OK?'

'Yes, lovely, thanks.' She moved the tiny wooden umbrella to the side of the cup and took a sip. The strength of the rum scorched the back of her throat as she swallowed. It certainly didn't taste as nice as she remembered a pina colada tasting, or maybe that was just because she'd never had it with so much rum.

'Nice, aren't they?'

'Really good, thanks.' Jenny gave a thumbs-up and took another sip. The music track changed, and the dancers became energised, jumping up and down, seemingly without a care in the world.

'I see Gav and his mates over there.' Ashley pointed to the far corner.

'I know, Scarlet spotted them. Don't make it obvious!'

Settling back against the cushions, Jenny half-listened to the conversation as she watched dancers exchange looks, smiles and short conversations before one of them inevitably sidled up to the other. She observed as fresh groups of teenagers and young adults filtered through the door, heading to the bar and then either straight to the dance floor or to stand in groups around the edge of the room.

'Do you want one, Jenny?'

'Sorry, what?' Shaking herself from her thoughts, she focused in on Tara, who was standing with her hand on her purse.

'We're getting shots in, want one?'

'No, it's fine, thanks.' Jenny waved her plastic cup in the air before looking around the table, while she'd only just begun her second cocktail, it looked as though everyone else had already finished.

* * *

'Look, look, they're up. Gav and his group are up and dancing.' Tara nudged Poppy.

'Right, come on. Tonight is the night, Poppy. Let's go and dance.' Standing up, Ashley slid out from behind the table, holding her hand out for Poppy.

'I don't know...'

'You only live once.'

'I know, I know, but...'

'No excuses. Come on, girls.'

'I'll just finish my drink before I come over.' Jenny smiled. She didn't really want to dance. She hadn't danced since she'd begun dating Anthony and that had been, what, seven years ago. The only dancing she did nowadays was dancing along to nursery rhymes with Grace. She'd only embarrass them.

'OK, then you'll come up, right?' Ashley paused, her forehead creasing with worry.

'Yes, I will.'

'Are you sure? You're having a good time, aren't you? Are you glad you came out or did I force you?'

'I'm having a great time, thanks. I'd only have been sat at the flat feeling sorry for myself.' Jenny grinned and took another sip of her drink.

'OK, cool. See you in a bit then.'

Jenny watched as the girls made their way to the dance floor, the clip of their high heels on the wooden floor lost in the beat of the music blaring from the DJ booth. Giggling away, they began dancing, a little unsure of themselves at first and then as the song slipped into a different one Jenny could see their confidence grow. Soon Gav and his friends had made their way across to them. Jenny was unsure which one was Gav but one of them paired off with Poppy, moving slightly away from the main group.

'Can we sit here?' A girl with a high ponytail and large silver hooped earrings indicated the table.

Nodding, Jenny smiled as three girls and a boy surrounded her, chattering loudly and excitedly.

Jenny closed her eyes, she wanted her bed, well, Helen's bed. She wanted to be curled up in her scruffs on the sofa or to be reading in bed. She didn't want to be here. She didn't want to be surrounded by young, thin, beautiful people. She just wanted to be comfy.

She took a gulp from her pina colada, not that she was even certain that's what it was, not as she consumed more of the bitter drink. She couldn't leave though. Not yet. Ashley was obviously worried she wasn't enjoying herself. She needed to stay a bit longer; she needed to reassure her. It had been lovely of Ashley to think about her, to not want her to be wallowing in the flat. And Jenny should be grateful for that. She knew she should.

Finishing the last of her drink, she excused herself from the table and made her way to the bar. She needed a gin and tonic. The bartender couldn't mess a simple G&T up, could he?

Slipping through the groups gathered around the bar, Jenny

made her way to the front and placed her elbows on the sticky surface. Holding her money out, she tried to catch the bartender's eye.

Shifting on her feet, she watched as drinks and money were exchanged until she was finally served.

'What can I get you, love?'

'Just a gin and tonic, please?'

'Coming right up.'

'Jenny, hey.'

'Nick?' Jenny shook her head as he edged towards the bar, slipping his way between a group of drunken teenagers to come and stand next to her.

As the bartender placed a plastic cup in front of Jenny, clear liquid sloshed over the edges.

'I'll get this.' Nick turned to the bartender. 'And a pint please, mate?'

'You don't have to do that.'

'It's fine. I want to.'

'OK, thanks.' Jenny slipped her money back into her purse and took a long drink from the plastic cup in front of her, letting the familiar light flavour of gin and the tickle of bubbles from the tonic hit the back of her throat.

After grabbing his pint, they turned and made their way through the crowds to a quiet corner of the club. Standing to face the dance floor they both fell quiet. Jenny shifted her boots on the sticky carpet.

'So, your mates managed to drag you out in the end then?'

'Yes, they did. I came more to keep them quiet than because I wanted to come. I'm just waiting until they're completely drunk and I can slip away unnoticed.' Nick held his pint up to a group of men chatting around a table. 'How about you? What brings you to the delightful local club?'

'Ashley. She felt sorry for me, I guess. She didn't want me wallowing at the flat so she dragged me out. It's very sweet of her, but I'm not really in the mood, to be honest.'

'No? I know exactly what you mean.' Leaning against a pillar behind them, he took a long gulp of lager.

'Did you used to come here when you were younger?'

'You mean I'm too old now?' Nick chuckled and wiped froth from his lips. 'No, I'm not originally from around these parts. I spent all my clubbing days in West Yorkshire and then in London where I went to uni.'

'Ah, I thought you had a bit of an accent. I couldn't work out where it was from.' It was a very subtle twang and she probably wouldn't have noticed it if he hadn't been hanging around the parlour so much.

'Yep, that'll be the Yorkshire boy in me. It's nowhere near as strong as it used to be, though.'

'What brought you down here then?'

'Well, that's a bit embarrassing, really.' Looking down at his feet, he gently kicked an empty plastic cup underneath a table to his left. There was a reason they handed out drinks in plastic cups then.

'Go on.' Jenny tilted her head. What reason could be embarrassing? 'Obviously, you don't have to tell me if you don't want to.'

'No, it's fine. I met this girl in London when I was at uni. She was specialising in equine veterinary, and I proposed, she said yes, and so after our courses had finished we moved to be near her family. They live in one of those cottages on the edge of town.'

'That's not embarrassing. A lot of people move to be closer to their partner's family.'

'That's not the embarrassing bit. We arranged the wedding, moved in together and everything, like you do, and then the wedding day finally came and she didn't turn up. Turns out she'd been in a car accident.'

'Oh no, that's awful.' Jenny raised her hand to her mouth. 'I'm so sorry. That must have been heartbreaking, the day that you were supposed to get married as well.'

Nick ran his hand through his hair. 'Oh, she didn't die. Nothing like that.'

'Sorry I just assumed, because you didn't get married.' Jenny shrugged. 'Or did you? Did you marry her in the end?'

'No, she was in the car with my best man, going in the opposite direction to the church. They'd been having an affair ever since we'd moved back.'

'That's rubbish. I'm so sorry to hear that.' It couldn't have been that heart scarring for him though, or else he wouldn't have cheated on Helen. Jenny shook her head. She was being unfair, he and Helen hadn't been about to get married. Helen hadn't been left standing, waiting at the altar for him. But then, did that matter? Infidelity was infidelity, wasn't it? Yes, it must have been a hundred times more humiliating and hurtful to have your fiancé string you along and then run off with your best mate on your wedding day, but what he had done was still pretty bad. If not worse because he knew how it felt. 'I take it they moved away together. After the accident, I mean?'

'They did, for a while, yes. But they're back now. They've recently moved back and are staying with her parents, saving for a house, I believe. I'm not sure what's happened, but from what I understand, they had their own business, big house and all that and then went bust a few months back and are starting from scratch again.'

'That must be hard, them being back?'

'Yes, and no. I'm completely over her. It happened years ago, and you know, the past is the past, right? But it's the way they've been acting. That's why the lads brought me out. They heard that me and Rob, he was my so-called best man, had a bit of a run-in a few days ago and decided a night on the town would take my mind off it all.'

'Right.' He and Rob had had a run in. What did that mean? Had it been his ex-fiancé who he had cheated on Helen with? That would make a lot of sense and would be a reason for Rob to try to pick a fight or whatever it had been. 'Has it worked?'

'Not really. That's them over there.' With his pint in his hand, Nick pointed towards a couple on the dance floor at the opposite side of the club. A thin woman with a stark dark bob danced up close to a clean-shaven man with a bottle of something or other in his hand.

'Ahh.'

'Ahh, indeed.' Taking a swig from his plastic cup, Nick turned to look at Jenny. 'Anyway, that's enough about my pathetic excuse of a life, how are you finding it here? Have you settled into Helen's flat yet?'

'Yes. Mostly anyway. Grace seems to be enjoying nursery, and I don't think I'm quite running the parlour into the ground. Not yet anyway.' Jenny laughed.

'That's good to hear then.'

'Yep. I'll try not to lose you any money.'

'Cheers for that.'

'You're welcome. Do you want another?' Jenny held out her empty cup.

'Yes, go on then.' Nick checked his watch. 'I reckon another half an hour and I can bolt.'

'Same here!' Jenny glanced over at Ashley, Scarlett, Tara and Poppy. They seemed to be having fun. Her clubbing days, on the other hand, were definitely over.

* * *

'So, tell me something else. A secret, something not a lot of people know.' Jenny giggled and leaned in closer to Nick, her leg brushing his under the table.

'What like?' Laying his hands, palms up on the table in front of him, he looked at Jenny. 'I don't think I have any secrets. I've told you my most embarrassing moment already.'

'Haha, yes, you have! I'll bring that up next time you're annoying me in the parlour. I'll shout it across the shop floor and tell the world that you still like to wear earphones when you go for a morning jog even though you don't play any music. They'll know then that you can hear them and you're just ignoring them.'

'Not ignoring them. I just like to have some peace and quiet.' Nick grinned and pointed at Jenny. 'And, it's only when I'm in a bad mood. Most of the time I don't.'

'Well, it sounds funnier if I just tell them it's all the time!' Jenny laughed. 'Anyway, tell me something else.'

'I don't know what. Ask me something.'

'OK. OK, I've got this.' Pausing, she took a long gulp from her gin and tonic. 'If you could change anything, anything at all, what would it be?'

'Umm, literally anything? Could I make something not happen?'

'Yep, literally anything.'

'Right, well that's quite a serious question. I'll have to have a think.' Staring forward, he pursed his lips and scrunched his eyes up. 'I would have chosen the winning numbers on the lottery last week and built myself a self-sufficient home in the middle of a forest.'

'Seriously? That's it? That's what you'd change if you could change anything?'

'Yep, that's what I would change.'

'Fair enough, but it would probably take you longer than a week to build it.' Jenny laughed.

'Hold still.'

'Oh no, what? Have I got a spider on me?' Sitting as still as she could, she grimaced. She didn't mind spiders, but she didn't like the thought of one crawling over her.

'No, you've just got a loose eyelash.' Putting his pint down, he leaned forward and used the pad of his thumb to gently brush it off.

'Thank you.' She could see the reflection of the lights from the dance floor dancing in his eyes.

'You're very welcome.' Trailing his thumb from her cheek, he snaked it around her chin and up to her lips.

'Thanks.' Closing her eyes, she leaned in closer, the tingle of expectation deepening the closer they became. His lips were surprisingly soft for someone who spent so much time out at sea, his kiss strong but gentle.

'Is this OK?' Pulling back, millimetres from her lips, Nick looked her in the eye. 'Is this what you want?'

'Oh yes.' Cupping the back of his head with her hand, she pulled him closer again.

'Haha, I knew it! I knew something was going on between the two of you.'

Jumping back, their teeth jarred. Jenny rubbed her teeth with her finger as she turned to face Ashley. She could feel the crimson heat rise from her chest to her cheeks instantly.

'Sorry, I didn't mean to startle you.' Ashley grimaced. 'But I knew it. From the moment you both met, I could sense the electricity between you.'

'Really?' Jenny looked across at Nick, who was sat rubbing his teeth too. She'd only felt hatred when she'd first laid eyes on him, literally nothing else.

'Yes, definitely. Anyway, it's so sweet. You two make a really lovely couple.' Ashley pointed from Jenny to Nick and back again, the alcohol from her drink sloshing onto the floor. 'Are you coming to dance?'

'No, no. I'd like to keep the use of my legs, thank you very much.' Nick slapped his thighs and grinned.

'Oh, charming. Thanks very much!' Twisting around, Jenny faced him, her face screwed up in mock betrayal.

'No, I meant me. Not you. I can't dance to save my life!' Holding his hands up, he laughed.

'Glad to hear it. I'm a very good dancer, I'll have you know. I know all the cool moves to "Twinkle Twinkle Little Star"!'

'Maybe you can teach me some time then.'

'I most probably can't.' Laughing, Jenny watched as Ashley zigzagged across the club to find her friends.

* * *

Drying her hands on a paper towel, Jenny looked at her reflection in the mirror. She pulled her hair out from behind her ears and let it swoop across her shoulder. Taking her lip balm from her small handbag she applied it, coating a very slight pink tint across her lips. She should have brought some proper lipstick.

She shook her head and frowned at herself, Nick had seen her in tears earlier at the parlour with her hair shoved on top of her head sporting an apron. He obviously liked her for being her. She didn't need to worry about not applying lippie. Picking her bag up from the small shelf behind the tap, she stood back to let three girls teetering on their high heels past before joining Nick out in the foyer.

'Is this one yours?' Holding up Jenny's thin jacket, he grinned. 'I don't think it will fit me.'

'Haha. Yes, it's mine. Thanks for getting it.' Taking the jacket, she put it on before slipping her arm through his.

'Are you ready?'

'Yes. Let's escape the unbearably loud music and sticky carpets.' Smiling, she let him lead her down the stairs and out into the cool night air.

'It was loud, wasn't it? Louder than it used to be.'

'In the good old days, you mean?' Throwing her head back, she laughed. 'No, I think we're just getting old.'

'I think you're probably right.' Laughing, Nick led the way across the road to the taxi rank.

'You know when I first met you, I didn't really like you at all.' Shoving her hands in the pockets of her jacket, she looked up at him.

'Thanks! And now?'

'And now, I think I do. Really like you, I mean.' As she swayed into his side, Nick put his arms around her and rubbed her shoulders.

'That's good then because I really like you too.' Leaning down, his lips met hers again, stronger this time, surer of himself.

9

Plaiting her hair and throwing it over her shoulder, Jenny looked in the mirror. The person staring back at her today certainly looked a little more worse for wear than when she'd studied her reflection in the club toilets. That, or, she had been too tipsy to notice the wrinkles around her eyes and dark bags underneath them.

Turning away, she picked up her toothbrush. What had she been thinking last night? Nick? Anyone but Nick. Yes, she had moments when she thought that her initial hatred for him was wearing thin, but still, Nick?

Squirting the stripy blue, white and red paste from the tube, she watched as a perfect pea-sized blob was expelled onto the bristles of her toothbrush. She could still feel his lips upon hers, the comfort she'd felt when he'd wrapped his arms around her as they'd waited for the taxi.

She shoved the toothbrush into her mouth and closed her eyes; she needed to stop thinking about him like that. He was off-limits. Nothing should have happened between them. He was Helen's ex, her boss, and he was a cheat. She didn't need to get involved with someone like that, however 'lovely' he appeared to be, she knew what he was really like.

Spitting out the toothpaste, she turned the tap on and watched as the bubbles washed away. At least the tablets were beginning to work, her hangover was slowly subsiding.

* * *

'Morning!'

Holding her hand to her forehead, Jenny bit down on her bottom lip. Maybe those tablets hadn't started to work after all. Closing her eyes, she waited as the door swung shut behind Ashley. 'Hi.'

'Looks like we're going to have a super busy day today. The sun is beating down already.' Smiling, Ashley slipped her apron over her head and began taking the chairs down from where they had been stacked on top of the tables.

'Great.' Trying to fake the same amount of enthusiasm Ashley exuded, she winced as each chair leg scraped against the floor. Grabbing the dishcloth and spray, Jenny followed Ashley around, wiping the newly clear tables. 'How come you've got so much energy? What time did you lot leave last night? You were definitely later than me.'

'We stayed until four when it closed. Well, me, Tara and Scarlet did. Poppy ended up going off with Gav about two.'

'Four? It's only half-eight now. You couldn't have got much sleep!' How on earth was Ashley so awake now?

'No, a couple of hours maybe. I find that's the best way after a big night out, though. I'll have my lie-in tomorrow when we open up late.'

Jenny shook her head. 'And I'm assuming you don't have a hangover or anything?'

'Nope, not me. Oh sorry, are you suffering?' Looking across at Jenny, Ashley placed the chair she was holding onto the floor very gently.

'I'm all right. I've just got a bit of a headache, but I'm hoping my tablets will kick in soon.' Jenny shook her head. 'Oh, how I miss the days of no hangovers. Enjoy it while you can, as you get older the hangovers seem to catch up and punish you for drinking a heck of a lot less than you could when you were younger.'

'I intend to!' Ashley laughed as she placed the menus in the middle of the tables. 'So, tell me, how long have you and Nick been seeing each other? I mean, there have been so many times that I've figured something was going on, so it wasn't a surprise. But, tell me!'

Washing the dishcloth under the tap, Jenny looked down, hoping Ashley wouldn't see the blush creeping across her face. What did she mean she'd figured something was going on? Nothing had been going on, until last night anyway. 'There's nothing going on. We'd just had a bit too much to drink, that's all.'

Pausing, menus clasped in her hands, Ashley looked across at Jenny. 'I don't believe you for a second! The amount of chemistry between you both is unreal. There's definitely something going on.'

'There isn't. Honestly.'

'OK.' Holding up her hands, palms forward, Ashley grinned. 'You don't have to tell me, but if you're worried about Helen finding out, you really don't have to be. She'd be happy for you and Nick.'

'There's no me and Nick.'

'OK, but she would be totally cool with the idea. Especially after the way their relationship ended... Sorry, I shouldn't have said that.'

'Don't worry. Helen told me what happened.'

'There you go then, you know she wouldn't mind.'

'I'll go and pop the sign out.' Gripping the heavy sign, Jenny dragged it outside and positioned it on the pavement. Ashley was right about one thing; it was heating up already. She took a deep breath, letting the warm salty air fill her lungs. Ashley was wrong about the other, though, Helen wouldn't want Jenny to get into a relationship with Nick. She wouldn't want Jenny to risk getting her heartbroken too.

* * *

Pulling out another tub of ice cream from the freezer, Jenny balanced it on top of the other five. Ashley had been right, they had been busy ever since opening up. She'd have to stay up late tonight to make more batches of ice cream; they were running low on at least four flavours. Anyone would think they were the only ice cream parlour for miles around, but despite the fact that her feet were throbbing from standing up all day and her headache was still clinging to the inside of her skull, it felt good. It felt good to know that people were coming to the parlour and buying the ice cream that she was making. A few months ago she'd never have dreamt this would be where her life would have taken her, but she was glad it had.

Kicking the freezer door closed, she picked up the tubs. Clinging onto the bottom one, she leaned back so the tower of freezing plastic didn't topple forward.

Pausing at the door, she listened as the familiar tone of Nick's voice floated through from the parlour. Slumping her shoulders, she bit her lip. That was all she needed, Nick to turn up. Taking a deep breath, she circled her shoulders back. She needed to be strong, whatever feelings she thought she had for him she needed to banish. She wasn't going to get hurt again. He wasn't worth it. It wasn't worth having him cheating on her for a few weeks, months maybe, of happiness. No, she knew she didn't know the real Nick yet; she knew she hadn't seen the side of him that had sent Helen running to the other side of the world. Leaning her hip against the kitchen door, she pushed her way through to the parlour.

'Jenny, hi. Ashley tells me you're suffering with a hangover?' Standing up from the stool he'd positioned himself at, he leaned towards her.

Ducking from his peck on the cheek, Jenny placed the tubs on the counter and rubbed her hands together, trying to warm them up and get some feeling back. 'Hello. Sorry, Ashley, are you OK for a few minutes? I just need to pop upstairs and sort something out.'

Frowning, Ashley nodded.

'Thanks. See you, Nick.' Turning on her heels, Jenny walked towards the door to the flat. She could feel the heat creeping across her face, her stomach-churning. Keeping her eyes on the floor in front of her, she tried to push the image of Nick's crestfallen face out of her mind. It was for the best. Avoiding him was for the best.

10

———

'And this one too.' Laughing, Jenny caught Grace's right foot as she squirmed away from her, her high-pitched giggling infectious. 'Are you looking forward to going to nursery today? I bet you're going to have so much fun! Do you want to do a painting for me? We can put it up in the parlour with the others.'

'Yes! Painting!'

'What are you going to do a painting of?' Pulling Grace onto her lap, she slipped the pretty pink sock on before tickling her under the arms.

'Mummy!' Jumping down, Grace ran to the other side of the bedroom, throwing her head back with laughter. 'Me going to paint Mummy, Daddy, Annie and Grace.'

'Ooh, that will be a nice painting then.' Jenny shifted on the bed and folded Grace's pyjamas.

'For Annie. Want to give Annie my painting.' Clapping her hands together, she jumped up and down before running into the living room.

'Lovely.' Jenny swallowed. Ever since Anthony had brought

Grace back yesterday evening, all she'd been talking about was Annie.

'Look.' Running back into the bedroom, Grace held up a princess doll.

'Your new princess.'

'Yes, Annie gaves it me. I can cuddle her and be like Annie cuddle me.' Grace waved the doll in the air, its bright blue hair wafting behind it before gripping it to her chest and kissing it on the head.

'What do you mean, Gracie?' Placing Grace's pyjamas under the pillow, she looked back at her daughter.

'Me cuddle princess and like me cuddle Annie.'

'Oh, OK. That's nice.' Smiling, Jenny blinked back the tears stinging her eyes. 'Did she tell you that? Is that what Annie said to you when she gave you the princess doll?'

Grinning, Grace nodded.

'Right. That was nice of her then. Why don't you run and get your nursery bag, Gracie?'

'OK, Mummy.' Placing the doll on the bed next to Jenny, Grace turned and ran back into the living room.

Picking up the small plastic doll, Jenny turned it over in her hands. How dare she? How dare Annie say that to Grace? She was *her* daughter, not Annie's. Annie had no right to plant an idea like that in Grace's mind, to assume that Grace would miss her and need comfort. But Grace *had* missed her. She had cried for her when Jenny had been trying to get her to sleep. And if Jenny was honest, that was what had hurt the most, not Annie's assumptions and overstepping the mark but the way Grace had missed her, had cried for her, for someone she barely knew. Jenny was her mum, not Annie, and she didn't want Grace to have such a strong bond with anyone apart from herself.

Standing up, she went to the window. The courtyard needed weeding again. They grew up through the slabs quicker than Jenny had the time to pull them out. Pushing the heels of her hands against her eyes, she waited for the world to turn black and starry. She was glad Grace liked Annie, or at least she knew she should be glad. It meant that Grace would be happy to go and stay there every other weekend. But, it was tough, really tough. It was tough to see Grace think so highly of someone else.

'Got it, Mummy. Look!' Skipping back into the room, Grace turned to show Jenny her pink backpack swamping her small body.

'Brilliant, well done. Are we all set now?'

'Yes, Mummy.' Pausing, Grace looked around, a shadow flitting across her face. 'Where's Princess Annie?'

Swallowing hard, Jenny tried her best to keep her voice steady. 'Here she is. Here's Princess Annie.'

'Me take her to nursery.' Grabbing the doll from Jenny's hand, Grace hugged it to her chest.

'OK.' She knew she was being paranoid. She knew no one would come between them, and she knew this infatuation with Annie was only because Grace hadn't known her long and they'd no doubt done lots of lovely things together. She knew it was just a novelty, a phase. Even so, she couldn't help but hope the thing would get lost and forgotten amongst the other toys at nursery.

'Me having lunch with my friends?'

'Yes, you're having lunch at nursery today.' Holding out her hand, she let the warmth from Grace's tiny hand soothe hers. As soon as she thought it, she knew it sounded immature but she just couldn't shake the feeling of jealousy and unfairness. Anthony had moved on straight away, if not before, and here she was, the only person she can think of is her best friend's cheating ex. She shook her head, she needed to forget him. She needed to focus on her and Grace. She didn't need a man to be happy. She and Grace were doing just fine and were happy by themselves. Yes, finding that special someone would be the icing on the cake, but she didn't need them. And she could put Nick out of her head, she knew she could. She'd just be slightly more confident if he didn't keep turning up at the parlour.

Jenny groaned, she had to pick Smudge up from the vets today. It was impossible to avoid Nick. Completely impossible.

Jenny stared at the poster in front of her before checking her watch again. She'd left Ashley to lock up the parlour, but she needed to go and collect Grace in half an hour. If she was kept waiting much longer, she'd have to arrange another appointment to collect Smudge. Tapping her foot against the tiled floor, she read the poster for the thirteenth time in the past five minutes and wondered, for the thirteenth time also, when Smudge was due to be wormed. She'd have to check with Helen next time she spoke to her.

The sound of hushed laughter made her turn around and she watched as a couple and two children came out of the vet's room, the small girl in front carrying an even smaller fluffy puppy. The perfect little family with their perfect new pet.

'Miss Weaver, the vet will see you now.'

Standing up, she smoothed her T-shirt down over the top of her jeggings. Please don't let it be Nick. Please don't. Apart from that one close call, she'd managed to avoid him since Friday night. He hadn't come near the parlour yesterday, so hopefully, that was a good sign. Hopefully, he realised it had all been a mistake.

Making her way down the dim corridor to the room at the end, Jenny paused before placing her hand on the door handle. Taking a deep breath in, she walked into the room.

'Jenny, hi.'

'Hi, Nick.' Crumpling up her forehead, she smiled. She just needed to act normal. To act as though nothing had happened. 'I've come to collect Smudge.'

Nick nodded and grinned at Smudge who sat hunched up in front of him on the table, a cone of shame around his neck to prevent him from licking his wounds.

Jenny shook her head, how could she not have noticed the cat was right there in front of him. Not that it mattered if she looked daft in front of him, of course. 'Thanks. I found this carrier in the shed. It should be OK to get him back to the flat in, shouldn't it?' Jenny lifted an old wicker carrier up onto the table.

'Yes, of course. Now, I've sorted out some pain relief for the next few days which should keep him comfortable and you can book an appointment for the end of the week for a check-up.'

'OK, I will do. Thanks. How long does he have to keep that thing on for?' Jenny pointed to the plastic cone around Smudge's neck.

'It depends really. Some cats need them on until the wound is completely healed, others don't seem bothered by the stitches at all and don't have to wear them. He's been a bit of a pain, haven't you, Smudge?' Nick stroked Smudge's ears. 'So, you might want to keep it on for a couple of days, that being said once they're back in their home environment some cats cope better so he might be OK.'

'Right, I'll see how he gets on.' Opening the door to the carrier, Jenny held open her arms. 'Come on, Smudge, let's get you home.'

'Here , let me help.' Lifting Smudge up, Nick gently popped him in the carrier, his hand brushing against Jenny's.

'Thanks.' Strapping the carrier door shut, Jenny lifted it from the table. He was heavier than he looked.

'Look, Jenny. Have you got a minute?'

'Not really. I need to get him home and collect Grace by half-past.'

Glancing at the clock on the wall, Nick walked around the side of the table towards her. 'I finish soon, I can drop Smudge off at yours then if it helps? That way you'll be able to go straight from here to collect Grace?'

'No, it's fine. I can cope. Thanks though.' Jenny smiled and headed towards the door.

'Jenny, have I done something wrong?'

Looking back, Jenny took a deep breath in. It wasn't the place to have this conversation. Plus, the longer she spent stuck in this small room with him, the quicker she could feel her resolve melting. She needed to be strong. She needed to remember that he couldn't be trusted. In fact, the puppy dog eyes and the way he spoke to her as if he really did want to help was probably all just an act anyway. If he could cheat, he could lie. 'No, I'm just in a hurry.'

Outside in the car park, Jenny picked up her pace. She had less than ten minutes to walk to the other side of the town centre to collect Grace. Smudge would just have to come. 'OK there, Smudge? We're just going on a little adventure and then we'll get you home and settled.'

'Jenny, Jenny, hold up.'

Using her free hand to wipe the tears away from her eyes, she looked around. Hadn't he got the hint?

'You forgot Smudge's medication.' Running towards her, waving a white paper bag in his hand, he slowed down. 'Are you all right? You look upset?'

'I'm fine. I think I've just got a bit of hay fever, that's all.'

'Oh right. I didn't know you suffered with that.'

'It must just be some plant that's come out now. Thanks for this.' Taking the bag from him, Jenny turned back and made her way back down the path, quickening her pace. She could do this. She could.

11

'We're out of the mint-choc-chip too. Could you grab one of those, please?' Jenny called over her shoulder to Ashley who had disappeared into the kitchen to refill some other flavours.

'Will do.'

'Hi, what can I get you?' Turning back to the customers in front of her, Jenny smiled.

'Two strawberry and kiwi smoothies, please?'

'Coming right up.' Jenny smiled at the couple in front of her. She was sure she recognised them from somewhere. Turning around, she scooped the fresh strawberries from the small under-the-counter fridge and began chopping the kiwi. They'd probably been in before. It was amazing how many faces she recognised and how many people greeted her when she was out and about with Grace. After years of living with Anthony and hardly knowing anyone locally, it was strange to think she'd befriended this many people in such a short amount of time.

'Can you just leave them on the counter? We'll be back for them in a moment.'

'OK.' Jenny called over her shoulder.

'Oh no. When did they get here?' Plonking the tubs of ice cream on the counter, Ashley nudged Jenny.

'Who?' Jenny looked to where Ashley was indicating. 'Oh, them. Just a few minutes ago. They're the ones who have ordered these smoothies but they're coming back for them, apparently. I'm sure I recognise them from somewhere.'

'Yep, so you should.' Folding her arms and leaning against the counter, Ashley ignored the small queue which had formed.

Placing the smoothies at the end of the counter, Jenny watched as the couple stepped outside, waving at someone across the road. 'Is that Nick?' Jenny squinted. It looked like him, although with the sun glaring off the windows, she couldn't be sure.

'Yep, that's Nick and those two are his ex-fiancé and so-called best man.'

'Oh.' Turning to the next customer, Jenny fixed a smile on her face. 'What can I get you?'

'A mint-choc-chip cone and a chocolate scoop in a tub, please?'

'Good choices.' Turning back to Ashley, Jenny sorted through the small pile of tubs of ice cream, putting them away as she went. 'I wonder what they want then.'

'I don't know, but I don't think it will be anything good. They've been hassling him ever since they returned.'

'Yes, he said about that.' Jenny scooped the chocolate ice cream into a small cardboard tub.

'I just don't understand how someone could do that. Not to Nick, he's one of the good guys, isn't he? I don't mean what happened with Helen...'

'Umm.' How could she say he was one of the good guys who didn't deserve to be cheated on, when he had done exactly the same thing.

'It's awful, though. He's been through so much. And for them to have the nerve to come back after all this time and try to run him out of town! It's his home now.' Ashley shook her head.

Looking in the direction Ashley was staring, Jenny watched as Nick wiped his hand across his forehead before plunging his hands in his pockets, his shoulder slumping. She frowned, she'd never seen him look so defenceless before. She'd always thought of him as a strong, happy-go-lucky person. The Nick that was standing across the road looked beaten. She forced herself to stand her ground instead of rushing over to check on him. He wasn't all innocent, was he? 'Do you think he's OK?'

'No. These are their smoothies, right? I'm going to take them and go over there.' Grabbing the smoothies as she passed, Ashley strode out of the parlour.

'Could I have sprinkles on the chocolate one, please?'

Looking back at the customers in front of her, Jenny tried to concentrate. One mint-choc-chip cone and one chocolate scoop now with sprinkles. 'Yes, of course.'

* * *

Passing across a strawberry cone and a chocolate milkshake, Jenny looked up. The queue had finally subsided and the parlour was relatively quiet. A group of teenagers sat gossiping at the table by the window, but apart from that everyone else had taken their purchases away with them, probably to eat in the sunshine.

Bringing her hand to her eyes to shield the glare of the sun's reflection on the windows, Jenny watched as Nick's ex and so-called best man finally walked away from Nick and Ashley. Grabbing the dishcloth, she walked towards the front of the parlour and watched as Ashley led Nick to the low wall separating the beach from the pavement and sat down, their heads together, deep in conversation. Wringing the dishcloth in her hands, Jenny chewed on her bottom lip. Should she close up and go over? She wanted to. She wanted to make sure he was all right. He looked pretty shaken up.

Yes, she would. She'd close up for a few minutes and go and check on him. Walking back to the counter, she flung the dishcloth down and turned back.

'Jenny, sorry about running off like that. I just couldn't watch them have a go at him like that.'

'Ashley, I was just about to come over. Where's Nick? Is he OK?' She was too late. She'd dithered and worried for too long.

'He's gone home. I told him to go and get some rest. I doubt he will, though. He said he was on a lifeboat shift this evening, but the state that he's in I think he should call in sick.'

'Why? What happened? What did they say to him to upset him like that?' Drying her hands on the tea towel, Jenny pinched the bridge of her nose. Why did she still feel like this about him?

'They're basically trying to force him to leave town.'

'Leave town? How can they force him? He's not going to, is he?'

'I don't know. I hope not, but this has been going on ever since they moved back. They've been telling him the decent thing would be for him to move on because Steph, his ex, grew up here. I mean, how immature can you get? They're acting like a couple of school kids bullying someone in the playground.'

'I don't understand. Why do they want him to move out of town?'

'I don't know. If you ask me, Rob feels threatened. Maybe Steph still has feelings for Nick.' Ashley shrugged and made them both a coffee.

'That's pathetic.'

'I know. Plus, Rob is a vet as well, which doesn't help things.'

'Oh, I didn't know that.' Why would she though? Nick had barely said two words to her about what was going on.

'Yep, they trained together at veterinary school. Anyway, I think part of the reason is he wants Nick to sell his half of the practice to him so he can make a life for himself here.'

'That's awful.' Putting down her coffee, she grabbed her mobile from the shelf. She should ring him. She wanted to ring him.

'I think the worst thing for him was realising that her parents must be behind it all.'

'What do you mean?' Jenny slipped her mobile into the pocket of her apron.

'They've offered him quite a bit apparently, you know, for the veterinary practice, and there's been rumours that Rob and Steph came back to live with her parents because of financial problems, so it can't be them who are trying to buy him out. Her parents must be putting up the money.' Ashley turned to serve a new customer.

Frowning, Jenny watched as Ashley made up a strawberry and kiwi smoothie before turning back to her.

'I think that upset him more than Steph and Rob trying to buy him out. He used to be so close to Steph's parents. Even when Steph had moved away with Rob, they used to invite him over for dinner sometimes. They became his family and, now, since Steph and Rob have been back they've just dropped him, as though everything was his fault somehow.' Ashley shrugged.

Shaking her head, Jenny wiped the counter down. She knew exactly how he was feeling. It had been the same with her, one minute she'd been part of Anthony's family and the next, well, she'd felt as though she'd been discarded along with the rubbish. His parents, particularly his mum, had treated her as though she were her daughter. She'd even said to her that was how she viewed her, and yet when she and Anthony had broken up, poof, just like that, she'd become an outsider. It was as though she no longer existed. Gone were the long phone conversations, the offers of babysitting and the advice-giving. Instead, she was subjected to the type of small talk someone might give a complete stranger. All with a hint of aloofness, as though they didn't really care how she answered, what she felt.

Momentarily closing her eyes, she tried to push the image of Anthony's parents out of her mind. Looking back at them now, it was hard to believe how close she had once felt to them, how much a part of the family she had been. It must be even harder for Nick, his almost in-laws had carried on treating him as one of their own right up until Steph and Rob had returned. She couldn't imagine how he felt now, knowing that it was them who were giving or lending Rob the money to get rid of Nick.

Taking her mobile from her pocket, she looked towards the door. The parlour was quiet now. There always seemed to be a little slump at this time, Ashley would cope for a few minutes.

'You all right, Jenny? You seem very quiet.'

'I'm OK, thanks. I was just thinking about how Nick must be feeling. I might go and give him a quick call, if you can manage here a moment?'

'Yes, I'll be fine. You go.'

'Thanks.' Making her way through the kitchen, Jenny scrolled through her mobile and pressed on Nick's number.

Stepping out into the small courtyard, the heat and humidity in the air instantly warmed her skin. Standing still, she waited as the mobile rang through to voicemail. Hitting the End Call button, she rang again.

'Damn.' Again, the voicemail kicked in. Jenny cleared her throat. 'Hi, Nick, it's Jenny. I, umm, I was just ringing to see how you were. Umm, ring me back. If you want to that is.'

Rolling her eyes, she returned her mobile to her apron pocket. Should she have left that message? He would realise that she'd been speaking to Ashley about him now. She shouldn't have left it.

Untying her hair, she smoothed it back up into a ponytail. She really shouldn't have left it.

'How is he?' Looking up from the ice cream cone she was filling, Ashley glanced over at Jenny.

'His phone went straight to voicemail.'

'Oh.' Ashley leaned into Jenny and lowered her voice. 'I just hope he doesn't do anything stupid like give in to them.'

Looking down at the counter, Jenny frowned. 'I'm sure he won't. This is his home now.' He wouldn't let them run him out of town, she was sure he wouldn't. He had too much to lose, the veterinary practice, the parlour, not to mention his passion; the lifeboating. Plus, he'd lived here for years. This was his home now, more than it was Rob and Steph's.

'I know. I just hope you're right. He's just not been the same since they got back.'

* * *

'That's it, pop your arm through here and we'll be ready.' Jenny looked around the parlour, there was no denying that it wasn't busy. The rain had driven people to seek shelter inside. The queue wasn't too long though, most people had already been served and were loitering at the tables waiting for the rain to subside. It had been nice earlier. The hot weather and clear skies of the morning had enticed people to the beach before the clouds had opened, and with the holiday season came tourists who were forever optimistic that the little 'shower' would cease allowing them to once again enjoy the sun's warmth and rays.

Pulling Grace's hood up, Jenny smoothed down her lightweight waterproof, the pale green fabric emblazoned with bright pink flamingos lit up Grace's eyes. Slipping into her own dull blue waterproof, Jenny glanced out at the clouds. They weren't shifting any time soon. People would soon get bored of hunkering down and waiting for the rain to pass, then Ashley could enjoy a bit of peace.

'You sure you don't mind?' Grabbing Grace's lunchbox from the counter, she called across to Ashley.

'No, it's cool. You go. We've got that youth group coming in later so we'll be even busier then.' Turning on the smoothie machine, Ashley smiled at Jenny.

Drat, she'd forgotten they'd agree the youth group could meet at the parlour this week. The organiser, Lydia, had asked Jenny if they could meet at the parlour while their hall was being refurbished. She'd completely forgotten. Taking Grace's hand, she waved across at Ashley. She supposed at least they'd still bring some money in even if the rain carried on all day. 'Ready?'

'Yes, Mummy. All ready.'

'Good, good.' Glancing at the clock above the counter, Jenny turned and led Grace towards the door, careful to avoid the collection of bags, windbreakers and buckets and spades scattered between the tables. She'd have to get the mop out again when she got back, even though it felt like a futile battle against the rain dripping from the various paraphernalia the customers had brought in with them. Now though, she needed to try to get across town in less than seven minutes or Grace would miss the beginning of lunchtime at nursery.

'Right, hoods up, let's go!' Stepping into the street, it surprised Jenny how warm the rain was. She shook her head, of course, it would be warm, it was the middle of summer.

'Me getting wet. '

'I know, Gracie, but it won't take us long to get to nursery.'

'Don't want to go. Want to stay with you.'

'Oh, sweetie. Nursery will be great! Much more fun than staying at the parlour.' Looking down at Grace who had come to a standstill just outside, Jenny gripped her hand gently and inched her forward. 'I tell you what, why don't I make us some pizza for dinner and then we can snuggle up on the sofa when you get back and watch the film with the fairies in?'

'Umm...'

'And, hey, look at that giant puddle! Why don't you see if you can hop from puddle to puddle?'

'All the way there?'

'Yep, all the way there!' Jogging alongside her as Grace ran from puddle to puddle, Jenny tried to hold her hand at arm's length to avoid the worst of the splashes.

'Wow, look, Mummy. This one looks big!'

'Wow, it does.' Crossing her fingers, Jenny hoped it wasn't as deep as it looked, she hadn't brought any spare clothes for Grace so she didn't want the rainwater seeping over the top of her boots.

Slowly closing the door to the nursery behind her, Jenny paused, waiting until Grace's cries quietened. She'd asked her key worker how long it usually took for kids to settle in, but they'd just said it depended on the child which was the answer Jenny was half expecting, anyway. Having to hand Grace over to another adult, her small arms still encircling her neck, always brought a tear to her eye. Leaning closer, she laid her ear against the darkened glass, she could hear her sobs getting quieter by the minute.

Wiping her eyes, she turned away. She knew Grace usually settled after a few minutes and enjoyed herself. After each session, it was Grace who asked when she was going again, so Jenny knew she had fun there. It was just tough listening to her calling for her.

Plunging her hands into her pockets, she put her head down against the rain and began the walk home. Hopefully, it wouldn't be so busy when she got back and they could have a breather before the youth club invaded.

Taking the alleyway towards the marketplace, she quickly checked her watch. Ten minutes and she'd be back and Ashley could go on her lunch break while she took over.

Narrowly avoiding a massive puddle, Jenny strode out of the alleyway onto the High Street. The small town was almost desolate apart from a couple peering into the estate agent's window ahead and a group of teenagers sheltering in the doorway to yet another empty shop. It was strange, the seafront was lined with thriving businesses and yet even since they'd moved here at least three town centre shops had announced their closure. She supposed the tourists came for the beach, not for the shopping; there were enough retail parks within a short car journey that catered for the few who did.

'Damn.' Tripping over her shoelace, she grabbed hold of the window ledge to her right and steadied herself. Bending down, she gripped the soggy laces between her thumbs and fingers and began tying them.

A shout from the other side of the road startled her, and she looked back to see where the commotion was coming from. It looked as though the couple looking in the window of the estate agents were having a disagreement. The woman pointed to a photo of a house while the man stood, hands in his pockets and shook his head. The woman then proceeded to shake her umbrella about, spraying droplets of water on to the man who then wiped his jacket.

Standing up, she wiped her wet hands down the front of her coat, not that it helped much, it just meant her hands were now covered in clean rainwater rather than the muddy water her laces were drenched in. Peering across at them, there was something familiar about the couple. She was sure she'd seen them before, the woman's perfectly straight dark bob was quite distinctive.

Jenny shook her head, she had probably just seen them around town or in the parlour. Wiping wet strands of hair away from her face, she carried on walking.

No, that wasn't it. She did recognise them, not just as passers-by or customers, she was sure she knew them from somewhere.

She did. It was Nick's ex-fiancé, Steph, and Rob. She'd recognise her anywhere, with her long legs and salon-perfect hair. It was. She was sure of it. Ducking down, Jenny untied her other shoelace. Taking her time, she smoothed the laces out before tying them, slowly.

Scrunching her eyes up, she tried to make out what they were arguing about. Steph's voice rose and dipped while Rob's deep tone stayed steady.

It was no good, she couldn't make out a word. Straightening up, she shook her head. It was none of her business, anyway. None of it was. Plus, as Ashley had said, there was no way Nick would relent and leave town. He had his half of the parlour, and of the veterinary practice too. He wouldn't give those up, especially the vets.

Yes, she cared about him, but she was trying very hard not to. Jumping away from the kerb, she narrowly missed a car splashing her.

It was only natural to care in a way though, wasn't it? He was still her friend, if you could call him that. Besides Ashley, he was the only other person she really knew down here, of course, she didn't want him to leave. That was all. Looking down at her feet, her trainers muddy from the rain, she swallowed hard. He was just a friend. That was all he could ever be. She couldn't, wouldn't, risk getting hurt again. She couldn't put herself, or Grace, through that, not again.

* * *

Stepping into the Parlour, Jenny slipped out of her wet coat and wiped her feet. It was fairly quiet now, a couple of small family groups of people sat clustered around the tables by the window, but apart from them, the majority must have given up the hope that the rain would clear and gone back to wherever they were staying.

'Hi, Jenny. Did you get my message?' Coming out from around the counter, Ashley walked towards her, her voice quiet.

'Your message? No, sorry, I've not looked at my phone.'

'It's OK. I just wanted to warn you, Nick is here.'

'OK.'

'He's brought an estate agent with him. I think he's getting the parlour valued.'

'What? Seriously?' Jenny clasped her hands tightly around her coat. He wasn't going though, he couldn't be. 'Where are they?'

'In the kitchen. They're waiting for you to get back so they can look around the flat.' Ashley wrung the dishcloth in her hands.

'Oh, right.'

'They asked me to send you through when you came back.' Ashley looked over her shoulder towards the kitchen.

'Right. Of course. OK, I'll go and see them then.' Jenny watched as Ashley returned to the counter before taking a deep breath and heading towards the kitchen. Nick was probably just getting an idea of the value of the place. Just because he'd brought an estate agent round, it didn't mean that he was considering Steph and Rob's offer, let alone taking it seriously.

Jenny hung her coat up on the hook by the kitchen door and cleared her throat. 'Nick, hello. Can I help?'

'Jenny, hi. Ethan, this is Jenny. She's running the place while the other owner is away. Jenny, this is Ethan, he's just come to value the business.'

'Pleased to meet you.'

'And you.' Jenny shook his offered hand. With his floppy blonde hair and cheap suit still sporting creases down the legs, he looked too young to be an estate agent.

'We were just wondering if we could have a quick look around the flat to get a proper valuation? I'm sorry, I know legally I need to give you notice, so if you'd prefer, we can arrange another time.' Nick looked down at his feet.

'No, no, that's fine. I will warn you though, it's a bit of a mess. I've not had time to wash up after breakfast or tidy Grace's toys up from last night yet.'

'That's fine. I'm sure I've seen a lot worse. This way?' Ethan used his clipboard to point to the door to the flat.

'Yes.' Jenny fished in her pocket for her key and handed it to him. Nick looked tired. Really tired. Deep dark circles shadowed his eyes and the stubble on his chin suggested he hadn't been looking after himself. Holding the door open, she let them walk ahead of her, trying to catch his eye. It was no good, Nick walked behind Ethan, keeping his eyes fixed on the step in front of him.

'Is the living room this way?' Ethan indicated towards the living room.

'Yes.' Ducking ahead of them, Jenny opened the living room door, hurriedly picking up Grace's scattered toys. 'Again, sorry about the mess.'

'No problem.'

Standing in the corner, Jenny watched as Ethan quickly measured the room before turning and going into the kitchen. Maybe Nick *was* serious. Maybe he really was going to leave. Clasping Grace's dolls to her chest, she tried to catch her breath.

Why was she so bothered if he was going to move away? She barely knew him.

'All done. Thank you. I'll be in touch with the valuation later on this afternoon.' Ethan shook Nick and Jenny's hands before heading back downstairs.

'Yes, thank you, Jenny. And sorry it was so last minute.' Turning on his heels, Nick followed Ethan's footsteps.

'Nick. Wait.' Holding out her hand, Jenny touched his jacket before returning her hand to the pile of dolls in her arms.

Slowly Nick turned around, his face softening briefly.

'Nick.'

'Yes?'

'I... are you really leaving?' Jenny coughed, her voice croaky.

'It looks that way. Thanks again for letting us look round.'

'It's OK.' Jenny watched as Nick went down the stairs and disappeared through the door.

Shaking her head, she went into the living room and sunk into the sofa cushions. With the dolls on her lap, she pulled her mobile from her pocket and searched for Helen's name.

'Hello?'

'Hi, Helen? It's Jenny. I hope I've not woken you?' Jenny picked at a loose thread on the knee of her jeans. She'd fallen over in them a couple of months before and the hole was getting worse. She shrugged, they probably looked fashionable now.

'No. Hold on one sec.'

Jenny listened as Helen excused herself, her muffled voice floating down the phone line.

'Sorry about that.'

'It's OK. Sorry to disturb you, are you out?' She was sure she could hear music and laughter in the background.

'Yes, we came into town for a bite to eat and ended up staying here.'

'That sounds nice.' Jenny picked at the loose thread again.

'Hang on, two mins.'

Jenny listened as a voice, male, became clear before Helen must have muffled her phone and the voices and music became muted. She'd interrupted Helen having fun, hadn't she? She must have made a group of friends or something. Ever since they were kids, Helen had been good at making friends. They'd always joked that Helen could go into a supermarket for bread and milk and come out with a new group of friends. Maybe she shouldn't mention Nick selling up now? She should probably ring her back another time, she didn't want to spoil her evening.

'Right, I'm back with you. How's it going in sunny old England?'

'It's fine. The parlour is really busy with people visiting the seaside and Smudge is back home now. He's still recovering but should be able to be free of the cone of shame around his head in a few days, so that's good.'

'Aw, I do miss Smudge. Everything's going OK then?'

'Yep. Things are fine.' She couldn't tell her. Helen deserved to have some fun after the year she'd had.

'Come on, then. Tell me.'

'Tell you what?'

'What you're not telling me. I can tell something's wrong by the tone of your voice.'

'What's wrong with my voice?'

'Jenny.'

'OK, OK.' Straightening her back, she tucked a loose strand of hair behind her ear. 'When I got back from taking Gracie to nursery, I found Nick here, at the parlour, with an estate agent. I didn't want to spoil your evening by telling you, but he's thinking about selling his half of the business.' There, she'd said it.

'That was quick.'

'What do you mean?'

'He rang me earlier this morning and told me he wanted to sell up, but I didn't realise it was imminent.'

'You knew?' Why hadn't she told her? Had it not occurred to Helen that it was a big deal to her? She might be halfway around the world but it was Jenny, and Ashley for that matter, who would have to work with the new owners. Bile rose to her throat. She and Grace might well be homeless again if a sale went through and the new owners wanted to live in the flat themselves.

'Jenny, are you still there?' Helen's voice softened.

'I'm still here.'

'You're not worried about it, are you? You are, aren't you?'

'A bit. Me and Grace are just getting settled here and if he sells and the owners don't want me living in the flat or, even worse, don't want me working here either...' Jenny sighed. 'Then it's a big deal, for us. For me and Grace.'

'Hey, don't worry about that. I'll still be joint owners with them, remember? And we're writing you into the contract. It will be sold with you and Ashley as employees and you as a sitting tenant. They won't be able to just get rid of you.'

'Really? Thank you.' Jenny shook her head. She should have known that Helen would have thought about the potential consequences and come up with a solution.

'Really. Actually, it was Nick's idea. It hadn't occurred to me that any new owners would want to get their hands on the flat, to be honest.'

'Nick's idea?'

'Yep. It was one of the first things he said when he told me he was putting his half on the market.'

'Oh, right.' Excited shouting and more laughter wafted down the phone.

'Look, I'd better go now, but we'll catch up properly soon, OK?'

'OK.' And that was it, her phone went silent. Helen had already ended the call.

Jenny traced her finger along the edge of the sofa cushion. It had been good of Nick to suggest she and Grace stay as sitting tenants. He'd obviously thought hard about the logistics of selling his half.

Leaning down, Jenny scooped Smudge up in her arms and laid him on her lap. Nick *was* leaving then.

12

Pulling the buggy across the sand, Jenny turned it to face the sea and pushed the brake down with her foot, not that it was going to go anywhere, anyway. Sinking down onto the warm sand, she slipped out of her sandals and let the tiny grains trickle over her toes. Tipping her head back she felt the warm evening rays from the sun on her skin. Today had been particularly busy and her legs and feet ached from being stood up all day.

Looking across at Grace, she watched the slow rise and fall of her chest, her small fingers still gripping her pink blanket even in her sleep. Turning back, she watched the dancing waves roll onto the beach and back down, the tide slowly coming in. She couldn't imagine living back inland again. Yes, running the parlour was hard work and constant, but she wouldn't change it. It was difficult juggling spending enough time with Grace and running the business, but come the autumn they'd close for at least a day during the week and at the moment Grace was enjoying nursery and didn't seem to mind being in the parlour, 'helping' or playing with her toys sometimes. Plus, the benefits of her being able to provide a home and an income for Grace went above all the sacrifices they had to make.

Turning her head, she watched as the sunset slowly began turning the sky into a deep orange and red spectacle. This time of day was definitely her favourite, most of the tourists had gone back to their caravan parks or holiday homes and the beach became quiet again. Local dog walkers made their way across the sand, their dogs never tiring of the joy of running through the waves and the few tourists who still hovered were quiet, contemplating life like she liked to.

'Hey, do you mind?'

Shaking the thoughts out of her head, Jenny looked up. Nick towered above her, indicating the ground next to her. Shaking her head, she smiled at him.

'Thanks.' Lowering himself onto the sand, he put his arms around his knees, drawing them towards his chest. 'Lovely sunset.'

'It is.' He looked tired. Still. The dark circles beneath his eyes had grown since she had seen him last.

'I've been meaning to talk to you, but I haven't been able to catch you alone.'

'Oh right. I did wonder why you hadn't spoken to me about selling up. Are you still? Selling your half of the business?'

'Probably. I don't know. It kind of depends.' Rubbing his hand across his face, he looked towards the sea.

'On what?' So he might not be selling then? He might be staying after all.

'On a few things. I mean, Rob and Steph are trying their hardest to drive me away and that seems to be the easiest thing to do.'

'You can't let them make you leave, not if you don't want to. It's your decision.'

'I know, I know. It's difficult though. And, at the moment I haven't really got anything keeping me here.' Nick looked across at Jenny.

'That's not true. You've got your business. Your businesses. You've got the veterinary practice and you've got your share of the parlour. They're two pretty big reasons to stay by themselves. Plus, you've got your lifeboating and all your friends.'

'I know. And I'll miss the businesses and the lifeboating, but are they enough of a reason to stay? I don't know.' Nick shook his head and looked back towards the horizon. 'If I don't go, Rob will open a new veterinary practice and take half my patients. And the parlour, well, I don't really have any input in that, anyway. I only brought half off Helen to do her a favour.'

'There's the lifeboating...'

'I know and I'll miss that. Really miss that.'

'Stay then.'

'Rob's already signed himself up to the lifeboating team so that'll change the dynamics there.'

'Really? Why would he do that when he knows you volunteer there? It was him who wronged you, he should show a bit of remorse.'

Nick laughed, a hollow low chuckle. 'Remorse just isn't in his vocabulary.'

'I'm sorry. I don't know what to say, it seems very weird that he'd do that.' Digging her fingers into the sand, she picked up a handful and watched as the grains trickled down, instantly lost amongst the others.

'He's always been a bit like that. He's always wanted what I had, or that's what it seems. I'm probably being paranoid.' Glancing at her, he shrugged.

'Well, you've probably got more right than most to feel a little paranoid.' Smiling, she looked over at him.

'You're probably right, unfortunately.'

'I saw them the other day. They were stood outside the estate agents arguing, so it's not all roses in paradise.'

'Were they?' Crunching up his nose, he looked back out to sea before clearing his throat. 'Anyway, I didn't come over to talk about them. I came over to apologise about what happened last week.'

'Last week?' Looking down at the sand beneath her hand, she tried to concentrate on a small shell just in front of her.

'At the club, and after. I'm sorry if I did anything to offend or upset you. It wasn't my intention.'

'You didn't do anything wrong.'

'I must have done, you've hardly spoken two words to me since.'

'I know, I...'

'It's OK. I understand.' He rubbed his hand over his face. 'No, I don't understand, actually. I thought what we had between us was special, I felt a connection to you. We both had a good time on Friday night. I thought we'd shared quite a bit, got to know each more, and...' Pausing, he spread his hands out, palms up, in front of him. '...I guess I glimpsed the possibility of a relationship between us.'

Staring straight ahead, Jenny watched as a ship in the far distance slowly made its way across the water. He had felt like she had. He had felt something too. She shook her head; it didn't change anything. It couldn't change anything. 'I...'

'And I guess, I would like a relationship with you. I know things have been strained between us and we've probably both been a little unsure of how the other felt.' Looking down, he traced his finger through the sand. 'And I know I've been a bit weird recently. All this business with Steph and Rob coming back and trying to buy me out has affected me. Not because I have any feelings left for her, because I don't, but because I've been so unsure as to what to do. Do I leave, which will be the easiest thing to do? Certainly easier on my sanity. Or do I refuse to sell and stick around on the off chance that things might work out between you and me?'

Looking down, Jenny pinched the bridge of her nose.

'I guess what I'm saying, asking, is whether there's a future for us?' Turning to face her, he gently clasped her hands, his warm, strong fingers, linking hers.

Jenny looked down at their entwined fingers and then into his eyes. 'Nick, I can't. I can't risk it. I'm sorry.'

Taking his hand away from hers, he looked towards the sea and back down to his feet before clearing his throat. 'Right, of course. Sorry.' Pushing himself to standing, he brushed the sand from his jeans and began walking away.

Standing up, Jenny grabbed hold of his hand, pulling him back. 'Nick, please wait? I do feel we have a connection, and I do think of you that way, and if things were different...' Letting her hand fall, she took a deep breath. There was nothing she wanted more than to fall into his arms but she had to be strong. She needed to do the right thing for Grace, for herself. She had to. 'I can't risk you doing what you did to Helen. I just can't put myself through all of that and it wouldn't be fair on Grace either.'

Standing still, Nick looked at her and shook his head, his forehead creased. 'What I did to Helen? What do you mean?'

'I'm sorry. I shouldn't have brought that up. It's none of my business what went on between you and Helen.' He obviously hadn't realised how close she and Helen were, they told each other everything about their love lives. Well, Helen did, Jenny hadn't had much chance to recently. Even so, maybe she shouldn't have brought up her name, she must have embarrassed him, shamed him.

'You've said it now.' Shoving his hands in his pockets, Nick looked straight at her. 'What did you mean?'

'I just meant about why your relationship ended. I'm not

saying you'll do it again, but I just can't put myself through something like that, not so soon after Anthony.'

'I'd do what again?'

Jenny rolled her eyes. Did she really have to spell it out? Well, that was just another reason to walk away from him, wasn't it? If he really couldn't see what he had done was wrong, then there would be no hope for him changing. 'Look, just leave it. I need to go and get Grace to bed, anyway.'

'No, what did you mean? What did Helen say I had done to deserve her cheating on me like that?'

'What?' Did he really think she'd fall for that? 'You cheated on her, not the other way around.'

'I did not. I would never cheat. Do you really think that after what happened with Steph that I would inflict that pain on someone else?'

Biting down on her bottom lip, Jenny narrowed her eyes. What was wrong with him? He'd been rumbled so why didn't he just admit it? 'That's low, even for a bloke.'

Running his hand through his hair, he lowered his voice. 'Jenny, I... I need to get back.'

Jenny gripped her fingers around the handle of Grace's buggy, her knuckles turning white, and watched as he slowly turned and made his way up the beach. With his shoulders slumped and his head down, he made a good impression of being the one who had been wronged. He was a good liar, she'd give him that. She knew she'd had a lucky escape so why did she feel so awful, as though she'd hurt him.

Wriggling her fingers, she waited until the blood was flowing properly again before she turned and dragged the buggy across the sand towards the promenade.

* * *

Turning the key in the door to the parlour, she held it open with her foot and gingerly bumped the buggy up the front step. Safely inside, she peered over the hood. Good, Grace was still asleep. With any luck, she'd be able to carry her upstairs straight to bed without her waking.

Dropping down onto one of the hard plastic chairs, Jenny put her head in her hands. Nick had actually told her he'd wanted a relationship, and she'd knocked him back. Closing her eyes, she reminded herself of all the reasons she couldn't trust him. Whatever she felt, she had to be strong. She had to do her best to provide a stable home for Grace, and Nick couldn't be a part of it. He just couldn't. She couldn't be let down again. She wouldn't put herself in that situation.

Pulling her mobile from her jean pocket, she scrolled down until she found Helen's number. Helen wouldn't believe that Nick had tried to put the blame on her. She'd either be completely livid or find it hilariously funny, depending on what mood she was in.

No answer.

Pushing the chair back, she stood up. She'd transfer Grace into bed and try again.

'Come on, sweetie. Shhh... it's just Mummy. I'm going to take you up to bed now where you can get all cosy with Blankie.' Bending down, she scooped Grace into her arms, Grace's head lulling to rest on her shoulder.

Taking one step at a time, Jenny shushed as Grace stirred.

Tucking the bedsheet around Grace's small frame, Jenny kissed her on the top of the head and stroked her cheek. 'It's OK, you're in bed now. Go back to dreaming. That's it, good girl.'

Soon Grace's breathing became slow and regular again as she drifted back to sleep. Inching towards the edge of the bed, Jenny slowly stood up, hoping the movement wouldn't wake Grace again.

Leaving the door ajar, Jenny tried Helen again. No answer still.

Clearing her throat, she left a message. 'Helen, it's Jenny. Can you call me back as soon as possible, please? I need to talk to you.'

In the kitchen, she filled the sink with hot soapy water and began scrubbing at the tomato soup stains from the bowls. How could Nick have lied to her like that? Straight to her face? He'd looked shocked that she had known what he had done, really shocked, and the scary thing had been that he hadn't looked like he was lying when he denied it. He'd looked confused, upset even. Yep, she'd done the right thing. Anthony had been able to lie like that, she didn't need it again.

Clattering the bowls onto the drying rack, she tried to steady her breathing. Why had him lying affected her this much? Yes, she'd liked him. If she was honest, she'd felt drawn to him from the moment they'd met, she could see that now. Shaking her head, she pulled the plug and watched the bubbles squeeze down the plughole. She'd known what he was like from the moment she'd found out who he was, she shouldn't have let herself feel like this.

Her mobile buzzed along the work surface before ringing, its high-pitched ringtone piercing the silence of the flat. Drying her hands on the tea towel, Jenny grabbed it as quickly as she could. She didn't need Grace to be woken up. She'd been grouchy enough after nursery, she needed all the sleep she could get.

'Hello?'

'Hi, Jenny, it's me, Helen. Sorry, I missed your call. I've got so much to tell you! I've met this guy, well, I met him on the first day I got here, but it was only the other day that I found out he actually likes me. He is literally amazing! He lives next door, and it's so sweet all the neighbours help each other out, you know if they need any repairs doing or anything. So, two days ago now, there was me cutting the front lawn minding my own business, and he turns up, with his streamer, and only begins helping me!'

'He sounds nice. What's his name?' Pulling out a chair from the small kitchen table tucked away in the corner, Jenny sat down.

'Jude. He is just so lovely. He's got these eyes that you get completely lost in when he looks at you, and he's got such a great sense of humour. You'd like him, Jenny. You two would get on so well. Oh, and his best mate is gorgeous too, just your type. Hey, I'll set you up when we get married. You'll obviously be my maid of honour and he'll be Jude's best man... It'll be so cute!'

Jenny rolled her eyes. Helen always did jump straight into a relationship with both feet. 'Look, I rang because I need to talk to you about something.'

'Right, sorry, there's me rambling away and I haven't even asked you how it's all going there. It's just so exciting. I literally don't think I've felt like this about anyone before. At least not for a very long time, anyway. He's absolutely perfect.'

'I'm really happy for you. It sounds like you're enjoying it over there still then?'

'I sure am! It's great, really great. Now, what's up? Is everything OK with the business? How's Grace enjoying nursery? Is it making life easier having her go?'

'Yes, it's all fine. Business is good, we're really busy at the moment, actually. Grace is enjoying nursery and, yes, it makes working at the parlour so much easier knowing she's well looked after and happy.'

'Good, good. It sounds like it's all going well. Oh, I'm not sure if I've already mentioned this, but I normally pitch a stall on the beach for the Summer Festival. I normally sell cookies and hot chocolate, that sort of thing. It usually brings in loads of extra cash, and it's fun too, being in the midst of everything.'

'What's the Summer Festival?' Jenny closed her eyes, it rang a bell.

'You've probably seen posters around town? There are usually posters on every lamppost and roundabout. It's a big thing down there. There's usually a huge influx of tourists that weekend, and then on the Saturday evening, people dress up and walk through the town to the beach. On the beach, there are loads of stalls and usually a few fairground rides for the little ones. It's great, and there are fireworks over the sea too, which are absolutely amazing!'

'Oh, wow. It sounds really good.' That was it, she'd probably seen posters around town, just not taken much notice of them. It did sound good, but it also sounded as though it would be hard work, especially if they had to run a stall too. If there was going to be even more tourists arriving for that weekend, she dreaded to think how busy the parlour would be. She took a deep breath, she knew she was looking at it the wrong way, she knew she should be feeling positive about it. After all, it sounded as though it would bring more money in for the parlour.

'It really is. You'll love it and little Gracie will, too.'

'Umm.' She wouldn't even think about how she'd cope with looking after Grace whilst running the stall. On the one hand, it would be great if it fell on a weekend she was at Anthony's but then, on the other hand, it would be a shame for her to miss it. Jenny would have to check the dates on one of the posters on the way to nursery in the morning.

'Anyway, what was it you wanted to talk about?'

'Oh, that.' Running her finger along the edge of the table, she scratched at a drop of dried soup she'd missed earlier. 'It was about Nick. We were having a conversation, well argument, earlier, and he tried to make out that he hadn't cheated on you. He'd been adamant. It just really annoyed me that he lied about it, especially with you all the way in Australia, it's not as though you were here to defend yourself even.'

'Right...'

Clasping her mobile to her ear, Jenny listened to the silence.

She shouldn't have said anything. She'd upset Helen now. Why had she told her? She hadn't needed to. She shouldn't have. It wasn't as though it was affecting Helen, Nick telling lies. It wasn't affecting her at all. Or it hadn't been, not until Jenny had brought the subject up. 'I'm sorry. I don't even know why I felt as though I had to tell you. Just forget I said anything.'

'You just took me by surprise, that's all. I've not thought about Nick for so long now, not in that way. In fact, I think the last thought I had about him in the slightest way that way was that you two would end up together. You deserve a good man.'

A hollow laugh escaped Jenny's throat. 'Right, thanks. I'm not that desperate to date someone who I know has a track record of cheating, thanks. I think I'd rather be alone than go into a relationship, knowing there was a high possibility he'd do the dirty on me too.' Jenny shook her head. Of all the people she knew, she'd always thought Helen would look out for her.

'Ah, Nick's a good guy.'

'How can he be? He cheated on you! You literally had to move to the other side of the world to get over him!'

'That's not entirely true...'

'Well, it must have been a factor for you moving there. You made the decision shortly after you broke up with him, didn't you?'

'Well, yes I did, but he wasn't the reason why I moved here. Look, for all his faults, Nick's one of the good guys, really good guys. I mean, he helped me out by buying into the business, didn't he? I would have lost it completely if it wasn't for him.'

'Yes, but it couldn't have been very nice for you to have to constantly see him.'

'I didn't. He's a silent partner, he hardly ever used to come in.'

'Oh, right.' Then why was he always in there now, or why had he used to be? The only reason he'd come into the parlour since that Friday was to show the estate agent round. In the beginning, it had probably been to check up on her, and she didn't blame him, he hadn't known her. But the rest of the time? Well, he either really had felt a connection, or he'd really not trusted her with the business. Business had been going well, maybe he had been being honest when he'd said he'd felt a connection too.

'Go on, give him a go. Hey, you might be able to get together on the night of the Summer Festival, fireworks are always romantic.'

'Umm, you're forgetting he is still a cheat. You should be protecting me, not trying to force me into a relationship with someone who can't be trusted.' She closed her eyes. A relationship with Nick had to stay off the cards. Not that the option was even there any more, not after the way they'd had that argument.

'Jenny. He didn't, OK? He didn't cheat.'

'Yes, he did. I remember you telling me.'

'No, I didn't tell you he cheated.'

'You did. You specifically told me you'd broken up because of another person.' Why was she trying so hard to get her to go out with him?

'Exactly. I told you that we broke up because of another person. It wasn't Nick who had the affair.'

'It was you?'

'Yes, I'm not proud of it, but yes, it was me who had the affair.' Helen suddenly sounded very very far away.

'You? You don't cheat.'

'I did. It was with Dean, you know the bloke I dated a few years back and was totally in love with? Or so I thought I was, anyway. He came back into town. We were just going to be friends, but then one evening one thing led to another and I felt awful. I felt terrible for Nick, I really did. So I didn't say anything. I thought it was best to protect him from it.'

'So then he found out...?'

'No. Not about the first time, anyway.'

'The first time? You mean you carried on seeing him behind Nick's back? How long for?' Jenny wiped the dried tomato soup from her finger onto the tea towel in front of her and straightened the placemats. Helen had always been so against lying, let alone cheating on someone. What had happened to her?

'A while.' Helen cleared her throat. 'A couple of months, three maybe. Please don't judge me though. It wasn't meant to happen, it just kind of did. He'd ran into money problems, or that's what he told me, and when I lent him the money he didn't want anyone to know it had been me who had lent it him. He thought it best I carried on seeing Nick so no one would guess.'

'You lent him money? How much?'

'A lot. Too much. Of course, I found out eventually that he was just playing me and didn't want a real relationship with me.' Helen's voice cracked down the phone line. 'He was just using me.'

'For the money?' How could she have been so naïve? Helen was smart, smart enough to build up a successful business from scratch. How on earth had she found herself in that position?

'Yes, for the money. He just wanted me to bail him out of a few debts he'd run up. He had people on his tail for it and I guess in some weird way he probably was trying to protect me by insisting I carry on with Nick, so nobody knew where the money had come from.'

Shaking her head, Jenny pinched the bridge of her nose. Protecting her? He didn't exactly sound the sort to protect anyone, not if he was happy to take money from his so-called girlfriend, secret lover, whatever title she would have had. 'That's why you went to Australia, to get over Dean, then? It was nothing to do with Nick?'

'I know it sounds like I'm an awful person, and I was, I'm not saying what I did wasn't wrong. It was, it was horrible and the way I treated Nick...'

'Did you get the money back?' There was no point in asking really, Jenny knew that.

'No, I don't even know where he is now.'

'And Nick owning half the business, was that to bail you out after you'd bailed Dean out?'

'Yes. Nick was so lovely. Even after he found out everything about Dean. Obviously, we split up, and he was really hurt and I assume quite angry with me, but after a bit, we became friends again and when he found out what a mess the business was in, he offered to buy a share. He really is a good guy.'

'I'm starting to see that. Why didn't you tell me any of this? We must have spoken loads on the phone when all of that was going on. I think you even came and saw me for a weekend, didn't you?'

'Yes, I did. We took Gracie to the centre of London for the day, didn't we? She loved the train. I just couldn't bring myself to tell you. You'd split from Anthony and then found out he was dating that Annie girl so soon after. Do you remember you were saying that you didn't know if anything had been going on whilst you'd been together? I couldn't tell you I was one of those people. I didn't want to jeopardise our friendship.'

'So you decided to wait until I found out when you were on the other side of the world? Helen, we tell each other everything. Or we used to anyway.'

'Umm, that's not entirely true, though is it? You haven't told me how you feel about Nick.'

'What do you mean?'

'Well, there's obviously something going on or you wouldn't be ringing me up trying to get my side of the story.'

'What? How has what I feel about him got anything to do with you lying to me? Anyway, nothing is going on.' Helen and her lies had seen to that. Laying her free hand palm down on the table, she took a deep breath, trying to calm herself.

'If you didn't feel anything for him, you wouldn't be getting so angry with me now.'

'I'm not getting angry. I'm upset that you felt you had to lie to me, but I'm not angry. What you did, do, is your own business, not mine. It was between you and Nick.'

'Umm, but you do like him. Admit it.' Helen's tone softened.

Jenny shook her head. It didn't matter now, anyway. She'd completely ruined any chance she'd had of them getting together. 'He's your ex and you know I wouldn't date an ex of yours. Plus, you'd led me to believe he was a cheat. I wasn't about to go and get involved with him knowing, or thinking, that he'd break my heart. I've had enough of men letting me down, I wasn't about to walk into a relationship thinking he had a track record of sleeping with other women behind his girlfriend's back.'

Helen laughed.

'What? What's so funny?'

'How old are you? You seriously wouldn't get with someone just because he was my ex?'

'No, it's a moral thing, which it seems you probably wouldn't be so good at.'

'Jenny, I'm sorry. Seriously though, nothing's happened between you? I'd really thought you two would hit it off. In my mind it was a bit like setting you up on a blind date, only you were managing a business together instead of having dinner.'

Jenny tapped her fingers on the table, Helen could turn anything into a game. 'We spent the night together the other week, but that's it. You'd told me he was a cheat so I...'

'So you ruined your chances.'

'Yes, I brushed him off.' With her voice cracking, Jenny closed her eyes. It wasn't funny. It was her life. Helen's lies had ruined the one good thing that could have happened to her in ages before it had even begun.

'I'm sorry, Jenny. I really am. I just didn't think... Ring him, tell him I bent the truth. Blame me if you have to.'

'There's no point. He wants to leave anyway, doesn't he?'

'Oh, of course. All that business with Steph and Rob? Nothing's sold yet though. The parlour isn't even on the market yet and his house will take ages to sell. Speak to him.'

'Maybe.'

'There's no maybe about it. Just give him a ring. Or do you want me to ring him and explain?'

'No, no, I don't. Look, I'm going to go now. Have a good evening. Bye.'

'OK, sorry again. Bye.'

Placing the mobile carefully on the table, Jenny lined it up against the top of the placemat. How could Helen have thought it OK to lie to her? And what on earth had she been on about when she'd said she'd felt like she was setting them up on a blind date? She should have known Jenny wouldn't have wanted anything to do with Nick, not after Helen telling her he'd cheated. Helen had cut their chances from the beginning.

Standing up, she grabbed the dishcloth and wiped the table. She'd have to ring him. She'd have to apologise. Throwing the dishcloth in the sink, she slumped back into the chair. She really didn't want to have this conversation. How could an apology make up for calling him a liar and not believing him? It couldn't. And it certainly couldn't come close to making up for the fact that she had accused him of cheating. She shrugged. It had been so obvious that he had been telling the truth. Of course, he wouldn't cheat on someone. Like he'd said, he knew what it felt like to be the victim.

Calling his number on her mobile, she listened to the rings.

Nothing. It went straight to voicemail, a nasally woman instructing her to leave a message. She couldn't very well leave this as a message. It was too big, too important a conversation to have one-sided.

Replacing her phone on the table, she closed her eyes. He wouldn't want her now, anyway. She'd blown her chances. Completely blown them.

* * *

Pulling the sleeves of her pyjama top down over her wrists, Jenny pulled the throw over her, leaning her head against the sofa cushions. Even though the weather had been scorching earlier, there was a definite nip in the air tonight.

Flicking through the channels, Jenny sighed. It was no good. There was only one thing she had to do, and however much TV she watched it wasn't going to block it from her mind. Sitting up again, she grabbed her mobile from the coffee table. She'd try him again and this time she would leave a message. Just in case he was ignoring her.

'... please leave a message after the tone.'

We know, we know. Everyone knows you have to wait for the tone to finish before speaking, so why did every recorded message still insist on instructing the caller? 'Nick, hi, it's Jenny. I know you probably don't want to speak to me at the moment, but I want to apologise. I'd thought that you had cheated on Helen. I know that's not the case now. Helen told me what had happened. I'm sorry. Really sorry. I shouldn't have accused you. Umm, can you ring me back, please?'

Had that been enough? Should she have said something else too? There was so much to say. She'd rambled, hadn't she? Picking up a cushion she hugged it to her chest. There was nothing she could do about it now, anyway. She should just try to get some sleep before opening the parlour again in the morning. And she must remember to talk to Ashley about the Summer Festival. They would need to start preparing for a stall if they were going to have one. Would she have to book it? With whom though? The organisers? And would she need to apply for a licence so they could sell off premises? Unless because they had premises and actually had the parlour, maybe they wouldn't need a licence? Pulling the throw back over her, she tried to block all the thoughts rushing through her head. Ashley would no doubt know the answers to the business questions. As for Nick, she'd hopefully run into him or something.

13

—————

'Literally don't worry about the festival. Helen booked us in again straight after last year's and there's not much to do to get ready for it. We just need to bake some cookies and flapjacks or something and get the stuff from the wholesalers.'

Replacing the empty ice cream tubs, Jenny looked across at Ashley.

'Honestly, it will be fine. It's normally a really good night. It has a great atmosphere.'

Nodding, Jenny took the empty tubs back into the kitchen. It did sound as though it should be quite straightforward. Ashley had said it was in two weeks, so Grace would be at Anthony's. It was a shame that she'd miss out but she'd probably not remember it anyway, and running the stall and keeping an eye on her at the same time would have been near impossible. Next year, if they were lucky enough to be able to find a place to rent and stay down here when Helen came back, she'd take her. That way they could really enjoy it, and Grace was more likely to understand what was going on and be able to remember it.

'Are you OK, Jenny? You look shattered.' Leaning against the kitchen doorframe, Ashley folded her arms.

'Sorry, I'm fine. I just didn't get much sleep last night, that's all.'

'Do you want me to take Grace to nursery for you today? She's there all day today, isn't she? It's usually quite quiet first thing so you'll be able to grab a coffee and have a minute.'

Jenny smiled, blinking back tears which threatened to spill. Ashley wouldn't be being so nice to her if she realised what she'd accused Nick of. 'That would be great, if you really don't mind?'

'Of course not. It'll be fun, won't it, Gracie Girl?' She ruffled Grace's hair as she walked into the kitchen.

'OK, thank you. That'll be nice, won't it, Gracie? Ashley's going to take you to nursery today.'

'Yay! Ashley! We look at the birdies.'

'She likes to watch the pigeons and seagulls down the High Street.' Jenny filled Grace's water bottle and popped it in her bag.

'Oh, I'm sure we can do that, can't we, Gracie?'

Taking a sip of her mocha, Jenny could almost feel the caffeine filtering through her system. She looked around; the menus were on the tables and everything was in place for the rush of customers they'd no doubt have later in the morning. For now, though, it was peaceful. A couple of dog walkers had popped in to grab a coffee on their way home and the three joggers had treated themselves to their usual caramel milkshakes and green tea, but apart from that Jenny had been on her own.

Walking to the front of the parlour, Jenny picked up one of the daily newspapers they had started to have delivered. Back behind the counter, she laid it out and skim-read the stories. She hardly ever read newspapers, she couldn't even remember the last time she had looked through one. She always meant to get one. She'd always thought she'd be a proper adult, one who read the papers over the breakfast table, swapping papers with her husband when she'd finished. She coughed, that hadn't worked out. In fact, her life wasn't anything like she'd planned and dreamt.

Looking up at the sea in the distance, she reminded herself that, no, her life hadn't turned out the way she had hoped, the way she had expected even, but that didn't mean she didn't have a good life. She did. She loved being able to bring Grace up by the beach and she enjoyed running Helen's business. It was really freeing not having to work for anyone. OK, that wasn't strictly true, she was working for Helen, but she wasn't answering to her, not on a daily basis.

Jerking her head up as the bell above the door jangled, she caught her breath. 'Hi, Nick. Hello, Ethan, is it?'

'Morning.' Nick looked past her, seemingly focusing his attention on the menu choices on the back wall above the counter.

'Good morning. Nice to see you again.' Stepping towards her, Ethan shook her hand. 'We won't disturb you for long, I just need to take some photos of the establishment.'

Biting down on her bottom lip, Jenny tried to remember if she'd cleared away the breakfast dishes.

'Don't worry, we can take photos of the flat at a later date, that's if we need to at all. With yourself as a sitting tenant and the business being so profitable, I am confident we will have a fair few offers in no time. In fact, I wouldn't be at all surprised if we can close a deal by the end of the summer season.'

'That quick?' Swallowing hard, Jenny laid her hands against the counter.

'Oh yes, we'll make the process as quick and stress-free as possible.' Ethan nodded at her before pulling a small camera from his suit pocket. Walking towards the front of the parlour, he pulled open the door. 'I'll start with the frontage and work my way through.'

'Nick, wait.' Placing her hand on his arm as he walked past her, Jenny steadied her voice. 'Can I have a quick word?'

'To be honest, I'd like to go with Ethan and check the quality of his photos.'

Narrowing her eyes, she shook her head. 'Please? It won't take long.'

'OK. What can I help you with?' Folding his arms, Nick looked at her.

'Thanks.' Scratching the back of her neck, Jenny stepped back a little. 'I spoke to Helen. I'm so so sorry, I got it completely wrong. I just, I really thought it had been the other way round. I didn't mean to offend you or upset you.' Had he got her voicemail?

'Thank you for the apology.' Turning away, Nick began walking towards the front of the parlour.

'Nick, please?'

Stopping, he turned around, his arms by his sides. 'What do you want from me, Jenny?'

You. I want you. I want you to forgive me, to tell me you understand it wasn't my fault that Helen had bent the truth or at least implied it had been the other way around. I want you. 'I don't know. I guess I want you to understand why I said what I did. I guess I want you to give me another chance.'

'Look, honestly, thank you for apologising, and in some way, I understand why you thought it had been me who had been in the wrong. So I completely understand why you spoke to me the way you did and why you would want to push me away.' Running his hand through his hair, he looked down at his shoes before looking her in the eye. 'No actually, I just don't understand how you could have thought that about me, why you'd take someone's word the way you did. You pretty much know me and I guess I didn't think I came across as the sort of person who would treat another human being like that.'

'I feel I know you too. I just, I had thought... I mean thinking back to my conversations with Helen I realise she didn't actually say it had been you who had cheated, but she'd said a third person had been involved in your breakup and I guess I just jumped to conclusions. The wrong conclusions. I thought I knew her. I didn't think she would do what she did. I got it wrong.' What else could she say?

Nick nodded and glanced across at Ethan who had just re-entered the parlour.

'I'm sorry. I don't know what else I can say.'

'There isn't anything. I understand. You and Helen have been friends for years. I understand why you assumed the worst of me and the best of her. It's only natural.'

'Yes, it is. I am sorry and...' Could she bring herself to say it? 'It would be great if you could stay and we could maybe see how things go?'

Looking down at his shoes, Nick rubbed his hand across his face. 'I'm going up to Yorkshire to look at a practice next week.'

'Oh, right. Of course, sorry.' Tilting her head, she looked at him. This business with Steph and Rob was really taking its toll on him. Judging by his bloodshot eyes and the dark circles enveloping them, he couldn't be getting much sleep still. His whole physique had changed. Not so long ago he had seemed so full of energy and enjoying life, and now with his arms folded against his chest again, he just looked so closed, so defeated. 'Look, Nick. You don't have to go. Stay. Why don't you stay? You've achieved so much here, don't let them push you away. It's your home.'

Shaking his head, he drew in a deep breath. 'It was never my home, not really. I only moved down here to be with Steph. Yes, I've made a life down here for myself but...' Shrugging he glanced towards Ethan who was kneeling down in the front corner trying to get the best angle for a photo. 'I can make a life for myself back in Yorkshire too. It's only fair on Steph that she gets her happy ever after.'

'Do...' Shaking her head, Jenny swallowed her words. Even if she thought that Steph didn't deserve a happy ever after, not after the way she'd treated Nick, and was still treating him now, it wasn't for Jenny to try to control how Nick coped with the whole situation. 'She didn't look especially happy the other day, anyway. Will you moving away really affect how she lives her life? Do you think her happiness really depends on whether you're here or not? Loads of people carry on living in the same town as their exes. Why is it so different with you two?'

Standing there, Nick watched a dark blue saloon car parallel park outside the parlour. The tourists were arriving to spend their day at the beach.

'Sorry, I shouldn't have said anything. It's not my place to question you.'

'You're right though. Most people would be able to handle living close to their exes, most people do. I guess the truth is it's not so much about Steph. I haven't felt anything for her in a very long time, it's Rob. He was my best mate and now he's trying to evict me from the town I've made my home in. I just don't see how it'd work, not with us both working in the same field as well. Plus, more than him, it's the fact that Steph's parents have been treating me like a son for the last, I don't know how many years, and now they're lending Rob the money to buy me out. I... I suppose I'm weak. Maybe I should stand up to them and tell them I don't need their kindness, their support any longer, but it hurts.' Nick held his fist to his chest. 'They had treated me like a son and now...'

'Have you spoken to them? Since Rob's been trying to buy you out?'

'What's the point? I can see where their loyalties lie, and I don't blame them. Steph is their daughter and, of course, they'll want the best for her.'

'There might be a point. Surely it would be good for you to speak to them, to try to understand why they are doing what they are?'

Nick shrugged. 'Maybe.'

'Sorry to interrupt, but can I just ask you both to move towards the window so I can get some photographs of the counter, please?' Ethan waved them away.

'Of course. Sorry.'

'You mentioned you saw them arguing?' Nick looked up from the floor.

'Steph and Rob? Yes, they were standing outside the estate agent's window, looking at houses.'

Frowning, Nick sighed. 'Right, I remember you saying. I didn't think they could afford to move out, not unless her parents are lending them the money for that too.'

'Right, that's me done. I'll get these up on the website ASAP and arrange for a For Sale sign to go up. You never know, a sign might entice one of the tourists to decide they want a change of life, move down to the beach, etc., etc. And with the Summer Festival coming up there'll be thousands of people passing by.' Shaking Nick's hand, Ethan nodded at Jenny and left.

'I'd better be off too. Thanks for this.' Holding out his hands, he indicated the parlour.

'Stay.' Jenny cleared her throat and tried again, louder this time so he could hear. 'Stay.'

'My shift at the vets starts soon.'

'No, I mean, stay. Stay here. Don't move. You said you wanted a relationship. Stay and let's see where things go.' Looking into his eyes, she clasped her hands together in front of her.

Sticking his hands in his pockets, Nick looked at her, glanced towards the door and back at her. 'I'd love to, but I can't. I can't do it. I can't risk falling for you, we don't have that trust. It wouldn't work.'

'What do you mean we don't have trust? Is it because I got it wrong? Is it because I accused you of cheating on Helen?' Why had she been so stupid?

'No, yes, a little. I'm sorry.'

'Right, sorry. I'd better go and get the... refill the mint-choc-chip.' Turning on her heels, Jenny rushed towards the kitchen, letting the door swing shut behind her. Why had she asked him again? He'd already said he was going. He'd decided to up and leave, of course, he wouldn't stay just because she'd asked him. Who did she think she was, anyway? She hardly knew him, he hardly knew her. He wasn't going to completely change his plans, his life decisions, for her.

Placing the palms of her hands on the work surface, Jenny looked down at her ragged nails. It wasn't as though she was pretty, even. Steph was a lot prettier than her, and Helen was stunning. In what world had she even thought for a single moment that someone like Nick would look twice at her?

Yes, he had said he had wanted a relationship with her when they'd been on the beach, but he'd been visibly hurting, he'd probably just wanted someone, anyone.

Turning around, she leaned the small of her back against the edge of the work surface and held her hands to her cheeks. Closing her eyes, she waited until she was sure the fierce redness from her cheeks had died down.

'Morning! Anyone here?' A voice floated through from the parlour.

'Drat.' Of course, Ashley was taking Grace to nursery. Pushing herself away from the work surface, she wiped her eyes and plastered a grin on her face before opening the door to the parlour. 'Morning, sorry about that, I was just getting a few supplies.' Looking down at her empty hands, she placed them on the counter in front of her. 'What can I get you today?'

'I'll have a strawberry milkshake, please?'

'Coming right up.' Glancing at her phone on the shelf, she noticed she had three missed calls. All from Helen. Shaking her head, she hit the button to silence the ringtone as it began vibrating again. She could wait. She was the reason Jenny had lost out on having a relationship with Nick, well, a large part of it, anyway. Jenny had nothing to say to her at the moment.

* * *

'Wow, that must have been the busiest lunchtime I've seen here so far.' Throwing the tea towel down, Jenny turned towards the coffee machine. 'Do you want some caffeine?'

'Absolutely. I stupidly thought I'd wear these shoes in today, you know make them comfy. I brought them for the Summer Festival, but they're killing me. I'm sure I must have about a hundred blisters threatening to pop up anytime soon.' Leaning down, Ashley rubbed her ankle.

'They're nice though, really nice. Do you want to borrow a pair of trainers? I think we're probably a similar size.'

'Is that OK? That would be awesome, please?'

'I'll pop and get them now. I won't be long.'

Upstairs in the bedroom, Jenny reached underneath the bed and pulled out a pair of trainers. Holding them in her hand, she perched on the edge of the bed. That was one good thing about them being so busy, she hadn't had time to even think about Nick, not until now anyway. Even just the memory of her asking him to stay caused her cheeks to burn. But at least she'd asked him. She hadn't got the answer she'd wanted, but she'd asked him. If she hadn't taken that chance then she'd always have wondered.

'Jenny!' Ashley's voice pierced the silence in the small flat as she called up the stairs.

'Coming!' Pushing herself off of the bed, she ran down the stairs, they must have become busy again. Pushing the door open, she looked to see Ashley standing behind the counter, the parlour's retro red telephone in her hand, the mouthpiece covered.

'Here she is. Bye.'

'Thanks.' Jenny took the phone from Ashley and nodded. 'Hi, Jenny here.'

'Hi, Jenny.'

'Oh, Helen. Afternoon.' Scrunching up her nose, Jenny wound her finger around the telephone cord.

'I've been trying to get hold of you. Are you ignoring my calls?'

'What? No, of course not. We've just been really busy and I haven't had a chance to check my mobile, that's all.'

'I'd believe you but knowing you, you keep your mobile close just in case Grace's nursery calls. Look, I don't blame you for ignoring me. I deserve it after I misled you about what happened between Nick and I. And I'm sorry if it's made things awkward between you two. I never meant or thought that would happen.'

'Umm.' Jenny rolled her eyes. Made things awkward? That was an understatement. More like completely destroyed any chance of anything happening between them and any chance of Jenny actually finding any form of happiness after everything with Anthony. She took a deep breath, she knew Helen hadn't meant to ruin things between them but she had still lied, and they were friends, she shouldn't have lied to her, or omitted the truth as she called it. Helen knew how much Jenny hated lying after living with Anthony for so long.

'Anyway, look, that's not why I phoned. Well, part of it is. I mean, I would have rung to apologise again, but I need to ask you a favour.'

'Oh, right.' Great, she messes with her life and now she needs a favour.

'I've had Patricia on the phone.'

'Who?' Jenny shook her head, she didn't know anyone called Patricia. At least she didn't remember anyone called Patricia.

'Patricia, she's Steph's mum. You know, Nick's ex-fiancée, the one who left him for his so-called best man?'

'I know who Steph is, I just didn't know her mum's name.'

'Yes, well, it's Patricia. She's been on the phone to me and she's really worried about Nick. Apparently, he's stopped going round there, and she hasn't seen him for weeks. She was saying that the last time she saw him, he looked really rough. Tired and run-down?'

'Yes, this business with Steph and Rob has really got to him. I'm not surprised he hasn't been going round there. I thought Steph and Rob were living with them?'

'I know, that's what I thought, and she said they are but she was saying that Nick normally pops round at least twice a week. They had a really close relationship after Steph ran off with Rob. He didn't have family or friends around there so they kind of took him under their wing. I know what you mean, though. I thought it's not particularly surprising that he doesn't want to go round there with Steph and Rob living there.'

'No, it's a bit weird to expect him to.'

'Exactly. Anyway, I said that to her, and she said she understands, but she's been trying to ring him and he's not been answering.'

'I don't really blame him, do you?'

'It seems strange, though. When I was with Nick he always made a point of going round there, usually for a roast on a Sunday, but if we were busy, he'd go another time. I don't think he went more than a week without visiting them.'

'Maybe, but things have changed now, haven't they? I mean, Steph and Rob are back and staying there and her parents have given them money to buy Nick out, so things are bound to be different.'

'What do you mean?'

'Well, I don't think I'd particularly want to go and spend time with somebody knowing that they're basically the reason I was being made to sell my business and move on, would you?'

'That doesn't make any sense.'

Jenny shrugged. Surely Helen must see Nick's point of view? 'No, it does, Steph's parents have basically stabbed him in the back. They've been all nice and friendly to him for all these years but now that their precious daughter, Steph, has returned they've turned their backs on Nick. And, they've even gone one step further than most ex-in-laws, they've given their daughter and son-in-law a weapon to drive him away from the home he's made. I don't blame him in the slightest, not wanting to talk to them. I don't think I'd particularly want to talk to Anthony's parents now that they've dropped me as part of the family and welcomed this Annie in, and they've not done half of what Steph's parents have. You...'

'Jenny, stop. Hold up.' Helen interrupted her, her voice suddenly sounding very muffled.

'What? You OK?'

'Yes, I'm fine. What did you say about Steph and Rob's money though? They want to buy Nick out, I knew that, but what do you mean about Steph's parents giving them the money?'

'They've given Steph and Rob the money to buy Nick out. I thought you knew that?'

'No, no, I didn't. That doesn't make any sense. Are you sure?'

'Positive. Or that's what Nick's told me, anyway. Plus, where else would they be getting the money from? Steph and Rob had to go bankrupt, that's why they've moved back.'

'Yes, I knew that, but... No, you've got the wrong end of the stick. They haven't given them the money to buy him out. They've given them the money to buy a house. It's an early inheritance, that's what she told me.'

'Are you sure? Where are they getting the money to buy Nick's share of the veterinary practice then? If they've just been made bankrupt, it's not like they could get a loan or anything.' Jenny watched as an influx of customers swept through the door and pointed to the phone, mouthing to Ashley, 'Shall I ring back later?'

Shaking her head, Ashley gave her the thumbs-up, indicating that she could cope.

'No, that's really strange. Patricia wouldn't lie, though. She's a good person, she wouldn't want anything to do with a plan to buy Nick's half of the practice. She knows how much it means to him and she cares about him.'

'Well, they're getting the money from somewhere.'

'Not from her, she wouldn't do that. I believe that one hundred per cent.' The phone line went quiet. 'Unless they're using her money but she doesn't know yet.'

'What do you mean? You think they're using her money to buy in on the practice instead of buying a house?'

'I can't think of another explanation, can you?'

'No, I can't and thinking about it I saw them both arguing outside the estate agent's window the other day when I was walking back after dropping Gracie off.'

'Maybe that's it then.'

'Maybe.'

'Look, will you go and speak to Nick for me?'

'What? Me? Why?'

'That's what I rang for, Patricia had asked me to talk to Nick and see why he's not been answering her calls or going round, but to be honest, I think it would be better if you go and talk to him. Face to face. It's not the same over the phone. Especially now, when it sounds like Patricia hasn't got a clue about Steph and Rob buying the business. Someone needs to tell him.'

'Yes, but we might have it wrong. Patricia might know, or the money might be coming from somewhere else.' Scrunching up her forehead, she pinched the top of her nose. It wasn't her place to go and speak to Nick. What was she supposed to say to him? Just barge in and talk about his business? He'd know she'd been speaking about him behind his back.

'Fair enough. I'll ring Patricia and ask her and then I'll either ring or message you and tell you what she said. But you promise you'll go round and talk to him, won't you?'

'No, I can't. I don't think I can. It's really busy here and I don't feel comfortable talking to him about something that's none of my business.'

'Please, Jenny? For him? He deserves to know what's going on before he makes such a massive decision about selling up and moving away.'

Jenny shook her head. She'd have to be strong. 'No, Patricia can talk to him herself. It's not for me to do.'

A crackling noise buzzed down the line, Helen must have moved the phone or something. 'Jenny, please? She can't. I know her. She hates any confrontation or anything out of the ordinary. There isn't anyone else I can ask. And it would be so much better coming from you, rather than me ringing him. Please, Jenny?'

Slumping her shoulders, Jenny sighed. 'I suppose so, but not until I know for definite that Patricia's not got anything to do with it.'

'Thank you! I'll ring her now. Thanks again, I really do appreciate this.'

Placing the phone back in its receiver, Jenny rolled her eyes. Why did it have to be her? Nick had loads of friends here. Why hadn't Helen asked one of them to speak to him?

'Everything OK?' Shutting the till, Ashley looked across at her.

'No, I don't think so. Helen wants me to talk to Nick about Patricia.'

'Oh, what about her?'

'Look, it's quietened down again now, you sit down and I'll grab us some coffees and bring them over. My head's reeling and I'm not really sure what's going on. Maybe you can shed some light on it.' Turning to the coffee machine, Jenny inhaled the bitter aroma. That's what she needed, some caffeine to clear her head.

* * *

Clasping her hands in front of her, Jenny tapped her foot on the newly mopped tiles. Keeping her eyes down, she tried to avoid the gaze from the receptionist. Nick must have spoken to her and told her how Jenny had treated him. The woman hadn't stopped staring since Jenny had told her she'd wait as long as she needed in order to see Nick. She checked her watch, she'd been waiting for almost half an hour now. Who knew a vet could be in such high demand on a summer's day in a small coastal town?

Circling her shoulders, she tried to relieve some of the tension pulling on her neck. She was getting a headache, maybe even a migraine. After getting the text from Helen to say that Patricia definitely hadn't given Steph and Rob the money to buy Nick out, Ashley had insisted Jenny had left straight away to come and tell him. Jenny still didn't know why it had to be her, she'd suggested to Ashley she should speak to him because she had known him longer than Jenny, but, no, for some reason it was Jenny who was sat waiting while Ashley held the fort back at the parlour.

The clip, clip, clip of the receptionist's shoes echoed in the empty waiting room. 'He will see you now. Mind, he does have an actual patient due in a few minutes.'

'Thank you.' Standing up, Jenny smiled and hoped the flush of embarrassment would fade before she got to his room.

Taking a deep breath, she knocked on the door and walked in. Nick was sat on a stool on the other side of the treatment table.

'Jenny. Laura said you wanted to see me. The estate agent hasn't been bombarding you with viewings by any chance, has he?' A small grin briefly lit up his face.

'No, sorry.' Clearing her throat, Jenny positioned herself opposite him, her hands clasped in front of her. 'Helen rang me up and asked me to talk to you. I told her it's not really my place or anything and that someone else should talk to you, but she wouldn't listen.'

'OK.' Nick folded his arms and tilted his head, a slow smile emerging. 'So Helen has set up an intervention from the other side of the world then?'

'No, yes, I guess she has.' Jenny grimaced.

'Typical Helen.'

'Yep.'

'Go on, then. I'll listen.' Slumping his shoulders, he leaned forwards and put his elbows on the table in front of him.

'OK, well. To be honest, I don't really understand what I'm supposed to say but I'm guessing it will mean something to you.'

Nick nodded.

'Right, well, Patricia, is it? Steph's mum rang Helen up this morning, or earlier, whatever the time is in Australia, I don't know.'

'Patricia?' Sitting up straight, Nick narrowed his eyes. 'She hardly knows Helen. Why would she ring her up?'

'Because she's worried about you. Apparently, you used to go round there a couple of times a week, no exceptions, and you haven't been since Steph and Rob got back. Plus, she's said she's been trying to ring you and you've not been answering her calls?'

'Well, no. Of course I haven't. She's made it perfectly clear where I stand in her list of priorities now that Steph and Rob are back. She can't have made things any clearer than giving them the money to buy me out and get me to move away.'

'But she hasn't. That's not what's happened.' Biting the nail on her thumb, Jenny looked him in the eye. 'She's saying she's giving them money to buy a house. An early inheritance or something, but it's not to buy you out. It's for a house for them.'

Tapping his fingers on the table, he looked at her. 'But they *are* buying me out. The contracts are being made up as we speak, they must have got the money from her, Rob's parents would never be able to afford to give them that amount and they wouldn't be able to get credit or a business loan.'

'I know, I know, but there's got to be an explanation. It's not from her, or if it is then...'

'Then what?'

'Well, I saw them arguing in front of the estate agents the other day, didn't I? I don't know, unless they were arguing about buying a house. Maybe Rob didn't want to, I don't know. I really don't. I'm just trying to think of an explanation, but Helen's checked and Patricia and her husband have definitely only given them money to buy a house, not this place. They don't want you to leave.'

Pushing his hand through his hair, Nick looked down at the floor.

'As I said, it's not my place to say anything. I'm just... doing Helen a favour. I know how you feel. I know you want to leave, but now you know what's happening, that Patricia isn't trying to push you away, it's down to you to make your decision, no one else.' Looking down at her hands, she laced her fingers together, trying to resist the urge to bite her nails again.

Nick nodded.

'You OK?'

Looking up, Nick took a deep slow breath in. 'Yes, yes, I am. Thank you for letting me know.'

'Does that mean you're going to stay then?'

'As I said, contracts are being drawn up for this place, and my share of the parlour is on the market now as well.'

'You don't have to go through with selling them though.'

'And I've organised to look at that practice up in Yorkshire next week too.'

'You can tell them your circumstances have changed. There'll be others looking too. It might even go before you get up there, anyway.'

Shaking his head, he stood up. 'It doesn't change anything. I'll still have to live here knowing that Rob tried to force me away. I don't want that, I don't want to live feeling as though I'm always looking out for them and trying to avoid them.'

Pursing up her lips, she stared at him. He'd just found out Patricia, who for some reason he really cared about what she thought of him, wasn't, in fact, trying to push him away and he was still adamant he wanted to leave. 'OK.'

'I know that's not the answer you were after, but you're better off without me in your life, anyway. Look at me, I'm a mess.'

'No, you're not. You're just stressed out. Why don't you talk to her? To Patricia, I mean. Why don't you answer the phone when she rings next?'

Shaking his head, Nick walked towards the door and held it open. 'Thanks for letting me know but I'd better get on now.'

Nodding, Jenny walked out. Why did he still have his heart set on leaving? Yes, he'd still see Steph and Rob around and it wasn't a nice thought that his old best friend and ex-fiancée had tried to force him to sell and move away, but it wasn't uncommon for people to live close to their exes. It was just part of life, something to put up with. Most people weren't able to just up and leave on a whim.

14

'OK, that's the decorations for the stall. I'll just get those cookies out of the oven and I think we should be more or less set and ready to grab everything in the morning.' Jenny balanced a large cardboard box on top of one of the tables, before hurrying to the oven.

'Great. I'm almost done here, too. What do you think?' Holding the icing bag up, she looked across at Jenny.

'Wow, they're lovely. I love the way you've made the icing come out with the different colours, they've almost got a marbling effect.' The cupcakes not only looked good, but they smelled delicious too.

'Thanks. I learnt that from Helen last year. I'm going to put these on too. I thought they'd give them the firework effect.' Ashley shook a jar of brightly coloured sprinkles.

'That's a great idea. It's been hard work getting ready, but I'm really looking forward to it now.'

'Me too. You'll love it, the Summer Festival is always great.'

'It's just a shame Gracie is at Anthony's this weekend.' Putting the oven gloves on, she knelt in front of the oven and checked the cookies. They probably needed a couple of minutes longer. She blinked back her tears before standing up. She didn't think she'd ever get used to being away from Grace so much. And the thought of the three of them playing happy families...

'Yes, it is.'

Jenny cleared her throat. 'Anyway, it will be great. What time do you think we should start setting up?'

'The carnival part usually kicks off about two so we'd probably be OK if we started at one, then we'll be ready by the time people get down to the beach.'

'OK, great. Sounds like a good plan.'

The smell of onions from the hot dog stall to their left and the buzz of people around the pop-up bar to their right had driven a lot of people to their stall. With the sea in front of them and the sand underneath their feet, hundreds, if not a thousand, tourists had flocked to the festival.

Jenny hadn't seen the carnival but the music and people talking on microphones had echoed their way through the salt laced seaside air before the tourists and spectators had been directed towards the seafront to enjoy an evening full of entertainment, food and fireworks. Fire breathers, juggling clowns on stilts, and an array of other street performers mingled with the crowds.

'Two hot chocolates, please?' A couple stood in front of the stall, arms circling each other around the waist. They were clearly in the perfect rush of love felt at the beginning of a relationship.

'Coming up.' Smiling, Jenny poured hot milk into prepared cups and stirred. Shaking her head, she tried to block the thought that she and Nick could have been enveloped in the same warmth and security of love. 'Help yourselves to toppings.'

'Thank you.'

'You're welcome.' She watched them weave their way through the crowds before coming to a stop by the shoreline, where they stood watching the sun on its slow summer day's descent.

'Looks like we're running low on toppings.'

Switching her focus to Ashley, Jenny looked down. Sure enough, the jars of marshmallows, chocolate flakes and white chocolate stars were nearly empty. 'I'll pop back and grab some more then. You all right for a few minutes?'

'Yes, sure thing. Be quick though, the fireworks will be starting soon. You don't want to miss those!'

'OK, will do.' Balancing the jars in her arms, she turned and made her way across the sand towards the promenade and the parlour. She needed to grab her cardigan while she was there too. Although the sun had been blazing hot during the day, the chill of the evening was quickly closing in.

Shrugging into her cardigan, Jenny picked up the jars of toppings and cradled them in her arms. They were heavier now they were full. Shutting the door behind her, she waited until she heard the click of the deadlock before making her way back across the road. The street was empty and eerily quiet with only the music and babbling voices from the beach sweeping across the road.

Helen hadn't been wrong when she'd said the stall would bring in a lot of money. Even though they were surrounded by local businesses offering hot dogs, burgers, fizzy drinks and coffee, they'd had a steady stream of customers seeking the comfort of hot chocolate and cookies. She'd been worried about the bar being so close to them but if anything it seemed to have brought custom to them with parents treating their children while they had a sneaky alcoholic drink.

'Drat.' The shrill ringtone of her phone rang out. Swapping the jars to her other arm, she pulled her mobile from her back pocket. It was Anthony. 'Hi. Is Grace OK?'

'Hi, Jenny... Yes, just hang on a moment, Grace. Yes, it's Mummy.'

Hiccupping sobs filled Jenny's ear. Closing her eyes and biting down on her bottom lip, she tried to stop herself from joining her. 'What's happened? What's wrong with Gracie?'

'She's hurt her finger, and apparently, you're the only one who can make it better. Can you just talk to her or something? Calm her down. She's going to make herself sick if she carries on the way she is.' Anthony's voice was laced with irritation.

'Yes, yes. I'll talk to her. Put her on.' She couldn't do this any more. It wasn't natural to be so far away from Grace. She shouldn't have to be. Grace needed her and she needed Grace. 'Gracie, sweetheart. Have you hurt your finger?'

'It hurts.'

'OK. What happened? How did you hurt your finger?'

'Door. My finger went in the door.'

'Oh, darling. Did you get your finger trapped in the door? What a naughty door. Has Daddy run it under cold water? That will make it feel better.'

'Yes, and Annie gave me a cold flannel.'

'That's good.' Shaking her head, Jenny tried to block out the image of Annie holding a cold flannel to Grace's finger. She knew Annie was only trying to help but it still hurt that she was there, doing the things Jenny should be doing. 'Wrap it super tight around your finger then and that should make it stop hurting so much.'

Grace's sobs slowed.

'Have you done that, Gracie? Have you wrapped the cold flannel around your finger?'

'Annie has.'

'That's good.' Jenny swallowed the bitterness rising to her mouth and told herself it didn't matter who was comforting Grace as long as someone was. 'Is it a bit better now, sweetie?'

'Yes.'

'That's good then.'

'Mummy. Want to come home. Grace wants Mummy.'

'Oh, sweetie. I want you too, but you're at Daddy's this weekend, aren't you? Have you been doing anything fun?'

'She can't see you nodding. You need to talk.' Jenny could hear Anthony's muffled voice in the background.

'We had a BBQ and going swimming tomorrow.'

'Oh, wow. That sounds fun. You're going to have a lovely time then, aren't you?'

'Yes.'

'Do you feel a little better now? Is your finger a bit better?'

'Yes.'

'Good, good.'

'Got to go now.'

'OK. I tell you what, I'll blow a kiss down the phone and you can catch it and put it on your finger, OK?'

'Yes, Mummy. Can I have one for my cheek too?'

'Of course, you can, Gracie. Are you ready to catch?'

'Yes.'

Pursing her lips, Jenny blew two kisses down the phone. 'Did you get them?'

'Yes, Mummy.'

'Hi, it's Anthony. Thanks for that. She got herself into a bit of a state.'

'That's OK. Bye.' Putting her mobile back into her pocket, she juggled the jars around again and stood, watching as more people began descending onto the beach. A bonfire had been lit further up and Jenny took a deep breath in, letting the smoky smell of burning wood hit the back of her throat. She had fond memories of her dad burning a fire in the back garden, getting rid of unwanted furniture and old bills usually. As she'd got older, he'd sometimes used to let her roast marshmallows over the flickering flames.

This one though was huge. The Festival Team, as Ashley had referred to them, had been collecting spare wood from around the town for weeks now and the fire stood at least nine-foot high. A huge barrier encircled it, with members of the team standing watch, guarding the tourists from danger.

A family rushed past in front of her, calling to two teenage boys dragging their heels that the fireworks were going to start soon.

Shaking herself from her thoughts, she followed them across the road and down to the beach, weaving her way through the crowds back to the stall.

'Brilliant, you got them.' Taking the jars from Jenny's hands, Ashley grinned. 'The fireworks are going to start in a minute. It's never long after they light the bonfire.'

'Whereabouts do they do them?' Looking up and down the beach, apart from the barricaded area off where the bonfire was, the beach was packed. She couldn't imagine anyone being brave enough to light fireworks so close to the milling crowds.

'Over the water.'

'Really?' Jenny nodded. She supposed it made sense to keep them as far away from the beach as possible.

A crackling noise filled the air before a voice boomed over the sound system that had been rigged up. 'Ten seconds until the fireworks. Ten, nine, eight, seven, six, five, four, three, two, one!'

A loud cheer spread through the crowds as the first rocket squealed into the sky. A huge bang echoed along the shore and an array of lights cascaded from the sky, reflecting on the surface of the sea.

Unanimous oohs and ahhs filled the air as fireworks hissed and popped in the evening sky, illuminating the faces of fascinated children and equally enthralled adults. Music began playing through the sound system, the fireworks seemingly dancing to the rhythm. As the song tempo quickened so did the light show, short bursts of bangers popping. As the song slowed, the fireworks steadied, a colourful fountain representing the soothing tones of the song.

Pulling her cardigan tighter, Jenny watched as the next song played and then another. It was probably a good thing the Summer Festival had fallen on one of Anthony's weekends, Grace wasn't a fan of fireworks, bangs and sharp squeals of the rockets always made her jump. Hopefully next year she would have grown out of her fear and they could enjoy the Summer Festival together.

As the final song came to an end, two huge rockets screeched into the sky. They angled towards each other forming a bridge in the heavens before exploding and spraying a fountain of confetti sparks across the sea. Applause spread through the crowds as people cheered and clapped their appreciation.

'Wow! That was amazing. I don't think I've ever seen such a big firework show.'

'I know. It is awesome. You wait until Bonfire Night though, that's pretty amazing too.' Grinning, Ashley filled two cups with steaming hot chocolate and passed one to Jenny.

'Thanks.' Wrapping her hands around the warm cup, she took a sip, letting the scorching liquid hit the roof of her mouth. Their hot chocolate was pretty great too, even if she did say so herself. 'What happens next? Do we take down the stalls now?'

'We normally keep it open for another hour or so. Most people will get going off home pretty soon, but a fair few just hang around, listen to the music and sit on the beach. Enough usually stay to make it worth keeping the stall open for a bit.'

'OK, cool.' Sipping her hot chocolate, Jenny watched as the crowds dispersed. People headed back to their cars but, as Ashley had said, a fair few people stayed. The more prepared families laid down picnic rugs and settled in front of the waves, listening to the music while others threw themselves down on the sand or began paddling in the sea.

'Ashley, hi. Are you meeting us later? We're heading down to the pub in a bit.' A group of girls made their way towards the stall.

'I might do.'

'Why don't you get off? There's not many customers now.' She didn't recognise the girls from the night they went out. It must be a different group of friends.

'You sure? What about packing it away?'

'I'll cope. You go. You deserve it.'

'Thanks.' Grinning, Ashley downed the rest of her hot chocolate, grabbed her bag from underneath the stall and headed down the beach with her friends.

Taking a deep breath, Jenny breathed in the warm salty air. The bonfire was still burning, though not as brightly as before, and a team of people were making their way methodically down the beach clearing up any rubbish left behind from the festival-goers. She assumed they'd just let the bonfire burn out. It wasn't causing any harm or danger where it was, anyway.

'Two hot chocolates, please?' A man stood in front of her, holding out his money.

'Of course. Coming right up.' Filling the cups, Jenny indicated to the jars of toppings. 'Help yourself to any you want.'

'Thank you.'

She watched as he spooned a generous amount of marshmallows into both cups. A screech and a steady stream of laughter came from the sea.

'There's always someone. You wait and see, loads of them will join her now.'

'Are they swimming?' Peering across the beach, Jenny could

just about make out a figure in the water. 'It must be freezing in there now.'

'After the hot day we've had, it shouldn't be that cold. It's the tide they forget about. At this time it's surprisingly strong and the sea looks deceptively calm, but with us being so close to those rocks out there, it's a dangerous game to play. Ever since we moved down here seven years ago, there's always been people swimming after the festival. I used to think they'd move it down a few hundred metres, but for some reason, the planners like to have it here.'

'Oh, I wonder why? It seems odd having it so close to the rocks if they know people go swimming.'

'Ay, it does. Though, to be honest, I think they set some of the fireworks off from those rocks so I'm guessing that's the reason. Never mind, those chaps and ladies will keep an eye on them.' The man pointed across to the bright orange tent the lifeboat volunteers had set up.

'I'm sure they will.' She waited for the man to go before looking across at the tent. She hadn't noticed it there before, probably because the beach had been so crammed full. She couldn't make out who was on duty though, the dusk was setting in too much for that. One of them may have been Nick but she couldn't tell.

Glancing across at the stalls surrounding her, she realised most of them were beginning to pack up. She glanced down the beach; it looked as though the people who were staying had settled. They'd sold out of cookies and cupcakes hours ago and there were hardly any toppings for the hot chocolates left, anyway. She might as well join the other stallholders and shut up shop.

'That'll be great there, thank you again.' Leaning the table against the wall, she smiled at the barman who had helped her across the road.

'You're very welcome.'

Shutting the door behind him, Jenny surveyed the parlour. She should stay and put everything away but the music was still playing down on the beach and she didn't really want to shut herself away inside. Filling a small flask with coffee, she ignored the mess. She could deal with it later. She'd go and sit on the beach for an hour and try to relax. She checked her mobile. She hadn't heard back from Anthony so she assumed Grace had calmed down. Tucking it back in her back pocket, she resisted the urge to ring him and check, he'd only complain that she didn't trust him. No, he would have rung if Grace was still upset, she knew he would have. After all, he had before.

Pulling the door shut behind her, Jenny stepped onto the path and made her way back to the beach. Even though she didn't know anyone, it somehow felt more acceptable to be alone here. She didn't feel quite so lonely. She shrugged, maybe it was because she didn't know anyone so there was no expectation or possibility of meeting up with friends. She hadn't made any here, apart from Ashley of course, and so she didn't have the feeling that she was missing out when she knew others were meeting up or just spending family time together. She was alone, independent, if you like, but not lonely.

Yes, she could do this. She could be happy here. She *was* happy here. It was a shame things hadn't worked out with Nick, but it was probably a good thing, not with him being Helen's ex. It would have just been weird when she got back from Australia.

Lowering herself down onto the cool sand, she crossed her legs and leaned her head back to look at the sky. She couldn't see any stars, not with the glow from the bonfire and the numerous fairy lights that had been strung up between the lampposts behind her on the street, but she knew they were there and she could sense the clearness of the sky.

Shouts from the shore refocused her mind, and she laughed as a group of teenagers gingerly waded their way into the water. There was no chance she'd be brave enough to join them at this time though, however long she and Grace stayed here for. No chance, and after speaking to that man earlier she wouldn't be letting Grace either.

Taking a sip of her coffee, she closed her eyes. She could see what the attraction would be to set up camp and sleep under the open sky. Maybe when Grace was older, they could do just that. Bring some sleeping bags down to the beach and stay awake as long as they could. She wanted to make some fun memories for Grace, partly to cancel out the months of arguing her and Anthony had subjected her to and partly simply because she quite liked the idea of being a fun mum.

She could just picture Grace growing up by the seaside. Maybe she could get her into surfing or something. There was a surf school up near the lifeboat station. She'd taken Grace to watch a couple of times on a Saturday when they'd had a lull in customers and Grace had been captivated. Yes, she'd start lessons for her when she was old enough.

A scream pierced through the music and general chatter on the beach jolting Jenny from her daydream. Twisting her head, she tried to locate who had screamed. There it was again. It was someone out at sea, one of the swimmers. Standing up, she squinted her eyes, trying to see what was happening.

Walking towards the shoreline, she realised that the screams were coming from a couple of teenagers a few metres out. As the screams continued, more people gathered around her.

Shaking her head, she turned to the person next to her, the man who she had served the last hot chocolates to. 'What's going on?'

'Looks like those young girls are being swept by the current. It's been an accident waiting to happen.'

'Oh no. Has someone called for help?'

'They're already on the case.'

Following his pointing finger, Jenny could see a lifeboat emerging into the sea from the estuary.

Stepping forward, she watched as the lifeboat sped towards the group of teenagers. Nick *was* on duty. She could just about make out him out. He must have been at the festival the whole time and yet he hadn't come across to their stall. She shrugged, he was on duty, maybe they didn't rotate and get breaks. Plus, after the way they'd left it at the vets, he probably felt awkward.

The watching crowd was growing; people were abandoning their evening picnic teas and spots on the beach to gaze at the unfolding drama. One of the girls kept ducking under the waves now, her arms waving as she drifted closer to the rocks. Three others from the group were trying to swim towards her, but they too kept being dragged by the current, forcing them to pause and tread water.

'If they're not quick, she's going to be bashed against the rocks.'

Glancing at the man, Jenny frowned. The lifeboat crew were going as fast as they could, which looked pretty quick to Jenny. Looking back out to sea, Jenny could see that they had reached her now and were throwing a lifebelt out towards her.

The girl reached out towards the lifebelt before ducking under the water out of view. What was happening? Why hadn't she just grabbed the lifebelt? Squinting against the setting sun, Jenny held her breath, she couldn't see the girl at all now. Where had she gone?

One of the people in the lifeboat stood up, was it Nick? Yes, she could see it was. What was he doing? Jumping from the boat, he dove into the sea, instantly dipping beneath the surface to look for the girl. Moments later, he rose to the surface again, this time supporting the girl's head with one arm. He had rescued her!

Jenny held her breath, she could see Nick was having to work hard against the current. The sea was becoming rougher now, the waves a little bigger and the swell against the boat a little quicker.

'Come on. Why don't they lean down and pull them up?' Jenny bit down on her thumb nail.

'They're trying to. They just can't get close enough.'

The bobbing of the lifeboat on the sea was being interrupted by waves crashing forward. Being pulled slowly in the direction of the tide, it seemed to be inching away from Nick and the girl rather than towards them. Jenny could see Nick trying his hardest to swim towards the lifebelt which was still floating on the surface, being thrashed this way and that way by the waves.

After what felt like ages but in reality was probably only a few minutes, if that, the lifeboat managed to get close enough for two crew members to lean across and haul the girl over the side.

A cheer arose from the crowd surrounding Jenny. Dispersing and returning to their picnics and positions on the sand, a general excited chatter swept across the beach as people praised the lifeboat crew and shook their heads at the group of teenagers who had re-emerged from the sea, red-faced and quite likely more than a little embarrassed.

Still standing by the shoreline, Jenny looked on, her eyes not leaving Nick's figure in the distance. Come on, Nick. Your turn now. The same two men held their hands out to Nick at the same moment a wave pushed the boat out of reach and pulled Nick under the water.

Jenny raised her hand to her mouth, where had he gone? Why was he not coming straight back up to the surface? Scanning the area between the lifeboat and the rocks, Jenny watched as Nick's body rose back to the surface, further away from the lifeboat now and closer to the rocks. Another wave swelled beneath him, pummelling him into the side of a rock. Gasping, Jenny took a step forward, not noticing the cold rush of water seeping into her trainers.

As the sea relentlessly pounded the rocks, Jenny could just about make out Nick swimming furiously towards the lifeboat which was desperately trying to reach him. With each stroke forward he made, the current seemed to pull him back twice as far.

'Come on, Nick. You can do it.'

'You know him?'

Jerking her head to the side, Jenny realised the crowd was back, standing along the beach watching the events unfold. Focusing her attention back on Nick, she nodded.

The sea swelled behind the lifeboat, racing towards them. Biting her bottom lip, Jenny watched as the boat was flung forwards and Nick's body was hurled against the rocks again.

Taking another step into the shallow waters, Jenny squinted. She couldn't see him. Where was he? Where was Nick? He wasn't coming back up. He wasn't coming to the surface. The fear in her stomach rose to her mouth, suffocating her.

The man who had been standing next to her gingerly stepped into the water and gripped her elbow. 'Come back, love. They'll get to him. You watch.'

Slowly stepping back until she was on firm ground again, Jenny watched as someone from the lifeboat jumped into the waters, a rope trailing behind him. Why had Nick not had a rope attached? If he had, then none of this would have happened.

The crew member shot forward through the space between the lifeboat and where Nick had last been seen. Jenny watched as they ducked under the sea, them too disappearing from view for what felt like too long. Coming back to the surface, the crew member took a deep breath and dove back under.

Where was he? Why couldn't they find him? He couldn't have gone far. Not unless... Jenny shook her head, she wouldn't let the worst-case scenario enter her head, she couldn't. She just couldn't. Nick would be fine. He had to be. He was strong. He would be fine. He would.

Again and again, the man repeated his actions, rising to the surface to take a breath and then disappearing below the surface of the water again.

Holding her hands against her cheeks, Jenny ignored the salty tears raining from her eyes. He was gone. Nick was gone. They couldn't find him and that only meant one thing.

Dropping to her knees, Jenny heard her voice, strangely detached from herself, a raw hollow noise involuntarily escaping her mouth. 'Find him. Find him.'

Dropping her head into her hands, she closed her eyes. This couldn't be happening. Nick couldn't be gone. He couldn't be. A sharp pain shot through her chest.

'Look, look. They've got him. They've got him.'

Opening her eyes and looking up, Jenny focused on the man, his face close to hers, his arm around her shoulder, gently pulling her to standing.

'Look. They've found him. They've rescued him.'

Turning back towards the ocean, she scanned the surface of the sea again, her eyes coming to rest on the crew member who had jumped in after Nick. He had him! He did have him. The man half swam and was half pulled back to the lifeboat to be met by a multitude of arms reaching out towards them, pulling them both across the side to safety.

Immediately the roar of the lifeboat echoed across the beach as it turned and sped back towards the estuary leaving in its path a trail of white foaming bubbles.

Turning in the direction the lifeboat was going, Jenny ran as fast as she could along the sand, slipping and sliding on the damp ground. Falling down, she pushed herself back up and ran upwards, past picnic rugs and cups left abandoned on the sand, their owners having formed small groups to chat and dissect what they had just witnessed. She ran past the still burning bonfire, embers catching the breeze and illuminating the air around her. Not caring for the barricades, she weaved her way through the orange fences surrounding the bonfire. She had to get there. She had to get to Nick as quickly as she could.

Climbing the concrete steps towards the promenade two at a time, she gripped the handrail, flinging herself around to face the estuary. As she ran towards the metal railings lining the path at the side of the estuary, she could see the flash of orange as the lifeboat zipped across the water.

Making her way towards the lifeboat station, she could hear sirens in the background, quiet at first and then becoming increasingly louder, its urgency piercing through the evening's silence.

Running down the concrete ramp, Jenny waited as the lifeboat was hauled onto dry land. The blue lights from the ambulance flooded the area, mingling with the bright white lights of the lifeboat station. Crew members jumped from the lifeboat, reaching back to lift a stretcher out. As they hurried Nick towards the ambulance, the paramedics jumped from the ambulance to meet them halfway.

Rushing towards him, Jenny halted. 'Nick...' His face was ashen, his lips tinged blue and blood seeped from a wound on his forehead, just above his left eye. 'Is he OK? Is he going to be OK?'

'We'll know more when we get him to the hospital.' Speaking gently, the paramedic put her arm on Jenny's elbow and carefully moved her out of the way.

15

Brushing the drying sand from her damp jeans, Jenny looked up at the posters emblazoned on the wall opposite her. She couldn't concentrate, all the words mingled together, and the beaming faces blurred in front of her eyes. What was taking them so long? Was it a good sign or a bad sign? It was a bad sign, wasn't it? If Nick was OK they wouldn't have kept him in resus.

The tap-tap of sensible footwear refocused her attention, and she looked around. A doctor left the room next to where Nick was being looked after, shouted some orders to a nurse and disappeared back inside. Nurses, doctors and even patients had come and gone from that room, but no one had come out of the room they were treating Nick in. Not a nurse, a doctor, or a porter. No one who she could ask if he was OK, if he was still even alive.

Wringing her hands in front of her, she reminded herself that there wouldn't be a whole host of people in there with him if he wasn't alive still. Plus, Nick was Nick. He was strong; he'd be fine. He had to be.

Standing up, she peered through the small reinforced window in the door for about the hundredth time since she'd arrived. She still couldn't see anything. The stark blue curtain was still pulled around his bed, shielding him and the team who was working on him from unwanted eyes.

He would be fine. He would. Jenny shook her head. She couldn't get the image of his pale face, the blood dribbling down his cheekbone from his forehead out of her mind. What if he wasn't? What if he wasn't OK? She knew how she felt about him now. For sure. She'd suspected, but now that she might actually lose him, she knew for sure.

Sitting back down, she rocked gently on the chair. He would be fine. He would. Brushing her jeans again, she looked down at the tiled floor beneath her. A thin layer of sand grains covered the bright white tiles.

Hearing the swoosh of a door being opened swiftly, Jenny lifted her head. It was a nurse, and she was coming out of Nick's room.

Jumping to her feet, Jenny rushed towards the middle-aged woman dressed in a pale blue uniform. 'Is he alive? Is he OK? Is Nick OK?'

The nurse led her back towards the row of chairs and held her hand. 'He's going to be just fine. He's been extremely lucky by all accounts. He took a nasty knock to the head and so we'll need to keep him in for observation. He'll have a CT scan to rule out any internal bleeding to the brain but all the initial signs are good. We'll also need to keep an eye on him to make sure there aren't any complications.'

'What do you mean by complications?'

'Some people who have had such a close call in the water develop pneumonia or respiratory distress.' She patted Jenny's hand. 'All of his vital signs are good at the moment, we just need to keep a close eye and make sure they stay that way.'

'Right. OK, but you think he's going to be OK?'

'The doctor has assessed him and is happy that his condition is stable at the moment. Do you want to go and see him?'

'Can I?'

'Yes. We'll keep it just to you, his partner, for the next hour or so until he's been for his CT scan. I'm sure his team members will no doubt be along after their shift, but we'll try to keep it quiet for him.' Standing up, the nurse patted her on the shoulder, indicated the door and walked away.

His partner? Jenny looked around before realising the nurse had been referring to her. Walking towards the room Nick was in, she peered through the small window again. This time she saw that the curtain was now pulled back revealing Nick's bed. Pushing the door open, Jenny inched into the room. His face was covered with an oxygen mask and he had an IV line snaking its way from the back of his hand to a bag of saline hanging beside his bed.

As she approached the bed, she could see he had a bit more colour in his cheeks. He was still pale but not the deathly iridescent white he had been earlier. His lips had pinked up underneath the oxygen mask and the wound on his forehead now sported a brilliant white dressing.

Jenny quietly cleared her throat. 'Nick?'

Flickering his eyes, Nick looked at her before closing them again.

'It's OK, you sleep. I just wanted to see that you were all right. You gave everyone quite a scare.' Laying her hand on his, she smiled at him. 'And that's an understatement. You gave us a real scare.'

Momentarily opening his eyes again, Nick smiled at her before reaching his hand up to his oxygen mask.

'No, you keep that on. You need it. You can tell me how soppy I'm being another time.' Standing still, Jenny watched as his eyes drifted closed again. Blinking her eyes, she pinched the bridge of her nose. She could have lost him. Taking a deep, shaky breath in, she wiped the tears away.

'Sorry to bother you, but it's time for his observations now.' Opening the door ajar, a nurse popped his head around the door before entering the room.

'Shall I go?' Jenny pointed to the door.

'No, you're fine where you are.'

'Thanks.' Standing still, the warmth from her hand still warming Nick's, she watched as he busied himself checking Nick's IV and blood pressure. 'Do you know when he's going for his CT scan, please?'

'I believe he's next in the queue so it could be any moment now. After that, we'll have him transferred to the ward.'

Jenny nodded.

'Ah, here they are now. Are you here to take him down?' Turning to face the door, the nurse grinned at two porters who stood in the doorway.

'We sure are.'

'There you are.' The nurse smiled at Jenny, pointing with his pen. 'I'll show you where to wait for him, if you like?'

Jenny nodded before leaning down and kissing Nick's forehead, careful not to touch the dressing. 'I love you.'

16

Blinking her eyes, Jenny jolted awake. Drat, she must have fallen asleep. Straightening her back against the hard plastic chair, she circled her shoulders. She checked her phone and shook her head. It was nine in the morning. She must have been asleep for hours. After popping in to see Nick after his CT scan, she'd decided to wait in the corridor outside his side room and let him sleep properly.

Shaking her head, she tried to work out what had woken her. His side room was positioned at the back of the ward and although the ward was quite full, it was still relatively quiet. With the majority of the patients still sleeping, the creak of the medicine trolley was about the only noise, that and a couple of TV's running.

She looked over at Nick's door. There was somebody in there with him. She could just about make out the voices now, a woman's and his. She recognised his voice even though he sounded croaky presumably from the combination of having swallowed too much water and having had an oxygen mask on all night. She didn't recognise the woman's voice though. It didn't sound like the overly friendly tones of the night shift nurse who had been popping in every hour to carry out his observations. Maybe the nurses had swapped over again. That was probably it, the nurse covering the night shift had presumably gone home.

Raking her hands through her hair, she tried to smooth out the flyaway strands. Now he was awake and fully conscious she didn't really want him seeing her in this state. She shrugged, she supposed it didn't matter and at least the majority of the sand that had been clinging to her jeans had gone.

'This way? Thank you.' A deep voice echoed down the corridor.

Looking up, Jenny rubbed the sleep from her eyes. Was that Rob? Yes, she was sure it was. She had only seen him a couple of times, but because of the way he had upset Nick she had his features embedded in her mind. Had he come to see Nick? She didn't think they got along. She closed her eyes momentarily, maybe the shock of what had happened had caused him to want to apologise for everything he'd done or something? Shock did funny things to people, or that's what her Nan had always said.

Leaning her elbows on her knees, she watched as he paced up and down, every now and then peering through the window into Nick's room. Why didn't he just go in? Maybe he was waiting until the nurse had finished.

Stretching her arms above her head, she checked the time again. She'd wait until Rob had been in to see him and then she'd pop in before getting back to open the parlour. It wouldn't matter if they were a little late opening up. The nurse had told her the lifeboat crew were popping in late morning anyway, so at least he wouldn't be on his own for long.

'Has she been in there long?'

'The nurse? A while I guess.'

'Steph. Has Steph been in there long?' Rob indicated Nick's door.

'Steph? Oh, umm, I didn't realise she was in there. I've not been awake long, I assumed it was a nurse who was in with him.'

'No, it's my fiancée, Steph.'

Jenny nodded. What was she supposed to say? Why didn't he just go in there with her? Pushing herself to standing, she bent down to get her bag. 'I'm just going to grab a coffee. Do you want one?'

'No, thank you though.'

Why had she even offered? Standing in front of the machine just around the corner, she rummaged in the bottom of her bag. She was sure she'd felt some loose change when she'd been looking for Grace's box of raisins the other day. Yes, there it was.

Putting the coins in the slot, she listened for the telltale clink as the metal fell to the bottom. She hadn't seen such a limited choice of drinks in a long time. She shrugged, no doubt she wouldn't be able to tell the difference between a latte or an Americano, anyway. Whatever she chose would probably taste of cardboard, they always did from these places.

'Well?' Rob's voice penetrated the quiet.

'Well, what? You knew I was coming to see him. I told you,' a woman answered him.

Frowning, Jenny picked up her cup of dull brown liquid and lifted it to her lips. Steph had obviously finished visiting Nick. A strange edge to Rob's voice stopped Jenny from returning to her seat. Wrapping her hands around the hot plastic cup, she looked at some coffee granules spinning on the surface of the liquid. She'd give them a couple of minutes to talk and then go and see Nick.

'Even so, I had asked you not to.'

'You don't own me, Rob. I can see who I like.'

'I know I don't own you.' Rob scoffed. Jenny could almost imagine the smirk on his face. 'I do, however, expect you to consider my wishes. I do for you, so it's the least you can do for me.'

'No, you really don't. I told you weeks ago that I wasn't happy with the way you're trying to muscle in on Nick's practice and buy him out, and yet you still went ahead with everything.'

'I'm doing it for you, for us. You don't want your ex-fiancé hanging around your hometown, do you?'

'It's not me who has a problem with him, though is it?'

'Don't start that again, Steph. I don't have a problem with him being here. It will make your life easier though without him living here, you've got to admit that. It's not as though he's just living here and minding his own business, he was always hanging around your parents' place. That can't have been very nice for you.'

'Like I've told you over and over again, it doesn't affect me in the slightest. Admit it, it's all been about the business for you.'

'The business? Yep, bring that theory of yours up again, won't you? You just think I want to get my hands on the practice, that's it, isn't it?'

'Well, don't you?' Steph's voice rose a little before she checked herself and lowered it to a harsh whisper. 'Admit it, it's not to make my life easier or anything, you want rid of Nick so you can step into his shoes at the practice.'

So it was all Rob's idea then. She'd been right, Steph's parents weren't in on the plan. Jenny shuffled forwards, still staying behind the corner so she couldn't be seen.

'You've told him, haven't you?'

'I can't believe you managed to talk me into it this far. It needs to stop. We need to drop this. Talk to him, tell him you don't want to buy his half of the practice any more.'

'Why would I do that?'

'Because it's the right thing to do, that's why. We shouldn't be pushing him out of the town he now calls home. It's my fault he moved here after uni instead of going back to Yorkshire.'

'Yes, well, maybe he should have done.'

'He was your best mate remember.'

'That was a long time ago. The way you're talking, anyone would think you still held a flame for him.'

'What? Are you being serious? I'm just trying to be a decent human being, something you're finding increasingly difficult to be these days.'

Frowning, Jenny held her cup tightly between her hands. Should she go out and say something? What could she say though? The argument was between the two of them; it had absolutely nothing to do with her.

'I take it you've told him?'

'Told him what? That my parents have nothing to do with your plan?'

'Well, have you?'

'Yes, I did, and I also told him that I'm not having anything to do with it any more and that I think he should stay. I'm done, Rob. Literally done. I can't stand back and watch you break another person like you're doing now. You're on your own.'

'Steph, wait.'

Biting her lip, Jenny listened as Steph's shoes tapped away down the corridor and a thud came from around the corner. Closing her eyes momentarily, Jenny took a deep breath and headed back. Rob had disappeared, leaving a small bin on its side in his wake. Shaking her head, Jenny tutted. There was no need to take his frustration out on hospital property. Picking it up, she set it back to the side of the corridor and knocked on Nick's door.

'Hi, how are you feeling this morning?' Walking to his bedside, she was relieved to see how much better he looked.

'Hi.' Pushing himself up on his elbows, he smiled.

'Hey, just rest.' Placing her half-empty coffee cup on the stark bedside table, Jenny puffed up the pillows behind him, gently guiding him to lean back against them. 'So are you feeling any better? You look a bit better.'

'I'm OK, thanks.'

'You gave us all quite a fright last night.'

'I know. You said that last night too, didn't you?' Relaxing his shoulders, he relaxed into the softness of the pillows.

'Umm, yes, I probably did.' Picking her coffee cup back up, she held towards her lips, hoping it would cover some of the embarrassment which was blushing its way across her cheeks. 'I didn't think you were with it when I saw you last night?'

'It's all very patchy, but I remember you coming to see me.'

'Right.' If he remembered her saying that to him, did he remember what she had whispered to him before she'd left? No, of course he didn't. He wouldn't have.

'Thank you.' Sitting back up, he reached for the small clear plastic glass on the bedside table.

'Here, let me.' Passing him the glass, she searched his eyes for any clue that he'd heard her.

'It meant a lot, knowing that you were there.' Taking a sip of water, he looked at her. 'You've not been here all night, have you?"

Putting the glass back down, Jenny bit her bottom lip and shrugged. 'I didn't have much else to do.'

'Thank you.'

'I'm just glad you're all right.'

'I'll live. I'm not looking forward to the crew coming in though.' Nick grimaced. 'I'll get a good telling off for not having my guide rope on when I jumped into the water.'

'And so you should. You could have died.'

'I know, I know, but if I'd waited even just a minute more, that girl... Is she OK? Have you heard anything?'

'She's fine. The paramedics checked her over at the beach and she walked away from the whole thing.'

'Oh, good.'

'Yes. You're quite the hero, even if you did put your own life in danger.'

Nick's cheeks pinked up, and he looked towards the door before clearing his throat and changing the subject. 'Steph came to see me. You were right. Her mum didn't have a clue about them buying the practice.'

Jenny nodded.

'I'm sorry I was so horrible to you. I don't know what I was thinking. I wasn't sleeping and everything just kind of got on top of me. I know it's no excuse, but I guess I just felt everyone was against me and I couldn't see what was right in front of me.'

'Don't worry, I know you were having a bad time. I hope that things start to get better now you've spoken to Steph and she's explained her side of the story.'

'So do I.'

'I heard them arguing in the corridor and I think Steph's trying to call a halt to the whole plan of buying you out.' Jenny looked at the floor. 'Maybe you could stay?' He will, he had no reason to go, not now that Rob wasn't going to buy him out. Jenny crossed her fingers, please stay.

Nick nodded. 'I guess I'll just have to wait and see. I'm going to give myself a bit of time to get over this and hopefully clear my head a bit.'

Jenny nodded.

'I am really really sorry for the way I treated you, though. Some of the things I said...' Shaking his head, he took Jenny's hand in his.

Smiling, Jenny closed her fingers around his, the warmth of his hands reassuring after the way he'd looked barely a few hours before. Swallowing hard, she told herself she wouldn't think about what could have happened.

A loud knock on the door echoed in the small room and Jenny jumped back, her hand falling to her side.

'Helloooo...?'

Grinning, Nick sat up a little more. 'Hey, come on in.'

'I'll get going now. I'll pop in later.' Turning around, she smiled as the lifeboat crew filed in and headed out to the corridor.

Closing the door on the laughter and teasing, Jenny crunched her coffee cup up and threw it in the bin.

* * *

Pulling her mobile out of her apron pocket, Jenny checked the time.

'That must be the twentieth time you've looked at your phone in the past half an hour. Why don't you pop up to the hospital and check on Nick? I'll cope here for a bit.'

Jenny watched as Ashley turned to serve another customer. They had been quite quiet all day. People were probably relaxing in their holiday homes after the excitement and bustle of the Summer Festival yesterday.

'Go on. We'll be closing in a couple of hours, anyway.'

'Are you sure?'

'Yes. I wouldn't have offered otherwise. Honestly go. Say "hi" from me.'

Smiling, Jenny untied her apron and grabbed her bag. 'I'll make sure I'm back before closing.'

'No hurry.'

* * *

Walking through the hospital corridors, Jenny took a deep breath of the unmistakable bleach and disinfectant fragrance of a deep clean. She turned towards Nick's ward, turning her back on the memories of the horrific events of last night in the Accident and Emergency where he had been brought in. They had literally saved his life.

Pushing the door to his ward open, Jenny made her way through the beds and bays towards the side rooms. Swallowing, she tried to calm the nerves in her stomach, a slow grin making its way across her face as she got closer to him.

'Afternoon. Can I help you, love?'

Jenny smiled at the petite greying nurse. 'I've just come to visit Nick. He's in one of the side rooms.'

'Our town's own hero? He's gone, love. The doctor discharged him about lunchtime, I think. A young woman came to pick him up. Sophie or Steph, I think.'

'Oh, right. Thank you.' Frowning, Jenny turned and made her way back through the hospital corridors and back into the fresh air. It was good that he had been discharged, it meant he was better, so why did she feel as though she'd been kicked in the stomach? And why had Steph taken him home? Why would he have rung her and not Jenny, or anyone else for that matter?

17

'We're almost there now, Gracie. Just a bit further.' She should have brought the buggy. Anthony had dropped Grace off late last night and she hadn't settled until well past her usual bedtime.

'No, Mummy. Carry me.' Stamping her foot, Grace pouted.

Standing still, Jenny looked down at her daughter. There was no chance she'd get her to walk the rest of the way to nursery. 'Come here, then.' Reaching down, she let Grace circle her arms around her neck and picked her up.

'Love you, Mummy.'

'Love you too, cheeky.' Ducking her face against the nape of Grace's neck, she blew a raspberry.

'Mummy!' Squealing with laughter, Grace clapped her hands.

'Right, sensible faces on now, we're almost there and I think today you're making decorations for the nursery's summer fayre on Saturday.'

'You come. Me and you go to fayre.'

'Yes, of course, we will. We'll shut up the parlour for a few hours and go and have some fun, shall we?' Laughing, Jenny pointed to the bakery window. 'Ooh, those cakes look good, don't they? Shall I see if I can pop out some time and get us one each?'

'Now. Get them now.'

'We can't, sweetheart. It's too early. Nowhere is open yet.' She loved walking Grace to nursery. Although it was before opening time, there was still so much going on, so much hope in the air for the day ahead. Standing there, they watched as the baker filled the window with more freshly baked cakes and cookies. 'Which one do you want if I can get you one?'

'That one with the pink flower on, please, Mummy.' Holding Jenny's shoulder with one hand, Grace leaned down, pointing to a small sponge cupcake lavishly decorated with pink and blue piped flowers.

'Ooh, that one does look good, doesn't it? I'm not sure which one I'll get, they all look so yummy.'

'Look, Mummy, look. Nick.'

Straightening her back and jerking her head towards the road, Jenny watched as a white car pulled up in the lay-by a short distance ahead. 'Is he in that car?'

'Yes, look.'

Shifting Grace's small body onto her other hip, Jenny watched as Nick stepped out of the passenger side and Steph slipped out of the driver's side, quickly coming round to Nick's side of the car.

'Where they going?'

'I don't know, sweetie.' Turning back to the bakery, Jenny pointed at a large doughnut. 'I like the look of that one.'

'Yummy.'

'Yes, it looks good, doesn't it?' Glancing sideways, Jenny watched as Nick and Steph went into a small café. With its speciality being cooked breakfasts it was the only place that opened early, trying to catch the retail workers before they had to start their shifts, no doubt.

'And this one.'

'Yes, yes. We'll see. We'd better get going before you're late for nursery.' Walking quickly, Jenny kept her eyes focused on the path in front of her.

* * *

'Enjoy your milkshake.' Smiling, Jenny passed the glass to the lady in front of her before turning to wipe the counter down.

'Here, I've made you a latte.'

'Thanks.' Looking up, Jenny took the latte from Ashley.

'Are you OK? You've been really quiet since you dropped Grace off.' With a quiet lull in the parlour, Ashley leaned against the counter and sipped her drink.

'I'm OK. Grace didn't get to sleep until quite late so I'm just a bit tired.'

'It's been a hectic few days, hasn't it?'

'It sure has.' Jenny wrapped her hands around her latte glass and tried to keep her voice steady and casual. 'So, have you heard if Nick's still selling up?'

'His half of this place? I don't know. I might pop over to Steph's parents' place after work and see him. He's staying there for a few days so they can help with his recovery.'

'Oh.' Why would he be staying there? Yes, he had a close relationship with Steph's parents, but with her and Rob there too? Surely that would be a bit awkward? And how did Ashley know and not her? 'With Rob there too?'

'No, he's moved out. Apparently, he and Steph broke up and he's left. So I'm assuming Nick will have a rethink about selling and moving on now Rob's out of the picture. Hopefully, anyway.'

Jenny nodded. So Rob had moved out and Nick in. Steph didn't hang about, did she? But she supposed they'd almost got married, it wasn't as though Nick was a stranger to her. 'I'm just going to go and prepare some more ice cream whilst we're quiet.'

'OK. I think it's just bubble-gum and fudge we need.'

'Right.' Placing her latte glass down, Jenny walked into the kitchen. It wasn't as though there had been anything going on between her and Nick. And now he'd made it perfectly clear where his loyalties lay.

* * *

Placing the last of the containers in the freezer, Jenny headed back out of the kitchen. With her hand on the kitchen door, she paused. It was Nick, she could hear his voice. He was talking to Ashley. Standing up straight, she took a deep breath and tightened the belt of her apron before going out.

'Hi, Nick. How are you feeling?' Beaming, Jenny made her way behind the counter and washed her hands.

'I'm feeling much better, thank you. I almost feel like my normal self now.'

'Good, it sounds as though you're being looked after well then.' Refilling the ice cream cones, she hoped he hadn't heard the fact that her voice had been laced with sarcasm.

'Yes, I guess I am.' Tilting his head to one side, Nick looked at her. 'Everything all right with you?'

'Of course.' She ducked her head down and straightened the cones.

'Nick's got some great news! Tell her, Nick. Tell her.' Ashley grinned and tapped the palms of her hands against the counter mimicking a drumroll.

'What?'

'I've decided not to sell up. This place or the veterinary practice. I'm staying put.'

Nodding, Jenny shuffled the paper napkins. She could never get them to look neat. 'That's good then. I'm pleased for you.'

'Thanks. And thank you again for being there for me at the hospital.'

Jenny looked up at Nick as he gently touched her forearm, the warmth from his fingertips tingling her skin.

'Nick, are you about ready?' The bell above the door tinkled as Steph walked through.

Nodding at Jenny, Nick removed his hand and turned towards Steph. 'Yep. Just coming. See you both later.'

'Bye.' Ashley waved as they left.

'I'm just going to pop upstairs, if that's OK?' Throwing her apron down on the counter, Jenny turned and made her way up to the flat.

Sitting down at the top of the stairs, she pushed the heels of her hands onto her eyes. She would not cry. She would not. She was being completely daft. She knew she was. She knew she shouldn't feel this upset over something that never was, anyway. She and Nick had never really had anything going on, so why did she feel as though she'd had her heart ripped in two?

Closing her eyes, she took deep slow breaths. It wasn't as though she'd moved down here to find love. She'd moved down to provide a better, more stable environment for Grace to grow up in. The last thing she needed was a man to confuse things. Especially being as Anthony had already introduced Annie into Grace's life. No, Grace needed stability. Men were incapable of providing stability. Even Nick. He'd told her he'd wanted a relationship barely a week ago and now he had moved in with Steph. No, she didn't need him. She didn't need anyone. She and Grace would be just fine, happier even, on their own.

Standing up, she shook her arms by her sides. She could do this. She'd smile at Nick and Steph when they came in next and wish them well in their relationship.

18

Cupping her coffee, Jenny watched as Grace sat cross-legged on the grass in front of Magic Mike from Merlin's Magic Show. The nursery had put on a good show for their summer fayre. Besides Magic Mike who had been putting on repeat performances and wowing the children all morning, there was a bouncy castle and some donkey rides alongside the usual craft stalls and games for children to play.

As the show came to an end, Grace's nursery teacher stood up and clapped. 'Let's hear a huge round of applause for Magic Mike!'

Grace clapped before standing up and running towards Jenny.

'Wow, that was good, wasn't it?'

'Good, good, good.' Grace's eyes were shining from all the giggling she'd done when Magic Mike had miraculously pulled two stuffed bunnies from his hat and then squirted water from a plastic carnation at her teacher.

'What do you want to do now?'

'Lucky dip! Lucky dip!' Grace pointed to a stall surrounded by children and adults at the other end of the field.

'Good choice. Come on, then.' Holding out her hand, Jenny

waited until she felt Grace's small hand in hers and led her towards the lucky dip. It was so nice being able to spend some quality time with her. Normally they only had the early mornings and evenings uninterrupted. She must speak to Helen about hiring some cover, both her and Ashley could do with some time off. Not that Ashley would admit to it. Although she knew as the summer season wound down, business would become quieter and they'd be able to close up earlier and maybe even close for a whole day once a week.

'Hello, Grace. Have you come for a go on the lucky dip?' One of the nursery nurses smiled at Grace and held her hand out. 'That'll be one pound, please?'

'Here you are, sweetheart. You can pay.' Placing a coin in the palm of Grace's hand, Jenny watched as Grace paid before digging her hand into the large box filled with shredded paper.

'She's settled in so well at nursery, haven't you, Grace?'

Jenny smiled. 'She seems to enjoy it. Her favourite thing at the moment seems to be going on the slide. That's all she talks about.'

'Oh, yes. You like the slide, don't you, Grace? She's always asking when it's her group's turn to go outside. That's it, dig a little deeper, Grace. See if you can find a little present hiding in there.'

'Got one! Look, Mummy, me got one!' Pulling her hand out, she held up a small parcel wrapped in yellow paper.

'Wow, so you did. What did you get?'

Ripping the paper off, Grace revealed a small book. 'Look, look, an elephant book.'

'Ooh, that looks good. We can read that when we get home, if you like?'

'Yes, Mummy. Yes.' Waving at the nursery nurse, Grace gripped hold of the bottom of Jenny's top and pulled her away. 'Bouncy castle. Can I go on bouncy castle?'

'Yes, OK.' Jenny followed Grace back across the field towards the bouncy castle.

'Me going to do lots of jumps.'

'That will be good.' Bending down, Jenny helped Grace slip off her sandals and watched as she stepped up onto the castle.

'Jenny, hi.'

'Nick, hi. How are you?' Pulling her handbag up higher onto her shoulder, Jenny turned to him.

'I'm good, thank you. I'm glad I ran into you. I wanted to have a quick word, if you've got a minute?'

'Umm, yes. OK.' What now? Had he changed his mind about moving away? Was he looking to sell up again?

'Mummy. Come on.' Jumping from the bouncy castle, Grace ran over towards Jenny, gripping her hand, she pulled her towards the bouncy castle.

'Hold on, sweetheart. Mummy's just talking.'

'No, Mummy, come on with me.' Stamping her foot, Grace pulled her harder.

'OK.' Jenny glanced behind her. After all, this was the only bit of free time she'd had with Grace during the day for a long time, Nick could tell her yet some more bad news another time. 'Sorry, I'll catch up with you another time.'

'Quick, Mummy, take shoes off.' Grace paused and pointed to Jenny's trainers.

'Yes, OK.' Slipping them off, Jenny kicked them to the side before dropping her handbag on top.

'Up.' Climbing onto the front part of the bouncy castle, Grace pulled Jenny's hand.

Stepping up, Jenny smiled as the surface sank beneath her weight. She'd always loved bouncy castles as a kid.

Giggling, Grace let go of Jenny's hand and ran to the other side of the castle, her small body bouncing up and down as she ran over the dips and hills. When she'd got to the other side, she turned back to face Jenny and waved her across. 'Your turn, Mummy. Your turn.'

Laughing, Jenny ran towards Grace.

Grace clapped her hands before turning and pointing. 'Nick.'

Turning around, Jenny laughed. What was he doing? Nick had climbed up onto the bouncy castle and was making his way towards them.

'Jump, Nick, jump.' Bouncing across to him, Grace held onto his hands and jumped as high as she could.

'What are you doing?' Leaning against the side wall, Jenny shook her head.

'I told you I wanted to talk to you.'

'Yes, but you shouldn't be on here. You've not long been out of hospital.'

'I'm fine.'

Letting go of Nick's hands, Grace jumped towards the opposite side of the bouncy castle before flopping her body against the bouncy floor.

'Really? Here?'

'Yes, I need to tell you something and, hey, I figure this is as good a moment as any. Plus, you're always busy at the parlour and I wanted to talk to you without loads of customers around.'

'As opposed to there being a ton of other people, like here?' Jenny indicated to the people milling around the field, buying things from the stalls, riding the donkeys and watching the magic show.

'OK, so maybe it's not as quiet as I'd like, but to be honest, I don't care any more. I need to tell you something and if I have to tell you while jumping on a bouncy castle then so be it.'

'Oh no. It's something bad, isn't it?' Why else would he have to tell her so urgently? 'You've decided to sell up and have found a buyer? Or worse, Helen is selling up too and I'm out of a job?' Even as she said it as a joke, it hit her that it could actually be possible. When they'd spoken on the phone, Helen had been asking less and less about the parlour, she was obviously losing interest in it. Would her and Grace be without a home again?

'No, I'm not selling. And neither is Helen, as far as I know, anyway.'

'Then what is it?' Jenny gnawed on her cuticle. Looking at him she realised he looked quite nervous, even as he was trying so hard to keep his balance he was rubbing the back of his neck.

'It's nothing bad.'

'OK.' He was getting engaged to Steph again. That would make perfect sense. He probably wanted to tell her before they made a big announcement which was why he'd resorted to following her onto the bouncy castle.

Positioning his legs slightly apart for balance, he took a deep breath. 'I heard you.'

'Heard what?'

'That night at the hospital, I heard you when you told me you loved me.'

No, no, he couldn't have. Lowering her hand from her mouth, she held on to the wall behind her. 'I'm sorry. I...'

'Mummy!' Giggling, Grace half sprinted and half jumped towards her, losing her footing and flying straight into Jenny's side. Flaying her arms out as she fell, Jenny somehow managed to grab hold of Nick's T-shirt pulling him down on top of her. Laughing, Grace jumped onto Nick's back, wrapping her arms around his neck.

'Sorry. Grace, Grace, sweetheart, off you get.' Reaching up, Jenny tried to pull Grace off of Nick. Grace tightened her grip around Nick's neck, oblivious to Jenny's protests.

Laughing, Nick turned towards Jenny, their faces millimetres apart. 'What I wanted to tell you is, I love you too. I think I have since the moment I first saw you and if you'd still like to give us a chance, I would too.'

Jenny laughed, a deep blush creeping up her neck. Had he really said that? Did he really feel that way? She nodded.

Smiling, Nick leaned down, their lips touching briefly before Grace rolled off his back, pulling him with her.

'Play tag. You're it.' Slapping Nick on the shoulder, Grace jumped up and bounced towards the far side of the castle.

Standing up, Nick leaned down and clasped Jenny's hands, pulling her up towards him. 'Is that a yes?'

'Yes, yes, it is.' Jenny grinned before Grace bounced towards her almost knocking her over again and informing her that she was now 'it'.

EPILOGUE

Putting her hand on the door from the flat to the parlour, Nick held her elbow.

'Jenny, wait. You've forgotten something.'

'Have I?' Turning back, she smiled. She still couldn't believe her and Nick were actually together.

'Yes, you've forgotten this.' Resting his hand on the door behind her, he leaned towards her and kissed her, her lips tingling with his touch.

'Jenny! Phone!'

Looking towards the door and back at Nick, Jenny smiled. 'I'd best get that.'

Nick nodded before kissing her on the forehead and opening the door for her.

'Do you know who it is?' Jenny mouthed at Ashley as she took the phone.

'Helen.' Ashley indicated the kitchen door. 'I'll go and sort the ice creams.'

Jenny nodded. 'Hi, Helen.'

'Hey, Jenny. How're things going with Nick?'

Jenny smiled as Nick came up behind her, putting his arms around her waist and resting his head on her shoulder. 'Good. Really good. How are things in Australia?'

'They're great. Actually, that's what I wanted to talk to you about.'

'Oh, yes?' Jenny watched Nick as he dropped his arms from her waist and went over to the coffee machine, holding a mug up to her and raising his eyebrows. Nodding, she made an 'L' shape with her fingers and mouthed, 'latte please' before blowing him a kiss.

'Yes. I'm really enjoying being out here, I've made some great friends and things are good. Things are going great between Jude and me too. I'm happy, I'm finally happy and I've decided to stay out here.'

'That's cool then. How long for?'

'Forever.'

Opening her mouth and closing it again, Jenny touched her lips. 'Forever?'

'Yes. I want to put down roots here, make this my home.'

'Wow. When did you decide this?'

'I've been thinking about it for a while now but I didn't want to say anything, not until I was certain.'

'I don't know what to say. I'll miss you.'

'I'll be back for the odd holiday here and there, and maybe one day you, Grace and Nick can come and visit me.'

'Yes, yes, I guess so.'

'I wanted to talk to you about the parlour.'

Opening her mouth, Jenny closed it again. Of course. Helen would have to sell up and that would more than likely mean that she and Grace would be out. Not unless she had something written into the contract like Nick did when he was going to sell his half. 'I understand.'

'I was wondering if you'd like to buy my half?'

'What? Me?'

'Yes, you. I was thinking now that you've been running it you'll probably be able to get a business loan out.'

'Umm.' Her? Buy Helen's share of the parlour? Could she really? Surely a bank wouldn't lend to her? But they might. As Helen said, she'd had experience of managing the place, she knew she could turn a good profit and she could show the bank the accounts. She might actually be able to buy it. Maybe.

'So, what do you think? Obviously, I'd give you time to find a lender and that, but in principle, what do you think? Do you hate the idea? You do, don't you?'

'What? No, I love the idea! Yes, I'd love to. I'd like to try and find out if I can, I mean.'

'Great. I was hoping you'd say that. Oh, and Smudge...' Helen's voice became quieter.

'Yes, I'll adopt him. Of course, I will.'

'Phew! OK, well I've got to go now, we're going on a boat ride around Sydney harbour in a few minutes.'

'OK, I'll speak to you soon.' Replacing the receiver, Jenny blinked. Had she really just had that conversation?

'Everything OK?' Putting Jenny's latte down on the counter next to her, Nick frowned.

'I think I might be buying Helen's share of this place.'

'Really?'

'Yes. I think so.' She looked at the phone and then back at Nick. 'She's staying out there and she's asked if I want to buy it.'

'That's great news!' Putting his coffee down next to hers, Nick grabbed her waist and pulled her towards him before lowering his head. As their lips met, Jenny could feel her heart swelling. Everything was working out.

'Mummy! Ready now.' Bustling through from the kitchen,

Grace wiped a smear of jam across her face and picked up her packed lunch box.

'Guess what, Gracie? How would you like to live here, properly, forever?'

'We already do.' Grace sat down and pulled her shoes on before standing back up.

Laughing, Jenny shrugged and looked at Nick. 'She's obviously taken it as given that we're here to stay.'

Nick grinned and made his way towards Grace. 'Come on, kid, let's get you to nursery.'

Stepping out onto the street, Jenny breathed in the warm salty air. She could definitely get used to this. She could definitely make this small seaside town her forever home.

'Swing, Mummy, Nick. Swing.' Holding both their hands, Grace ran forwards and lifted her feet.

ACKNOWLEDGMENTS

Thank you for taking the time to read The Seaside Ice-Cream Parlour. I hope you've enjoyed reading about Jenny's journey and her new beginning with Nick as much as I enjoyed writing her story.

A huge thank you to my wonderful children, Ciara and Leon, who motivate me to keep writing and working towards 'changing our stars' each and every day. Also to my lovely family for always being there, through the good times and the trickier ones.

And a massive thank you to my amazing editor, Emily Yau, who reached out and believed in me – thank you.

Thank you also to Shirley for copyediting and proofreading The Seaside Ice-Cream Parlour. And, of course, Clare Stacey for creating the beautiful cover. Thank you to all at Team Boldwood!

MORE FROM SARAH HOPE

We hope you enjoyed reading *The Seaside Ice Cream Parlour*. If you did, please leave a review.

If you'd like to gift a copy, this book is also available as an ebook, paperback, hardback, digital audio download and audiobook CD.

Sign up to Sarah Hope's mailing list for news, competitions and updates on future books.

https://bit.ly/SarahHopeNews

Why not try *The Little Beach Café,* another heartwarming novel from Sarah Hope...

ABOUT THE AUTHOR

Sarah Hope is the author of many successful romance novels, including the bestselling Cornish Bakery series. She lives in Central England with her two children and an array of pets, and enjoys escaping to the seaside at any opportunity.

Follow Sarah Hope on social media:

 twitter.com/sarahhope35

 facebook.com/HappinessHopeDreams

 instagram.com/sarah_hope_writes

Boldwood

Boldwood Books is an award-winning fiction publishing company seeking out the best stories from around the world.

Find out more at www.boldwoodbooks.com

Join our reader community for brilliant books, competitions and offers!

Follow us
@BoldwoodBooks
@BookandTonic

Sign up to our weekly deals newsletter

https://bit.ly/BoldwoodBNewsletter

Milton Keynes UK
Ingram Content Group UK Ltd.
UKHW040755040124
435437UK00004B/193